# Praise for Meg Benjamin's
## *Bolted*

"*Bolted* was an unexpected and delightful surprise... I am grateful for having discovered a great new author and will definitely check out more of Meg Benjamin's books, and until then I can't wait to read the next Promise Harbor Wedding books!"

~ *Book Lovers Inc.*

"I loved this story and how Greta discovered who she was and what she wanted to with the rest of her life. [...] Overall this is a great read and I can't wait for the next book."

~ *The Book Reading Gals*

# Bolted

*Meg Benjamin*

SAMHAIN
PUBLISHING

Samhain Publishing, Ltd.
11821 Mason Montgomery Road, 4B
Cincinnati, OH 45249
www.samhainpublishing.com

Editing by Lindsey Faber
Cover by Angela Waters

First Samhain Publishing, Ltd. electronic publication: April 2013
First Samhain Publishing, Ltd. print publication: February 2014

# Dedication

To the family—Bill, Ben, Josh and Molly—for all their support. And to my intrepid and long-suffering coauthors—Kelly, Sydney and Erin. Thanks guys, you made it happen!

# Chapter One

*Promise Harbor, Massachusetts*

Greta shifted slightly, trying to hold her bridesmaid bouquet and at the same time move the Crinolines from Hell away from the backs of her knees. This was undoubtedly the most ghastly bridesmaid dress in the history of mankind. The puke-green flounce around her shoulders stood out in a stiff ruff, while the paler green skirt looked a little like an inverted umbrella, thanks to the Crinolines from Hell. At least the length of the skirt meant that she could wear running shoes instead of the four-inch heels Bernice had originally proposed.

Bernice Cabot was a bridesmaid too, but somehow she'd ended up in charge of the bridesmaids' wardrobe rather than the bride, Greta's sister-in-law-to-be. Greta didn't really know Allie all that well—when they were kids, Allie had spent all her time with Josh, and Josh never wanted to be around his snot-nosed little sister. The age difference got in the way. Greta had a feeling Allie had asked her to be matron of honor just to be polite.

She wasn't sure why Bernice had chosen the bridesmaids' dresses rather than Allie herself, but she really hoped it wasn't because Allie liked Bernice's taste. They were undoubtedly the worst dresses Greta had ever seen, let alone worn.

She could still feel the crinolines' bite through her satin

slip, even after she'd managed to shift them slightly to the side (and when had she last worn a slip anyway? Middle school?). Gosh all hemlock, weddings were fun! Maybe she should just avoid them in the future. After all, she'd had her own experience with marital train wreck. Maybe she'd developed some kind of wedding jinx.

Her brother, Josh the Perfect, stood at attention as he watched her future sister-in-law, Allie the Even More Perfect, float down the aisle. In contrast to her bridesmaids', Allie's dress was gorgeous. Maybe because Allie had managed to choose her own dress instead of turning the task over to Bernice. However, Allie's shoes were...interesting. They had huge, green, artificial flowers on the toes. Every time she took a step the edge of her dress seemed to catch on them. Just on a wild guess, Greta figured Bernice had had something to do with those shoes. They showed her touch.

Just now Bernice was standing behind Greta, trembling with ecstasy in her very own bubblegum-pink version of the most ghastly bridesmaid dress in the history of mankind as she watched the bridal procession. The woman had a serious *Gone With the Wind* fixation. All three bridesmaids looked like they were ready for the barbecue at Tara. Or at least a barbecue at Pittypat's Porch.

For some reason, neither Josh nor Allie looked particularly happy, certainly not as happy as they should have been on the first day of the rest of their lives. Maybe they were both nervous. Maybe Allie's wedding foundation garments were as uncomfortable as the ones her bridesmaids had been forced to wear so that they'd look more like Miss Scarlett. Those seventeen-inch waistlines were a bitch.

Greta's mother gave a discreet sniff in her seat at the front of the church as Allie reached Josh's side and handed off her bouquet to Greta. Greta's mother had been sniffling for a week.

She must have gone through a case of Kleenex by now. Between sniffling and muttering "Lily would be so proud" every five minutes, her mother probably hadn't had time to notice the atrocity her daughter was wearing.

Greta studied Allie. She could swear her sister-in-law-to-be was swaying slightly. Granted, the bride had had one hell of a bachelorette party the night before, but she couldn't still be drunk. Could she? She looked really pale, too, so pale her makeup looked a little like a mask.

Josh leaned toward her, whispering. Probably sweet nothings, although judging from Josh's expression they were more likely to be sour nothings. Or worried nothings. Her brother looked sort of pale himself.

Greta had managed not to drink as much as the other bridesmaids the night before. It wasn't that she was trying to stay sober, but the stuff they were serving in that bar came in colors not found in nature. And she sort of remembered the bartender from elementary school. Being served drinks by the terror of the dodgeball court didn't strike her as a good idea.

Rev. Morgan cleared his throat. "Dearly beloved, we are gathered here today to unite this man and this woman in holy matrimony."

"Oh, hell no."

*What the fuck?* Greta swiveled toward the back of the room, along with everybody else in the church. She could approve of the sentiment in general but not when it was applied to her big brother's wedding in particular.

"*Gavin?*" Allie blurted.

Greta narrowed her eyes. She sort of recognized the guy standing in the aisle, but not exactly. He was from the harbor—that much she was sure of. Named Gavin, according to Allie-the-Even-More-Perfect. Probably the same age as Josh and

Allie, which made him too old for Greta to have hung out with in the past.

On the other hand, right now he looked a little like a refugee from the North Woods come to claim his mail-order bride. Beard, hair down to his collar, jeans, T-shirt, hoodie that was turning gray at the elbows. On second thought, he looked a lot like the Unabomber. Greta found herself edging discreetly to the side.

Josh's expression was somewhere between shock and fury. "This is *Gavin?*"

Allie gave a jerky nod.

"What do you think you're doing?" Josh snarled at the interloper.

*Oh come on, it's obvious what he's doing. He's breaking up your wedding.* Greta studied the Unabomber wannabe more carefully. Maybe the guy was another marriage survivor trying to stamp out the whole practice. Or maybe he'd been left off the invitation list. Hell, if that was the problem, Greta would gladly have given him her own.

"I'm here to talk to Allie."

Greta took another look at the North Woods refugee. Much as she loved her brother, she had to admit this Gavin had a certain...something. Which, of course, made his current actions even worse. Hunky guys were supposed to move on to the next girl instead of moving in on someone who was already taken.

Josh stepped between his fiancée and his competition. "We're kind of in the middle of something."

"Yeah, this can't wait." Gavin looked past Josh to Allie. "I need to talk to you. Now."

Allie's eyes were wide and she looked even more pale. Faint-at-any-moment pale. Greta stiffened. If Allie fainted, whose responsibility was it to catch her? Greta's own hands were currently full of two bouquets. She wondered if she could toss them to one of the other bridesmaids in time to keep her almost-sister-in-law from hitting the floor.

On the other hand, given how much Allie had had to drink the night before, there was also a very good chance she might be throwing up soon. Greta really considered taking care of that to be somebody else's responsibility. This wasn't anything she'd seen discussed in the various wedding guides she'd consulted before her own little trip down the Aisle Straight to Heartbreak. Nobody had said the matron of honor was in charge of cleaning up after the bride's mistakes.

Gavin started toward Allie, but Josh moved to block him. "I don't think so, Gavin."

Greta relaxed. At least one of the guys could catch the fainting bride if worse came to worst. And wherever Allie might be throwing up, it wouldn't be anywhere near Greta. She went back to studying Gavin-the-interloper. Definitely hunky. He seemed to have that whole tough guy with a heart of gold thing going. The opposite of her ex, the shifty guy whose heart was actually made out of polystyrene.

She glanced at the front pews. Her mother had dropped her Kleenex for once. Her bright blue eyes were wide, her red lips pursed in a grimace. Greta guessed this wasn't her idea of proper wedding procedure. She widened her survey to include the rest of the church. Holy crap, people were actually taking pictures of this fiasco. It looked like they were all going to end up on the Internet. Once this video hit YouTube, it should go viral in a matter of seconds.

"Listen, I can do this here in front of the whole town. I don't mind. I'm leaving here with Allie one way or another. But I think keeping some of this private might be appropriate." Gavin leaned around Josh to look at Allie. "I have some things I need to say before you say I do to another man, Al."

So now he wanted privacy? After stomping down the aisle in front of the entire population of the harbor? Well, at least no one could suggest the guy didn't have a pair, probably brass-plated too.

Josh sighed, lowering his own voice so that only the people at the front of the church could hear. "Don't do this, Gavin. Haven't you messed with her enough? Just let her be happy."

"That's exactly what I want to do. Is that what *you* want?"

"I'm standing next to her in a tux in front of a minister. What do you think?"

Greta half expected them to whip out their junk for a quick comparison. The wedding was rapidly descending into a shouting match.

"I think that if you don't let her talk to me, you know that she'll always wonder. You don't want that, do you? To have your wife wondering about another man?"

*Good question, actually.* Greta shifted the bride's bouquet to her other hand so that she could move a little closer. This was better than Lifetime. Who knew her brother's life had this much drama? Josh had always been Mr. Responsible, Pride of the Brewsters. He never screwed up. It was a rule. And now it looked like his life was headed south, not unlike Greta's.

She tried to dredge up some sense of outrage over Gavin Whatever His Name Was and failed completely. She'd had a suspicion Josh and Allie weren't all that right for each other to begin with, their personal perfection notwithstanding. They were affectionate enough, but not...hot. Not can't-wait-to-tear-your-clothes-off passionate. Of course, who was she to talk about passionate? She'd practically had to make an appointment for sex with Ryan.

Watching Allie chug a ridiculous number of really awful drinks the night before had cemented her impression—Allie just wasn't behaving the way a full-on, joyous bride should behave. Of course, that could have been because Allie was a lot more level-headed than Greta herself had ever been. You'd never see her running into something like a bad marriage. Except now it seemed like she had. Maybe Greta and her sister-in-law-to-be had more in common than she'd ever realized.

Josh blew out a long breath and shoved his hand through his hair. Greta wondered if she'd ever seen him look that frustrated before. Then he half turned toward his fiancée. "Allie?"

Allie turned toward Gavin the Hunk. She looked like she was trying to gather her wandering thoughts together again. "What would I wonder?"

"You'd wonder what I had to say to you so badly that I would fly over four thousand miles so I could rush in here to stop your wedding."

Allie stared at him for a very long moment, then shifted her gaze to the congregation that waited breathlessly for whatever the hell she was planning to say. There wasn't a sound in the church beyond the occasional snap of a camera shutter. Greta repressed the urge to scratch at her crinoline again.

"Allie?" The Hunk looked faintly worried.

"You're too late," Allie whispered.

Greta took a closer look at her almost-sister-in-law. She still looked immaculate, although slightly green around the edges—still more than perfect. But there were tears in her eyes. *Well, crap.*

In Greta's considered opinion, Josh was toast.

"Bullshit," Gavin Whoever He Was said. He stepped forward, dodging around Josh, bent and scooped Allie into his

15

arms, then headed for the side door, looking sort of like Rhett carrying Scarlett up those stairs. Bernice Cabot was probably ecstatic.

"Gavin!" Allie gave a couple of halfhearted kicks, but he seemed to have tightened his hold.

"Just a damn minute—" Josh started.

"Give me a chance," Gavin said, turning back again. "Let me talk to her. Let me tell her what I came here to say. Then if she wants to come back, I'll walk her down the aisle myself."

*And leprechauns will sing while unicorns frolic in the ferns.* That was probably the single most outrageous request Greta had ever heard somebody make at a wedding. It was also probably a mark of her own attitude toward marriage that it didn't seem that far out of bounds.

*Sure. Go off for a trial honeymoon with somebody else. If it doesn't work out, you can always come back for a second try with groom number one.*

On the other hand, the Hunkster was clearly delusional. Did he really think Josh would wait around while another guy made a pitch to his fiancée, and then take her back, no questions asked? Did Allie think that? Did anybody but the Hunkster really believe this was a workable idea? Greta leaned forward to see what would happen next, balancing the bouquets on her hip.

Josh stared at Allie, who had stopped struggling for the moment. Greta stole a glance at her mother. Her face was rigid with shock, the hand with the Kleenex curved into a fist at her side. *Terrific.* Greta had a feeling she'd be doing damage control with Mom as soon as this was over.

Gavin the Hunk murmured something in Allie's ear. In this case, it probably *was* sweet nothings, given the faint smile that drifted across her lips as she whispered something back.

Josh took a breath to say something else, but the Hunkster apparently felt the same way Greta did about the whole scene. Time for it to be over. He turned and strode toward the side door of the sanctuary, Josh's fiancée still cuddled in his arms. Mrs. Gurney, the pianist, obligingly opened the door for him— Greta figured she could kiss her wedding music fee good-bye.

The moment seemed to hang suspended in silence. Josh stared after his fiancée. Greta's mother stared after her future daughter-in-law. Or the woman who had been her future daughter-in-law until five minutes ago. At the moment, the prospect of Allie and Josh ever getting married seemed pretty remote.

Then Josh turned and stomped after them, throwing the door wide without Mrs. Gurney's help. Greta hurried after him, the two bouquets still clutched in her hands. Behind her the cell phone cameras clicked away, apparently recording every moment of this debacle for future reference. Greta managed to refrain from whirling back to flip off the photographers. She figured that would only make things worse.

Greta heard Josh cry "Wait," as she opened the door.

The Hunkster turned on the sidewalk outside the church, Allie still cradled in his arms while Josh strode near them, glowering. Greta wasn't sure she'd ever seen her brother glower before.

Josh balled his hands into fists at his sides. "What the fuck, Allie? Are you leaving with him?"

Gavin narrowed his eyes. "Allie called me last night."

Greta blinked. *Well, hell.* As the matron of honor she should probably have confiscated Allie's phone. But who knew she had that in mind? Most brides-to-be drunk-dialed the guy they wanted to yell *nyah, nyah, nyah* at, not the guy they wanted to have carry them up the aisle. The fact that Allie even

17

had someone she wanted to carry her up the aisle was maybe an indication that the wedding itself wasn't such a great idea.

Josh straightened, staring at Allie. "You did?"

Allie squeaked. She was losing perfection points by the second.

Gavin Whoever squared his already-square jaw. "She called and told me that she'd always love me."

*Oh, way to rub it in, Hunkster.* Now Allie groaned, closing her eyes. Greta had the feeling a groan or two wouldn't be enough to make her brother back off.

Josh folded his arms across his chest. "Allie? Is this true?"

There was another of those long pauses. "Well..." Allie murmured.

Josh shook his head. "Jesus Christ. Were you drunk?" He sounded like he was gritting his teeth.

"Maybe a little."

*A little?* Oh, Allie was losing those perfection points right and left now.

"You called Gavin the night before our wedding and told him you'd always love him?" Josh was staring at her as if he'd never seen her before.

Allie licked her lips. "Not *exactly*," she said. "I didn't tell him to come or anything. I didn't *say* that I loved him."

"Allie. We're getting married," Josh said flatly. "You don't just change your mind at the last second about something like this."

"I'm sorry," she whispered.

*Right.* Greta wasn't a lawyer, but she had a feeling that defense wasn't going to fly.

"That's all I need to hear." The Hunkster tightened his grip on Allie again, then headed down the sidewalk.

Greta pressed her lips together, watching a muscle dance in her brother's jaw. All of a sudden she really wanted this to be over. *Let it go. Just let it go.* She swallowed. Even with her own hard-won cynicism about marriage, it would be tough to top the last ten minutes in terms of marriage disasters.

Behind her, she heard someone catch her breath. *Great.* Apparently, she hadn't been the only one to follow them out of the church. Greta pivoted quickly—ready to tell whoever it was to go back inside and shut the hell up—and saw Devon Grant, Josh's ex, standing a few feet away.

Only judging from the way she was looking at Josh right now, she wasn't all that ex after all. Her dark brown eyes were wide, and she chewed on her lower lip as she watched the drama unfold in front of her.

Greta took another in a series of deep breaths. This was getting way too complicated anyway. She turned and slipped back inside the church. Let them figure it out for themselves— she was totally done.

Her mother stood in the middle of the aisle. Her lace fascinator had shifted forward over one eye and her navy taffeta was definitely showing creases. Greta figured if Mom had had an RPG, Gavin Whoever would be a grease spot by now.

She raised an eyebrow at Greta. Greta shook her head. The muscle in Mom's jaw danced like just like the one in Josh's jaw.

The noise level in the church grew to deafening. Then Mom pushed her fascinator back into place, her lips narrowing to a very thin line, like a general preparing to lead her troops on a suicide charge. She turned to the wedding guests, clapping her hands for attention.

"All right, everybody," she called. "There's food at the Promise Harbor Inn. It's all paid for. Go on and enjoy yourselves. There's no reason everybody has to have their day ruined. I feel a headache coming on."

She raised her head, surveying the crowd imperiously, then swiveled on her heel toward the same side door everybody else had used, throwing it open and then slamming it behind her without looking back.

As the noise level in the room rose to deafening again, Greta stared down at the bridal bouquet still clutched in her hands, wondering exactly what she was supposed to do with it. If she threw it to the crowd, would the person who caught it be the next one to have a traumatic breakup? Probably best not to find out.

She knelt and placed the bouquet in front of the altar, sort of like an offering, although she wasn't sure who it would be an offering to. Maybe the god of chaos.

Then she straightened again, glancing at the door where her mother, brother, prospective sister-in-law and various significant others had just disappeared. She had no intention of following them. Whatever was happening outside wasn't anything she wanted to be a part of.

And this probably wasn't the best time to break the news to her mother about her own divorce.

# Chapter Two

The room at the Promise Harbor Inn where the wedding reception was supposed to take place struck Greta as sort of downscale. It didn't face the water, for one thing. The windows had a great view of the parking lot at the inn—nicely landscaped, to be sure, but not exactly scenic. Still, there was a lot of food, including a fantasy wedding cake with lavender spun-sugar flowers. She gave it a quick critical survey. A little overdecorated, but okay. Sort of par for the course. Wedding cakes were definitely not her specialty.

She wondered if they could get a refund on the thing since nobody was going to be cutting it. Maybe the baker could sell it to a bargain-minded couple who didn't mind a little bad karma.

All around her she could hear the muttering of gossip moving into overdrive.

"Well, you knew about her and Gavin Montgomery, didn't you? Went on for years, I hear. I'm just surprised he had the nerve to show up at all."

The woman in the flowered dress looked vaguely familiar, in the same way most of the people in the room did—maybe a librarian, or somebody who worked in the post office. Right now, of course, she looked like the organizer of a lynch mob.

"Worked out for him, though, didn't it? Must have known she wasn't going to go through with it."

That sounded like Mrs. Grossblatt, from the insurance agency. Not that they were alone in saying what they were saying. Phrases floated by right and left.

"...must have been seeing him all along..."

"...always thought there was something wrong..."

"...kidnapped her right from the church..."

"...boy was always a bad seed..."

"...heard the law was after him for abduction—Hayley Stone..."

"...Lily must be rolling in her grave..."

"...poor Josh..."

"...poor Sophie..."

*Poor Greta.* She made a quick survey of the room, hoping against hope that her mother might have decided to show up after all. No luck, of course. The only family member she saw in the place was Allie's brother Charlie, propped in a corner with a beer and the kind of expression meant to discourage anyone from talking to him.

Greta had no intention of talking to him herself. In fact, she had every intention of sliding out the door again as soon as possible. She'd started edging in that direction when someone clutched her arm so tightly she worried about her circulation. She turned to see Mrs. Terwilliger from the grocery staring up at her with sharp black eyes, looking a little like a magpie.

"How's your mother Sophie holding up, dear?" Greta could swear she was salivating.

*You mean as opposed to my mother Tatiana?* "I haven't talked to her since the ceremony. I was heading there now." Greta tried to pull her arm loose from Mrs. Terwilliger's grip, but the woman hung on like an embedded barnacle.

"I'm sure she's just devastated. And your poor brother?

What an awful thing to have happen on your wedding day. He must be sick." Mrs. Terwilliger's fingernails dug a little deeper into Greta's arm.

Greta managed a thin-lipped smile. "No doubt. I'm just on my way…"

"So did anyone see it coming? I mean, Josh must have known about Allie and that Gavin Montgomery, didn't he? Did he know they were still seeing each other? They must have been, don't you think?" Mrs. Terwilliger's eyes snapped even brighter. She was moving from magpie to vulture.

Greta picked up her pace slightly as she headed for the door, dragging Mrs. Terwilliger along with her. "I really don't know anything about it."

"So did she tell him it was all over between her and Gavin? Looks like that wasn't exactly true, was it? Unless you think he kidnapped her?"

Greta could see the open door in front of her. She turned quickly, letting the full force of the Crinoline from Hell hit Mrs. Terwilliger in the knees. Mrs. Terwilliger jumped back with a squawk, dropping her arm.

"Sorry." Greta smiled at her sweetly. "Happy hunting. Or whatever it is you're doing." She turned and marched through the door, Mrs. Terwilliger's outraged "Well, I never" echoing in her ears.

Greta figured she probably wasn't doing much to shore up her reputation as a responsible person, but at that point her reputation was the least of her worries. She gathered up her skirt and trotted down the hall, doing her best to avoid all the people trying to get her attention. Bernice Cabot was stationed outside the door to the suite where Allie had gotten dressed, her arms folded across her more-than-ample bosom. The flounce around her shoulders could have served as a handy snack tray.

"Is Allie in there?" Greta nodded toward the suite.

Bernice shook her head. "I don't know where they went. I just thought somebody ought to keep the vultures from getting in."

"Sounds like a plan." Greta sighed. "Have you seen my mother?"

Bernice shrugged. "Maybe she went home."

"Maybe so."

Greta reversed course and headed for the parking lot, pausing only at the bridesmaids' room to grab the small purse that had her cell phone, her wallet, and her car keys. Going home made a certain amount of sense, although it meant she and her mother would be fending off all the Mrs. Terwilligers in Promise Harbor who managed to drop by and share whatever juicy details they'd been able to manufacture during the last half hour. She really should go home to help. Her mother shouldn't have to fight off the town gossips all by herself.

She climbed into her car, stuffing her skirt and crinolines around her like packing noodles. Her first order of business once she got back to her room at home would be to strip this monstrosity off and drop it in the largest trash can her mother owned. And after that, she would never, ever agree to be someone's bridesmaid again.

Which should be easy enough, given that she would never, ever be around another wedding. If pressed, she could always claim that chiffon gave her hives. Not that the most ghastly bridesmaid's dress in the history of mankind was made of actual chiffon. More like some fabric manufactured in the bowels of a cut-rate chemical company.

She turned the corner and pulled her car to the curb, studying the house where she'd grown up. The house that probably held a major complement of nosy neighbors at the moment. White clapboard, complete with gables and a wide front porch. It looked like her mother had gotten the shutters painted. The black lacquer shone in the sun. Probably trying to get the house fixed up for the wedding.

Greta closed her eyes, leaning forward to rest her forehead against the steering wheel. The Wedding That Wasn't. Her mother had spent so much time and energy on planning this wedding, and now it looked like she'd spent at least a fair amount of money too. All for nothing.

Her mother had sounded depressed for the year or so after Greta's father died, and she'd been worse when her best friend, Lily, Allie's mother, had died too. The wedding had definitely perked her up. Greta only hoped the unplanned elopement didn't send her back down again.

She turned her head and glanced at the driveway. Her mother's Volvo was parked next to the house, with two other cars behind it. One she didn't recognize, but the other was Owen Ralston's car. Allie's dad. *Great.* Well, at least they'd have something to talk about. And maybe Owen could help fend off the more aggressive gossips before they made her mother say something she might actually regret. Owen would be a lot better at doing that than Greta would be. He was, after all, a very nice man, while Greta had a long history of saying the regrettable.

She rubbed a hand across the back of her neck, staring at the front door. She should go in. She really should. Even though she couldn't think of anything she could do or say that would make her mother feel better. Even though her track record in terms of comfort or problem solving was spotty at best. Even though she would, at some point, have to drop yet another massive helping of crap in her mother's lap when she finally got around to explaining her own marriage, meaning, of course, her own divorce.

*Damn you, Ryan. This is all your fault.* Greta knew saying that was illogical, but it still made her feel better. At this point she was willing to blame Ryan for just about anything short of the Great Train Robbery.

*And Dorothy too*, she threw in. Oh yes, most especially Dorothy too.

She leaned back in her seat again, turning the key in the ignition. Really, she wasn't ready to go into that house with her mom and Owen and the neighbors and then give her mother another set of problems to deal with. Maybe later, like say tomorrow. She'd get around to it. She really would.

She turned the car toward the outskirts of the harbor, heading for Highway 1. Maybe an hour spent walking along the cliffs would help clear her head. And maybe when she went back, she'd have found a way to explain it all rationally to her mom.

*Yeah, right, Greta. Just like you always do.*


Hank Mitchell looked down at his foot, still wedged tight, still unmovable. The rocks in that part of the wall had looked sturdy enough when he'd stepped on them. By the time he'd realized how unsturdy they really were, and how ready they were to crumble under his weight, it was too late to jump back. He'd already tried pulling his foot out of his shoe, but the rocks on either side were squeezed too tightly to get it loose.

*Okay, how many times over the years did you tell the interns never to go to a dig alone?* Not enough times to drill it into his own thick skull, apparently. Now he stood at the base of a three-foot wall, the possible remains of a Wampanoag settlement, his foot jammed tightly in the midst of some Wampanoag rocks that had crumbled when he'd stepped in the wrong place. He didn't have the right angle to pry the rocks apart, and he didn't have any tools that might make it easier.

If he were a superstitious man, he'd say the Wampanoags were having their revenge on him. If so, they were doing a damned good job of it.

He checked around the dig one more time, hoping against hope that something might have changed in the three minutes since he'd last looked and that he'd find some kind of tool he could use to pry himself loose. His notebook and cell phone still sat where he'd left them next to the ladder, thoroughly out of reach, along with his trowel and his pick. He might try lying down full length to see if he could touch them, but he was guessing his knees wouldn't exactly bend in that direction.

Surely the sisters would miss him at some point. Even if Alice didn't, surely it would occur to Nadia that he hadn't been around when he should have been. Surely they'd call the cops to at least check on him. Of course, he didn't exactly have a regular schedule at Casa Dubrovnik. They might not even notice he hadn't come home until he'd been missing for a couple of days.

He'd get very hungry in two days, not to mention thirsty. At least the five-foot depth of the excavation would keep him from getting chilled by the wind.

Unless it rained. As it had regularly for the past month.

Hank sighed. He was possibly going to die here. At the very least he was going to get hungry, thirsty and probably wet. And it was all the result of his own idiocy, which made the whole thing that much worse. Alice would probably say she'd told him so, although he was fairly certain even her wide-ranging complaints had never covered this particular situation.

He tensed. For a moment, he could have sworn he'd heard something rustling. Probably a rabbit or something in the underbrush. And he couldn't think of any way to use a rabbit to rescue himself.

He paused, listening again. The rustling seemed more persistent than a rabbit, and it was coming closer. He ran through a quick list of large animals found in the Massachusetts woods. Bears and moose were possible, but unlikely. Coyotes were more likely but not particularly worrisome unless they decided he was easy pickings. Chances were it was some other kind of animal, though. Maybe a fox or a wild turkey.

By now he was curious enough about the source of the noise to try craning his neck so he could see above the edge of the excavation. Besides, a passing wild turkey would provide a little momentary distraction from his numb foot still wedged in the rocks.

For a moment, he thought he saw someone moving along the trail at the edge of the trees, a flash of color in the darkening underbrush. Hank blinked. The dig was clearly marked with *Danger* and *No Trespassing* signs. He'd wanted to put up a fence, but the state authorities had overruled him. Still, nobody was supposed to be back here. Unfortunately.

But if somebody was, they could at least pull him out of this hole. "Hello?" he called. "Anybody there?"

The rustling stopped for a moment, and then began again, coming closer this time. Hank strained to see beyond the top edge of the excavation. "Be careful," he called. "There's an excavation back here."

What he saw next almost convinced him he was hallucinating. The woman was dressed like something out of a movie: a huge bell-shaped skirt covered with ruffles, a wide sash at the waist, a low-cut neckline that stretched across her shoulders and revealed what looked to be more-than-respectable breasts. After a moment, she knelt at the edge, peering down at him, and he saw short, brownish hair and dark eyes. "Hi," she said.

"Hi." He took a quick breath, hoping to god she was real and not a particularly bizarre dream. "Could you possibly come down here and give me a hand? I'm stuck."

Her forehead furrowed slightly. "Possibly. What do you need exactly?"

"My foot's wedged in here." He pointed to his foot, still jammed between the two large rocks. "Maybe you could help me pull the rocks apart so I could get loose."

She frowned, considering. "How about just taking your shoe off?"

He shook his head. "I tried that. It's too tight. I can't get my foot out of the shoe."

"Oh." She was still frowning. "Okay, just a minute." She disappeared from the edge, and for a moment he was unreasonably afraid she'd gone. Then he saw the bell-shaped skirt at the top of the ladder. "Hang on. This may take a while," she said cheerfully. "This skirt isn't exactly made for climbing up and down ladders."

"That's okay. Take your time. Don't hurt yourself." He leaned back slightly against the side of the excavation. He still wasn't entirely sure he wasn't hallucinating, but at least it was more entertaining than standing there wondering if he could amputate his own foot with his pocketknife.

He watched the huge green skirt floating slowly down the ladder. Given the half of the girl he could see from the waist up, he assumed there were legs and a rear end under there somewhere, but there was no telling from what he could see currently. She looked a little like one of those dolls that had only a cone underneath the costume. He'd given one of those to his niece for Christmas a couple of years ago.

*Focus, Mitchell. Not the time to let your mind go wandering.* Maybe he really was hallucinating after all.

The girl in the green dress reached the bottom of the ladder, lifting up her skirt to step free. She was wearing white running shoes, he noted. Good thing, too. She probably couldn't have gotten down that ladder if she'd had to worry about her shoes along with her skirt.

She gave him a bright smile, pushing her bangs out of her eyes. "Now what?"

"My foot's sort of wedged in here at the base of the wall. Maybe you could push the rocks on one side and I could lead over to push on the other. I don't have enough leverage to do it all myself." In point of fact, he didn't have any leverage at all since he could barely reach the rocks as it was.

The girl frowned again. "Let me give it a try." She bent down at his feet, giving him a great view of her cleavage.

*Jesus, Mitchell, she's trying to help you. Do not ogle her.*

He tried to bend down too, dodging to avoid her when she raised her head suddenly.

"Look, just stay standing up, okay? There's not really room for you to bend down here too." She gave him a quick smile, then ducked her head again. "Am I right that you'd rather not have me do anything that would pull the wall down as we get your foot out?"

Hank closed his eyes for a moment. Two years of work gone in a jumble of stone. "That would be a big yes."

"Okay then, just relax. I should have this done in…" She leaned over further, doing something mysterious with the rocks that involved a lot of pushing. The neckline of her dress dipped dangerously. Hank forced himself to study the clouds.

"What is this place anyway?" she asked in a muffled voice.

"It's an ancient village. Fourteenth or fifteenth century."

"And the people who lived here built the wall?"

He shrugged. "Maybe. It's not entirely clear if the wall was part of the settlement or if it came later. Some of the caves around here were used for root cellars, and they may have been used for other purposes earlier than..."

"Got it!" she cried, and Hank staggered backward as the pressure on his foot was suddenly released.

"Whoa." She jumped to her feet, grabbing him by the arms to keep him from collapsing entirely.

"It's all right. I'm all right. Thank you." He started to step back again as she let go, but when he put his weight on the foot that had just been freed, the sudden surge of agony sent him to his knees. He repeated most of his extensive collection of obscenities before looking up to see her watching him with a faintly quizzical expression.

"I gather it hurts."

He nodded, drawing in a deep breath.

"Let me see. You might have broken it." She bent down to look at his foot, as if she could see the bone structure through his shoe. Maybe she had X-ray vision.

Hank shook his head. "I don't think so. I think it's just bruised. Or maybe sprained. Anyway, I don't think I can put much weight on it." He glanced at the ladder. The extremely short ladder that he sometimes avoided altogether, jumping down into the excavation without bothering to climb. All of a sudden it looked way too tall.

The girl followed his glance. Then she looked back at him, forehead furrowed.

"It's okay," Hank soothed. "I can make it." He started to

push himself up again, trying not to put any weight on his foot. He didn't seem to be making much progress overall.

The girl wiped her hands on her gauzy green skirt, leaving a couple of dirty streaks. "All right, here's what we'll do. You start up the ladder first and I'll come along behind you. I should be able to push you up in front of me so you won't have to use your bad foot."

Hank considered the relative positions of their bodies in the particular maneuver she was suggesting. Could be interesting. On the other hand, given the very real possibility that he'd fall off the ladder and land on her, copping a feel was probably not high on either of their lists at the moment. He sighed. "Okay. Let's try it."

He put a hand on her shoulder so that she could help him to the bottom of the ladder, then rested his good foot on the lowest rung. "Ready?"

"Oh yeah." She grinned up at him.

He started to turn away, then turned back. "Wait, one question. What's your name?"

She paused for a moment, as if she had to think about it. "Greta Brewster." She stuck out a hand. "And you are?"

He shook her hand. "Hank Mitchell. Thanks for getting me out of the hole."

She grinned again. Very nice grin. Gave her a sort of pixie look with her short hair, now somewhat mussed from the whole foot-freeing business.

"I haven't gotten you all the way out yet," she said. "Thank me when we get the top of the hole."

"Right." He sighed, turning back to the ladder again. He figured there were worse things than having a strange woman's hands on his ass.

# Chapter Three

Greta wasn't sure why she felt so cheerful all of a sudden. She'd just boosted a complete stranger out of a hole by pushing his ass up a ladder. Not exactly how she'd expected to spend her afternoon, but really a lot better than hanging around the harbor, dodging her mother and listening to everybody sneer about her brother and his former fiancée.

And for once it looked like following her impulses had worked out—after all, she'd just rescued somebody.

Now the rescuee, one Hank Mitchell, sat on a pile of dirt at the top of the hole, catching his breath. He'd pretty much pulled himself out by hand while she pushed from behind, and he looked beat. He also looked fairly hot, even in his disheveled state. Sandy hair, green eyes, well-developed chest and arms, probably from digging that sizable hole she'd pushed him out of. Those muscles had come in very handy when it came to pulling himself up from the excavation.

Along with her own efforts, of course. Seldom had she encountered a situation in which having both hands on a man's ass was an entirely altruistic activity. But fun though the afternoon had been, it was probably time to wrap it up. "Do you have a car here?"

He nodded slowly, gesturing toward a clearing at the side. "A truck. Over there. I'm not sure I can drive it, though." He glanced down at his injured foot.

Greta frowned. He had a point. Working the accelerator and brake would be a bitch. "How far away is your house?"

"About five miles. I've got an apartment in Tompkins Corners."

She tried to remember if she'd ever heard of someplace called Tompkins Corners before. She was pretty sure she hadn't. "I could give you a ride over there if you think your truck will be okay here."

He shrugged. "Probably. Not too many people come walking through these woods." He gave her a questioning look.

"I was on my way to the shore," she said quickly. Of course, she had been going in exactly the wrong direction if that were the case, but she figured he didn't need to know that.

"Lucky for me you took a detour."

"Right." In reality, she had no idea why she'd pulled off the road when she did. Maybe it was the allure of all those *Danger* signs. Just one more confirmation of her lack of common sense. Although this time, that lack had been a good thing, at least for someone else.

"Are you sure you wouldn't like me to take you to the emergency room in Promise Harbor?" she asked. "Shouldn't you at least get your foot checked to make sure it isn't broken?"

He shook his head. "I'm pretty sure it's not broken. Putting some ice on it should be enough."

"Okay, then. Tompkins Corners it is." She pushed herself to her feet again, brushing leaves and twigs off the ruffled skirt. At least when she went back home she could get rid of the dress and change into something that didn't make her feel like a refugee from a stately homes tour.

She reached a hand in his direction, helping him stumble

to his feet again. Or to his foot, since only one seemed to be working at the moment.

He balanced uneasily, resting a hand on her shoulder. "If you don't mind my asking, why are you wearing that dress?"

"I don't mind your asking," she said. "I was a bridesmaid. This is my outfit. My car's over here." She wasn't sure why she didn't feel like explaining any more. Maybe she just didn't want to get into the details of the Wedding That Wasn't. It would be hard enough to explain it to the people who'd actually been there.

They worked their way through the forest at the edge of the parking lot, Hank Mitchell hopping along with her as his anchor. It was almost too bad no one had seen them. She'd be willing to bet the sight would have been memorable. Eventually, she got him settled in the passenger seat. "Where to?"

"Turn left at the end of the road. Tompkins Corners is about five miles down the highway."

"I've never heard of Tompkins Corners. Is it very big?"

He shrugged. "A few houses. A hotel and general store. I'm not sure how many people live there all told—probably a few more farmhouses back in the hills."

They drove in silence for a while. She couldn't tell if he was naturally quiet or if he was still in pain from his foot. As she turned onto the highway she glanced his way. His eyes were closed, his head resting on the back of the seat.

Okay, probably pain.

A few minutes later, she pulled up in front of the only building in Tompkins Corners that looked like it might be a hotel, a two-story wood structure that extended along the town's only stretch of sidewalk. The walls were badly in need of a paint job, but Greta thought the building had once been white. A broad front porch extended across the front with a row of wooden rockers. "Hank? Is this it?"

His eyes opened. Then he glanced out the window. "Oh yeah. This is Casa Dubrovnik."

Greta blinked. "Casa Dubrovnik? That's what the place is called?"

He shook his head. "Officially, it's the Hotel Grand. Unofficially, it's Casa Dubrovnik. Or it is to me, anyway." He opened the door, slowly extending his injured foot toward the drive.

"Hold on. Let me help." She hurried around to his side, leaning down so that he could rest a hand on her shoulder again. Thanks to her stupid flounced neckline, he probably had a great view of her cleavage, but then he'd also had a great view when she'd been freeing his foot. By now he'd probably seen enough to make an informed guess about the size of her boobs and to confirm for himself that they were all hers.

He clamped one hand on her shoulder, hopping along beside her again toward the door of the building. Now that they were closer she could see the faded *Hotel Grand* sign at one side of the door. A little farther down there was another sign that said *Tompkins Corners Grocery* over a second door.

She raised an eyebrow. "Is this two separate businesses?"

He shook his head. "The sisters own the general store too. There's an entrance from the hotel inside."

"The sisters?" She frowned. "You mean like nuns?"

Hank Mitchell grinned for probably the first time since she'd pulled his foot free from the rock wall. "No. Absolutely not. No nuns here."

Nice grin. Worth the wait.

The front door swung open suddenly and a small cyclone came barreling through. "Hank. For heaven's sake, what happened? How badly are you hurt? Should we send for a doctor? Alice, Alice, come here, Hank's been hurt!"

The cyclone stopped talking long enough for Greta to get a good look. She was maybe five foot two or so, with hair the color of tar. Whatever dye she'd been using shouldn't have been allowed on the market in Greta's opinion, considering the color of the clumps of curls around her ears. Her rounded body was compressed into a long, gypsy-style skirt in a sort of purple paisley with a white peasant blouse. A purple pashmina drifted down off her shoulder. Greta checked for hoop earrings, but apparently the woman hadn't gone quite that far into character. "Alice," she yelled again as she pushed the door open.

Inside, the place looked more like a hotel. A very old-fashioned hotel that hadn't been renovated in the past fifty years. A front desk was tucked into an alcove with a row of empty mailboxes behind it. A slightly mangy couch and even mangier easy chair were placed in the front of the room beside the window. The wood floor looked clean and the Persian carpet in front of the desk looked ready to be retired. Another large, dark room opened off to the side, and a flight of stairs curved off to the upper story in the corner.

"Alice!" the small woman yelled a third time.

"Nadia, I'm okay," Hank soothed. "I hurt my foot, but it's not serious. I'm pretty sure."

"You should still see a doctor." The small woman, Nadia, nodded her black curls decisively. "It might be more serious than you think."

"It might be, but I doubt it. There's no need to call Alice."

"Now, Hank, you don't—"

"What the hell is going on now?" The voice seemed to cut through their conversation like a chain saw.

The woman who stepped toward the front desk looked as if

she'd made a conscious effort to be as great a contrast to Nadia as possible. Her blue jeans were so faded they looked like the ones that cost several hundred dollars in Boston, although Greta was betting they hadn't looked that way when new. Her blue plaid flannel shirt was rolled up at the elbows, probably because it was a size too big for her bony shoulders. If her gray hair had ever been close to any kind of dye, the dye had apparently lost the battle.

She narrowed her eyes, studying the three people standing in front of her. "So? What's the matter with the bone digger here?"

"And a good afternoon to you too, Alice." Hank sighed. "I hurt my foot, but it's not a big deal. Everybody can go back to doing whatever they were doing before."

"Humph," Alice grunted. She turned her sharp black gaze on Greta. "What the hell are you dressed up for?"

"Wedding. Bridesmaid." Greta figured Alice might appreciate brevity.

Alice gave her a slightly evil grin. "Jesus. What did you do to the bride?"

Nadia turned loose of Hank and stepped forward. "Hank needs a doctor, Alice. We need to call over to Merton. Maybe even Promise Harbor."

Alice raised a gray eyebrow in Hank's direction. "You need a doctor, Mitchell?"

He shook his head. "I just need to get off my feet."

"You can't take his word for it. He's just like you—doesn't want anybody to make a fuss. Well, let me tell you, sometimes a fuss is necessary. He might be badly hurt and all you're thinking about is convenience." Nadia propped her fists on her hips, her pashmina sliding to her elbow.

"If I was thinking about convenience, I'd have stayed back in the kitchen. Where, incidentally, you should be if we're going to have any dinner to serve." Alice's chin rose as her eyes flashed dangerously.

Nadia gave a slight huff. "I'll have dinner on the table, don't you worry about that. When have I not had dinner on the table?"

Alice's smile turned slightly sour. "Well, there was last Tuesday, for starters."

"Last Tuesday, we had a wonderful dinner. The macaroni salad was delicious."

Alice's smile disappeared altogether. "The macaroni salad was from Stop and Shop, and there was barely enough of it to feed Hyacinth, let alone the rest of us. If you'd spend less time working on that damn computer—"

"That damn computer brings in more cash—"

They were standing close together now, their voices dropping to snarls. Greta had the feeling this particular discussion had been run through before. Probably several times. Hank shifted beside her, grimacing.

"You got a room here somewhere, Ace?" she asked.

He shrugged. "Upstairs to the left."

"Then let's get you up there." She braced his shoulder against hers, sliding her arm across his back, and turned him toward the stairs at the side. "I don't suppose there's an elevator?"

He shook his head. "You're kidding, right?"

Behind them, the argument was beginning to pick up steam. "It's damn foolishness," Alice declared.

"You just think that because you don't—"

"Come on." Greta moved toward the stairs, waiting until

Hank had his hand on the banister, and then started to climb.

It took them around five minutes, all told, to go up the short flight of stairs to the landing, then turn to go up the next short flight to the second floor. By the time they got to the top, Hank was panting.

Greta glanced up at his face. He might have turned slightly pale. "You okay?"

He nodded. "Sure. It's the door on the end on this side."

The narrow hall had three doors on each side. Hank did the same supported hop to the end, then fumbled in his pocket until he pulled out a key. "Sorry about the state of the room. I wasn't expecting company." He pushed the door open and hopped inside.

Greta blinked. She'd been expecting a cubbyhole, but the room was surprisingly large. Late afternoon sunshine streamed through a bay window onto the papers and journals piled in front of the couch. A couple of rocks were placed on the coffee table, apparently for inspection, and some desiccated plants were tucked into jars on the windowsill. On the other hand, the bed in the far alcove was made, and she didn't see any dirty underwear.

Hank sank into the easy chair opposite the couch, extending his foot in front of him with a groan.

She glanced around the room again. There was a door on the far wall, probably the bathroom. At least he didn't have to share it with other, apparently nonexistent, tenants. "Got aspirin?"

He nodded. "In the bathroom."

"Got anything stronger?"

His eyebrows went up.

She grimaced. "I'm talking painkillers here. I'm not sure

aspirin is going to be enough to deal with that foot."

He sighed, shaking his head. "Aspirin is it."

The bathroom was Spartan, but at least it had a shower. There was a leather Dopp kit on top of the toilet. Greta picked through it gingerly, hoping she'd find the aspirin before she found anything really embarrassing, assuming Hank owned anything in that category.

She found the aspirin bottle and then filled a glass with water.

Hank was still as she'd left him, eyes closed, head back against the chair. The shadows picked out his finely sculpted cheekbones and the squarish lines of his jaw.

She placed the aspirin and water on the coffee table next to the rocks, then knelt in front of him. "Okay, Ace, we should probably take your boot off now. Do you want painkillers before, after or during?"

"How about all of the above," he mumbled. His jaw flexed tight.

Greta placed two aspirin and the glass in his hand, then bent to his feet, unlacing the battered work boot.

Hank managed to stay quiet until she pulled the boot off his heel. Then he moaned. "Ah, shit."

"Okay," she said hurriedly, "the worst's over." *I hope.*

She carefully pulled down the heavy sock, revealing a bright red foot with bruises beginning to appear on the sides. She sucked in a breath, managing not to comment on just how bad it looked.

Hank pushed himself up in his chair, staring down at the swollen surface that showed signs of darkening to purple. "Well, that sucks."

"Are you sure you don't want a doctor?"

He nodded. "I'm pretty sure it's not broken. And I'm pretty sure I don't have enough energy to get back in your car to drive to Promise Harbor."

"Okay. Do you want something to drink? I'm assuming the people downstairs might have something you could use."

"Nadia will have something. Alice will charge for it. Tell them to put it on my bill." He sank back in his chair.

"Are they sisters?"

He gave her a tired smile. "Sorry. I should have introduced you down there. Nadia and Alice Dubrovnik. Alice owns the hotel and general store. Nadia cooks. Sort of."

"Sounds ominous."

"Believe me, it's a lot more ominous than it sounds." He smiled again. "I didn't thank you for getting me here. Hell, if it hadn't been for you, I'd probably still be at the bottom of that hole."

His eyes were a dark green in the fading afternoon. The last rays of sunlight picked out flecks of gold beard stubble on his cheeks.

"My pleasure." Her breasts felt heavy suddenly, tingling. There was a faint jolt of heat in her stomach. Apparently her body was waking up after her long, post-separation drought. Time to move on.

"So anyway," she said quickly, "I'll go downstairs and see if I can get you a Coke or something."

"Or something," he murmured, closing his eyes. "Tell Nadia I want some of her lemonade. She'll like that."

"Right." She pushed herself to her feet and headed for the hall. Downstairs, she could still hear the sound of raised voices. Maybe the sisters hadn't yet noticed they'd gone.

She rounded the landing and headed down the stairs just

as Nadia apparently reached the crescendo of her argument. "Alice, you don't understand and I don't think you ever will." She wrapped her pashmina around her shoulders and made a majestic turn toward a door behind the front desk, stopping dead when she saw Greta on the stairs. "Oh. My. I'm so sorry— we forgot all about Hank. Does he need anything?"

"He'd like a glass of lemonade." Greta grabbed a fistful of ruffled green skirt so that she could descend the rest of the way without breaking her neck. "He said to put it on his bill."

Nadia grimaced. "Don't be silly. We won't charge for his lemonade."

"Oh yes we will," Alice said grimly. "Right now we charge for everything."

"Alice, don't be rude," Nadia snapped. She turned back to Greta. "Hank didn't introduce us, did he? I'm Nadia Dubrovnik, and this is my sister Alice." She gestured vaguely in Alice's direction. "I don't believe I got your name."

*I don't believe I threw it.* "Greta Brewster." She took Nadia's extended hand. "A pleasure."

Alice muttered something that sounded like "No it isn't," but they both ignored her.

"And how did you meet Hank?" Nadia smiled politely. "Was he at the wedding too?"

Greta blinked, trying to imagine Hank, in his dusty cargo pants and denim shirt, at any wedding she'd ever been to. "No. I found him in his excavation. His foot was stuck between some rocks. I helped him get out."

"Oh my, then you're a heroine," Nadia gushed. "We're so grateful to you for helping him. Hank is such a dear man. We're very fond of him."

"Seeing as how he's our only paying customer," Alice

muttered.

Nadia threw her an annoyed glance, then gathered the pashmina again. "I'll just go and get him his lemonade. Are you sure he doesn't need a doctor?"

Greta shrugged. "He says not."

"Well then, let's see if we can make him comfortable. I'll fix him something special for dinner."

"Oh, that'll perk him right up." Alice looked like she'd bitten into something sour.

Nadia threw her one more annoyed glance, then flounced through the door behind the front desk.

There was a long moment of silence while Alice and Greta studied each other. Then Alice shrugged. "You need a room for the night—Miss Whoever You Are? It's cheap, and it includes breakfast and dinner."

Greta paused to think about it. It was almost six thirty, but she could still drive back to Promise Harbor. She had nothing with her except a small purse with her cell, her credit cards, and about twenty bucks in cash. All the principles of logic told her to head back home.

But then, when had logic ever stood in her way before? Impulse was more her style when you got down to it.

"As I said before, my name is Greta Brewster. And yes, I'd like a room."

# Chapter Four

"Okay, then." Alice pulled out a battered hotel register as the door beside the front desk swung open again with a swish, apparently of its own accord.

"Grandma," a piping voice said, "Aunt Nadia wants to know how many dinners she should make."

Greta dropped her gaze. The child who stood just inside the door looked remarkably like an owl—brown T-shirt and shorts; short brown hair that framed a small, squarish face; huge, round glasses that made her eyes look several times normal size. She turned her gaze on Greta, looking almost as surprised as Greta herself probably did.

"Oh for Pete's sake, what does she mean, how many dinners?" Alice rested her hands on her hips, looking disgruntled. "Same number as always."

She glanced at Greta, then sighed. "On the other hand, we may have one more. Or one less. Is Hank going to be eating dinner?" She raised an eyebrow in Greta's direction.

Greta shook her head. "No idea. I can ask."

"Do that." Alice sighed again.

Greta turned and started back up the stairs.

"That's the most beautiful dress I've ever seen," the child blurted from behind her.

Greta wheeled around, staring. So did Alice.

The little girl regarded her with worshipful eyes. "You look like Cinderella. Or Belle in *Beauty and the Beast*."

"Oh." Greta stared down at her puke-green skirt, now ornamented with streaks of dirt from the excavation. Seldom had she felt less like a fairy-tale princess. "Thank you."

"I knew we shouldn't have gotten that damn DVD," Alice muttered.

"Aunt Nadia said I should give you this." The child extended one hand with a large glass filled with cloudy liquid that might have been lemonade.

Greta took it from her carefully. "I'll be right back," she said to Alice.

"Be still my heart."

Greta bunched her skirt in her fist again and climbed the stairs carefully, holding the glass of lemonade in front of her. She knocked lightly on Hank's door.

"Yeah."

He was still sitting where he had been when she'd left, but now his bruised foot was resting on the coffee table beside the rocks and his eyes were closed. She took a moment to study him. His sandy hair was mussed, and his foot was definitely ugly. He still looked yummy.

"I brought you your lemonade."

"Thanks." He didn't open his eyes as she placed it on the table beside his foot.

"And Alice wants to know if you're going to make it down for dinner."

He grimaced, opening his eyes to slits. "Nope."

"You want me to bring some up to you?" Greta rested her fists on her hips.

His eyes popped all the way open. "Christ, no!"

She blinked.

He sighed. "No. Look, I've got some peanut butter and crackers up here someplace. I'll just make myself a snack later."

"Okay. Um..." She tried to figure out exactly what she was supposed to say here as his apparently designated caregiver. "So how do you feel?"

He shrugged. "My foot hurts. Otherwise okay."

"Would some ice help?"

"Maybe." He shrugged again. "Look, just go have some dinner. Are you heading back to...wherever you were going before you ended up here?"

"Not exactly. I'll come check on you after dinner." She stepped quickly into the hall, closing the door behind her since she really didn't want to deal with the next logical question: *Why aren't you heading back to...wherever you were going before you ended up here?* She didn't really have an answer for that one at the moment. Whim?

She climbed down the stairs again, her skirt bunched in her hand. "Hank says no on dinner."

"His loss." Alice pushed the hotel register her way. The little girl had disappeared once again. "It's forty a night."

Greta opened her purse, digging out her credit card.

Alice narrowed her eyes, shaking her head. "Cash. Only."

Greta froze. "Is there an ATM around here?"

Alice gave her a dry smile. "What do you think?"

"I don't carry cash."

"Then I'd say you've got a problem."

Greta chewed on her lower lip. She could always head back to the harbor. And her mother. And the whole wedding disaster.

The idea of confronting that particular train wreck again made her head hurt. It would be so nice to have a couple of days without painful conversations, to say nothing of painful decisions.

Besides, Hank Mitchell needed her. Which was pretty much a total crock.

She looked down at her purse, wondering if she had anything worth bartering, assuming Alice believed in bartering, which wasn't necessarily likely.

She raised her head slowly. "Your granddaughter likes my dress."

"My granddaughter is nine years old." Alice folded her arms across her chest. "Her fashion sense isn't what you'd call infallible. Her name is Hyacinth, by the way."

Greta shrugged. "Nonetheless, she likes it. And it cost a lot of money."

Alice's brows went up. "You're offering me that dress to pay your rent?"

"Well, I—"

"Dinnertime," Nadia called gaily from the room at the side of the lobby. She switched on an overhead light that revealed a large dining room table made out of some dark wood. The chairs arranged around the sides had a faintly medieval look.

The little girl, Hyacinth, came through the door to the kitchen. "Aunt Nadia says come to dinner now while it's still hot." She skipped toward the dining room.

Alice grimaced. "We'll talk later."

"Right." Greta nodded.

The dining room looked like it had once served the hotel's guests. The table in the center of the room seated twelve, and another, smaller table near the window looked like it could hold five or six more. The medieval impression was reinforced by a dusty tapestry on the far wall that seemed to show a hunting scene or maybe a procession or possibly Valhalla. Distance and lousy lighting made it impossible to tell for sure.

Nadia stood next to the long table, smiling. A vase with bright red silk flowers sat in the middle, while flowered china plates were placed carefully at four of the chairs.

"Since we have a guest this evening, I thought we'd use the good china," Nadia trilled. "Why don't you sit here, dear." She gestured toward the chair across the table from Hyacinth, who sat poised, her folded hands resting in her lap.

Greta slid into place, beating the crinolines into submission, as Nadia disappeared through a door at the side. She reappeared almost immediately, bearing a platter of spaghetti and meatballs. "Hyacinth did the salad," she said, smiling.

Greta glanced at the pile of greens in the bowl next to her dinner plate.

"Dressing's on the table," Hyacinth murmured, nodding toward a couple of bottles at Alice's end.

Greta felt like sighing. Catalina and ranch, courtesy of Kraft Foods. Perfect.

"Eat up, everybody." Nadia placed the platter on the table and took her seat, unfolding her napkin with a flourish.

At one time in her life, Greta might have said that it was impossible to ruin spaghetti. Any dish where all you had to do was add boiling water should have been foolproof. Unless, of course, you were a sufficiently talented fool.

This particular version of spaghetti tasted like it had been boiled for a couple of hours. How it maintained its shape without collapsing into mush was a mystery. The sauce had probably begun as tomato soup augmented with ketchup. It

49

was hard to tell what it had originally tasted like, however, since it had been massively diluted with pasta water. The meatballs had so little actual meat that they could probably have bounced across the dining room, given a good shove.

After a few bites, Greta tried desperately to come up with a legitimate-sounding reason not to finish the rest of the plate. Alice was shoveling in bites of spaghetti with grim determination. Nadia sat at the head of the table, nibbling daintily. It looked like she'd given herself the smallest portion. Either she was being polite or she was being very smart.

Greta glanced across the table at Hyacinth and found herself nailed by a pair of huge, beseeching eyes. The child's plate was half-empty, and she was taking tiny bites of the rest.

Greta felt like sighing again. Why Hyacinth wanted her to finish her plate she wasn't sure, but the least she could do was accommodate her. She took three more bites of spaghetti, then concentrated on her salad. The lettuce was fresh and crunchy, and she'd been careful not to drown it in ranch dressing the way the sisters had. Between bites of salad, she managed to make it all the way through the incredible dreck on her plate.

Nadia touched her lips delicately with her napkin. "Who's ready for dessert?"

*Dessert?* The mind reeled. "I'm full," Greta said hastily.

"Nonsense." Nadia stood up, as Hyacinth collected their dirty plates. "We'll be right back, won't we, Hyacinth?"

Left alone in the dining room, Alice gave her a dry smile. "Having fun?"

"Loads."

Nadia reemerged from the kitchen, carrying a plate of brownies that she passed to Greta. "Fresh baked this afternoon. Enjoy."

Greta took a tentative nibble after passing the plate to Alice. She had to hand it to Nadia. Brownies were even harder to destroy than spaghetti, but she'd managed that too, mainly by burning them on the bottom. She could probably have managed to eat the tops alone, but Alice and Hyacinth were both taking sizable bites of their own brownies. Both of them must have developed cast-iron stomachs. Eating Nadia's food regularly would probably do that. Greta sighed and dug in.

Given that the brownies were smaller than the meatballs, they were finished more quickly. Greta managed an insincere smile. "Great meal. Thanks."

Nadia smiled serenely back. "You're welcome, dear. You should go up and check on Hank. Hyacinth and I will wash the dishes."

"We'll have our little talk first." Alice dropped her napkin on the table. "Care to join me at the desk?"

Greta gathered her skirts around her and headed back across the lobby to the front desk again.

Alice had the register open in front of her again. "As I recall, you were getting ready to offer me the clothes off your back."

"That was then," Greta said grimly.

Alice grimaced. "One meal and you're ready to head for the hills?"

"One meal and I'm ready to offer you something a hell of a lot more valuable than this atrocity of a dress." She leaned back, folding her arms across her ruffled chest.

"And that would be?"

"I'm a professional chef, a graduate of culinary school. I'll take over the cooking in exchange for room and board." That first statement fell into the "slightly shaky" category as far as being a professional chef went, assuming one was required to have actually worked in a kitchen to be considered professional. But at least Greta really was a graduate of culinary school. That much was accurate.

She didn't pause to wonder just when she'd decided to stay longer than overnight. But all of a sudden it seemed like a very appealing idea.

Alice's chin went up. "And why would I want to do that? I already have a chef."

"You have a cook. Sort of." Greta's smile was tight. "Wouldn't you prefer to have edible meals? Particularly when you could get them for free?"

Alice snorted. "It's not free. I'm giving up a room here."

"Yes, and that's undoubtedly a sacrifice. I mean, you've had so many guests clamoring for rooms since I got here with Hank." Greta gave her a level gaze.

Alice frowned. "I'm still not making money on this deal."

"I trained as a pastry chef." Greta allowed herself a faint smile. "I can make real brownies. From scratch. And chocolate chip cookies for Hyacinth."

Alice narrowed her eyes at her granddaughter's name, and Greta had to admit it was close to dirty pool bringing the child into it. But this was war. Sort of, anyway.

After a moment, Alice sighed. "What about the dress?"

"You can have it. Along with the underwear."

"You're going to cook naked?" Alice's eyes narrowed even further. "I'm not sure that's something Hyacinth needs to see."

"You have a general store there, right?" Greta nodded toward the door at the side that led into the shop next door, where she hadn't yet seen a single customer. "Got any jeans? T-shirts? Fruit of the Loom?"

"I'm going to be clothing you too?" Alice shook her head. "Look, before we go any further with this, I need to know—what exactly are you running from? I mean, is this a situation where the state police are going to show up on our doorstep tomorrow?"

Greta sighed. "I'm running away from a wedding disaster. And my mother, whom I'm not ready to face at the moment. No cops involved, so help me." Just the general population of Promise Harbor.

"So how long is this cooking arrangement going to last?"

She shrugged. "A week maybe. Call it a brief vacation."

Alice studied her a moment longer, then shook her head. "This probably qualifies as lunacy, but okay. Grab yourself some clothes from the store. There's not much there, but you can get the basics. I'll take it out of whatever pay you earn, if any. And I'll expect you to start cooking with breakfast tomorrow."

Greta headed toward the door. "Fair enough. Hyacinth really can have the dress and the petticoats."

"Right now all she could do would be to use them for a pup tent," Alice growled.

Greta shrugged. "Works for me."


An hour later, Greta unlocked the room across the hall from Hank. It was a little smaller, but at least it too had its own bath. She dumped the pile of jeans and T-shirts on the bed, along with a package of panties. Unfortunately, Alice's store didn't carry bras, so she'd either have to wash out the one she was wearing or do without. Given that the one she was wearing was one of the foundation garments doubling as torture devices that Bernice had supplied for the dress, she'd probably be going braless for the next week.

She started to drop her purse on the dresser, then opened it and took out her cell phone. She'd turned it off to save the battery. *Yeah, right, Greta.* After a moment, she turned it back on.

She checked the voice mail—nothing. Texts—nothing. Nice to know her absence had made such a dent in everyone's day.

Nine o'clock. Her mother might still be up. She started to punch in the number and then paused. What exactly would she say when her mother picked up? *Hi, Mom, I ran away because I couldn't bear to tell you your other kid's marriage is in the toilet too. I'll be back sometime. Don't wait up.*

Right. That would really work well. After a moment, she touched the text message icon, then the keyboard. *I'm all right,* she typed. *Don't worry.* Suitably vague but maybe enough to be reassuring. Her mother undoubtedly had other things on her mind at the moment. She turned the phone off again, dropping it back in her purse. Maybe one of the Dubrovniks had a charger she could borrow.

Or maybe Hank did. She paused, then stepped back into the hall again. A quick inspection showed no light under his door. Then again, he might be sitting in the dark. It was still relatively early. She knocked gently but got no response. After a moment, she opened his door.

Hank sat in his chair, head back, snoring faintly. His feet were stretched out in front of him. A plate on the coffee table held the remains of crackers and peanut butter.

She wondered if she should wake him and help him get to bed, then rejected the idea. She wasn't his mother, after all, and lugging him off to bed might seem like a bit much.

She studied his face for a moment. Good bones there. Not

exactly chiseled—more like sculpted. Skin slightly tan, probably from working in the sun. And that casually mussed, sandy hair, like he'd run his fingers through it.

She'd like to run her fingers through it too.

*Okay, Greta, time for bed. More than time, in fact.*

She turned back to the hall again, closing Hank's door softly behind her. If nothing else she was going to shuck off this dress and the Crinolines from Hell. And then she was never going to wear anything like them ever again.

# Chapter Five

It was the smell that woke Hank the next morning. He'd finally stumbled to his bed around one o'clock, vaguely disgruntled over the fact that Greta Brewster hadn't bothered to wake him to say good-bye, although he knew being disgruntled over that fact was stupid. Still. He'd hoped to get one more glimpse of those dark brown eyes before she sped back to wherever it was she came from.

Oddly enough, he didn't think she'd ever told him where she came from or where she was going during their adventures the day before. He knew it had something to do with a wedding, and judging from the dress, she and the bride hadn't been on the best of terms.

The buttery, sweet smell of something baking seeped up through the floorboards, reminding him his room was more or less over the kitchen. Of course, normally the smells that issued from the kitchen wouldn't have enticed him out of bed. They were more likely to make him put his head under his pillow.

He stood up cautiously, checking to see if his foot would bear his weight. Although he was fairly sure his foot wasn't broken, he wasn't absolutely certain and he didn't want to end up in a heap on the floor. Standing on his bruised foot was painful, but it was less so than yesterday. He could probably even make it to the dig if he wore loosely tied running shoes rather than his boots. It wouldn't be fun, but it would be doable.

After he had breakfast. Assuming that whatever he currently smelled turned out to be edible. With Nadia, you never knew. One fragrant concoction a few weeks ago had turned out to be a vat of hand cream she was getting ready to bottle.

He shuffled downstairs carefully, keeping most of his weight on his good foot. It seemed a little early for Nadia to be up, but the Dubrovniks were nothing if not unpredictable. Maybe she'd had some kind of inspiration during the night. He could only hope it had to do with actually learning to cook. Maybe she'd been visited by the ghost of Julia Child.

He headed through the dining room toward the kitchen door at the side. Odd that he didn't see anybody sitting at the dining table as he passed by. Nadia usually demanded that meals be served there, with china and silver. Maybe Alice had finally managed to convince her that meals eaten in the kitchen didn't result in the decline of Western civilization.

He pushed open the door to the kitchen and paused, transfixed.

Greta Brewster was taking a pan of what looked like muffins from the oven. She was wearing jeans and an oversize blue T-shirt that had *Tompkins Corners* splashed across the middle in red. Her feet were bare, and her hair looked slightly damp, as if she'd only recently stepped out of the shower.

She raised her head and caught sight of him, breaking into a sunny grin. "Morning. How's the foot?"

"Um...fine." He watched her walk across to the kitchen counter, where she placed the muffin pan on a trivet. Unless he was very much mistaken, she wasn't wearing a bra under that T-shirt.

He went hard almost instantly. *Well, crap.* Geez, it hadn't been that long since he'd been with a woman, had it? Apparently, the answer to that particular question was yes.

He sank into a chair at the sturdy oak table beneath the windows, covering his lap with a napkin. "So you're...staying?" He was still trying to find a polite way of asking what the hell she was doing in the kitchen.

"I am, yes." She gave him another grin. "Alice has hired me to cook. In exchange for room and board." She glanced down at her chest. "And clothes."

He narrowed his eyes. "I didn't realize you needed a job. Or clothes."

"I didn't exactly realize it myself. But here I am." Another grin. "Of course, the clothes thing was pretty obvious."

"Oh." He watched her upend the muffin tin on a plate. Suddenly he was salivating to go along with the whole sexual arousal thing. Interesting way to approach breakfast. "God, those smell great."

"Applesauce muffins," she explained. "Not exactly inspired, but I was stuck with what was in the pantry and the pantry doesn't have much. I'll troll through the general store today and see if there's anything better."

"Don't count on it," he muttered.

"Oh well, I saw a garden out back. Should be something I can scavenge out there." She brought the plate over to the table. "Eat up. There's coffee."

Nadia's coffee was sort of glorified dishwater. He regarded the pot with some suspicion. "What kind?"

She shrugged. "Supermarket generic. But I made it double strength. That usually helps. Let me pour you some. Rest your foot." She opened the cabinet next to the sink and pulled out a cup, then walked over to the automatic coffeemaker at the end of the counter. The coffeemaker that he suddenly noticed smelled really good.

She stood poised next to the counter, the cup in her hand. "Sugar? Cream?"

He shook his head and she set the cup on the table, followed almost immediately by a muffin on a plate. He tore off a small piece of pastry and placed it cautiously into his mouth. A month of Nadia's cooking had cured him of taking large bites of anything without first testing the waters.

He tasted apple and spice, cinnamon and a hint of something that might have been nutmeg. It was the best thing he'd tasted since he'd arrived in Tompkins Corners, but that wasn't saying much. Hell, it was probably one of the best things he'd tasted for a long time before that. Somehow he managed to keep himself from stuffing the entire muffin into his mouth in a single bite.

"This is really, really good," he mumbled around the crumbs.

"Thank you." She gave him a bright smile. "What else would you like?"

That particular question evoked a sudden flurry of lascivious images that he promptly suppressed. "This is fine. I'll just take another one to eat on the road."

She frowned. "You're going back to the excavation?"

"Sure." He shrugged. "We're behind now since I lost a day yesterday." Which was entirely his own fault, of course, although he didn't feel like bringing that up.

"But you're hurt. And what happens if you get stuck again?"

He grimaced. "Theoretically, I have an intern. Although he

didn't show up yesterday. With any luck, he'll show up today. Anyway, if I don't make it back by this evening, you can always come and rescue me again." He gave her a grin that was supposed to be winning but apparently wasn't.

Greta still frowned. "You shouldn't be out there by yourself."

"It's okay. Like I said, intern."

"Who didn't show up yesterday when you almost ended up spending the night in a hole." She rested her hands on her hips.

He sighed. "Look, it's a very small dig for which I have a very small grant that will run out at the end of the summer. I can't afford to lose a day because my foot hurts. I was stupid yesterday. I'll do my best not to be stupid again."

Greta rubbed her hand across her nose. She didn't seem to be wearing any makeup. It didn't make any difference. He still wanted to jump her.

One of her eyebrows arched up. "What if I bring you lunch?"

"Lunch?" He shook his head. "Alice doesn't provide lunch."

"So? I'm cooking. There'll probably be leftovers." She sat down beside him at the table. "Indulge me, okay? If I spend the day worrying about you out in that hole, it may affect my cooking." She gave him another of those grins, and his body once again went on high alert. *What the hell is it with this woman, anyway?*

He cleared his throat. "I wouldn't want anything to affect your cooking. Considering these muffins, I want to make sure your cooking works overtime."

She looked absurdly pleased. "Thank you. You're the first one to taste them. Hope everybody else feels the same way."

"I'd say that's more or less guaranteed." He started to push himself away from the table, then stopped, frowning. "Crap. I just remembered. I need a ride to the dig. I left my truck there yesterday."

"Can you drive it back by yourself?"

"Sure. Once I get there."

"If you can wait until everybody else gets up, I'll be glad to drive you. But I need to stick around to make sure they have everything they need."

"I can wait." In fact, he'd be glad to. He really wanted to see what happened when the Dubrovniks confronted edible food for a change.

As if summoned, the door to the Dubrovnik family living quarters swung open behind them. Hank couldn't see anyone, which told him immediately who it was. "Hey, Hyacinth."

The child approached the table somewhat warily. "Why are we eating in here instead of the dining room like we're supposed to? And where's Aunt Nadia?"

"I don't think she's up yet," Greta explained. "I just thought it was easier to eat in the kitchen, but I can set you up with a plate in the dining room if you'd like."

Hyacinth shook her head, climbing into a chair. "No ma'am. This is fine. What's for breakfast?" She sniffed the air cautiously, then with more enthusiasm.

"Muffins. And whatever else you'd like. Just tell me what you usually have."

"Usually?" Hyacinth gave her a contemplative stare. "Usually it's burned toast and cereal. Do I have to have that?"

Greta shook her head. "Definitely not. Would you like cereal? We can skip the toast since we have muffins."

"I'd rather just have a muffin." She began tearing one of them into decorous pieces, chewing them cautiously. After a moment the caution disappeared, and she reached for another muffin. She gave Greta a beatific, crumb-laden smile.

Greta smiled back. "Glad you like them. But I can still fix you some cereal or maybe some eggs if you want. And you need a glass of milk." She headed for the refrigerator while Hyacinth turned to Hank.

"Do you feel okay now?" she asked. "Aunt Nadia said you were sick."

"Sure. I'm fine." He smiled at her reassuringly and considered taking another muffin. There were only five left, though, and Alice and Nadia still weren't around.

The door swung open, and Alice walked in, iron-gray hair standing in stiff curls around her head. "What's that smell?"

"Muffins," Hyacinth and Greta chorused and then broke into mutual giggles.

Alice narrowed her eyes. "Muffins from where?"

"The oven." Greta's smile turned dry. "With the help of the pantry. There's also coffee. I couldn't find any juice, though."

"Never drink the stuff." Alice walked to the cabinet and took down a cup, then headed for the coffeepot. "Where's Nadia?"

"I haven't seen her."

"Aunt Nadia wasn't cooking with you?" Hyacinth's eyes widened.

Alice looked a little concerned herself. "I told her you'd be cooking yesterday, but I expected her to be up supervising."

Greta shrugged. "Like I say, I haven't seen her. Nobody was here when I got up this morning."

Hyacinth and Alice glanced at each other uneasily, apparently some kind of Dubrovnik secret code.

The child reached for her grandmother's hand. "It'll be all right."

Alice stared at her for another moment, then shrugged. "Of course it will. Now eat your muffin. It looks good."

As if on cue, the door swung open one more time, and all eyes turned toward Nadia. Who looked...pretty much like she always looked, as far as Hank could tell. She had on the same flowered silk caftan that she usually wore, along with the fluffy, wedged slippers that clacked as she walked across the kitchen floor. Her dark hair was pulled up on top of her head in a bow, with a few wisps hanging loose around her face. Her makeup was impeccable.

If she'd been forty years younger, he'd probably have wanted to jump her as much as he wanted to jump Greta.

Nadia smiled, picking up one of the muffins. "Oh my, these do look good." She dropped into a chair next to Hank, then beamed up at Greta. "Could you bring me a cup of coffee, dear? Everything smells delectable."

Hank had a feeling that all the people in the room had just let out the collective breath they'd been holding. Greta nodded and turned back to the counter.

"You going back to your hole?" Alice asked him, tearing into another bite of muffin.

He nodded. "If Greta can give me a ride. I left my truck there."

Alice shrugged. "I'll give you a ride—I need to go to Promise Harbor for supplies. What about that sorry excuse for an intern?"

Hank sighed. His intern was a constant trial. "I left a couple of voice mails for him. If he doesn't show up again today, I'll call his advisor."

Greta frowned. "Advisor?"

"Professor Mitchell works at Broadhurst College," Hyacinth

recited. "He's associate professor of arthropology." She gave him a glistening smile.

"Archaeology/anthropology," he corrected gently. "Thank you, Hyacinth."

"Not arthropology?" Her smile dimmed.

"No. But that would be sort of cool. Arthropods are invertebrates. I guess then I'd be a professor of bugs."

"That would be cool." Hyacinth's expression turned thoughtful. "Can I come along, Grandma?"

"All right, but everyone needs to get moving." Alice pushed herself to her feet.

Hank considered shaving so that he could wait around for Greta. *Forget it. Time to slow this whole thing down a little.* He really did have to get back to the dig, and waiting around for Greta might lead to more time-consuming activities. "Okay, let me get my hat and I'll join you."

Greta gave him another sunny smile. "See you at lunchtime. Don't work too hard."

He grinned back without really meaning to. The woman was infectious. "I never do. See you."

Only after he'd walked out the door did it occur to him that he'd just left Greta alone with Nadia. Which might or might not be a good idea.

Greta studied Nadia from the corner of her eye as she piled the dishes in the sink. She didn't look like she was ready to commit mayhem, but who knew? She was willing to bet that Alice hadn't been particularly sensitive in her explanation as to why Greta was taking over as cook. She really didn't want to rub salt into any open wounds.

Nadia sipped her coffee, staring out the window at the backyard garden. In the morning sunlight, the color of her hair looked even more unreal. Greta wondered if she'd be as gray as Alice without the not-particularly-effective dye job.

After a moment, Nadia put down her cup and picked up the remaining half of her muffin. "I'm really not angry, you know." She gave Greta a quick smile over her shoulder. "I've been trying to get out of cooking for at least two years, ever since Alice decided it was my job. You'd think two years of canned spaghetti and overdone peas would have convinced her, but she's always been stubborn."

Greta paused, then ran her dishrag around the muffin pan. "You did that on purpose?"

"Well, of course I did it on purpose." Nadia frowned. "You don't think I really enjoyed having my food taste like that, do you?"

"I didn't know for sure," Greta hedged. She stared down at the sink, trying to think of what she should say next.

As it turned out, however, Nadia didn't need her reply to keep talking. "Alice thinks I don't contribute enough to the household, which is bunk, of course. My creams and lotions are doing quite nicely, and I expect a much bigger bump in sales once my website is fully functional."

"Creams and lotions?" That at least seemed safe enough as a topic.

"Indeed." Nadia swiveled in her chair so that she was facing the sink. "I have a complete line of hand and body lotions. I'm planning on expanding into soaps, too, but that requires either lye or glycerin and I'm not ready to work with either one yet." She gestured toward the backyard. "I'm growing lots of herbs for the lotions, though, that I could use for the soaps as well. Rose geranium, verbena, lavender, sage and several others like basil that I haven't done much with so far. Perhaps you might like some of them for cooking too."

"Yes, I might." Greta managed to keep her expression bland. The woman had a garden full of herbs and she still cooked canned spaghetti and meatballs?

Nadia gave her a dry smile. "I know what you're thinking, dear, but it really was a matter of principle. Alice was trying to force me to accept her point of view, and I was resisting. It's nothing more than family politics, you see."

"I do see. I've been involved in a few family battles myself." Most of them stemming from her folks' fervent wish that she be more like Josh the Perfect. And her own insistence on being herself, flawed and screwed up though that self might have been. And possibly still was. More than possibly as a matter of fact.

"Really?" Nadia leaned forward. "What kind of family battles?"

"Oh, you know..." Greta shrugged, trying desperately to backpedal.

"Where are you from, dear?" Nadia narrowed her eyes slightly. "And how did you come to be here in a bridesmaid dress you didn't like? And why have you decided to stay here instead of going back home? Is this all part of one of those family battles?"

Greta blew out a breath. Alice hadn't bothered to ask anything beyond the basic question of why she was on the run, but apparently Nadia was more persistent. "I'm from Promise Harbor. Which is where the wedding was. Or wasn't, actually. And I'm staying here because I'm just not ready to walk back into the crap that's going on back home quite yet."

Nadia frowned. "Does your family know where you are and what you're doing?"

Greta shook her head. "I'll tell them. Maybe today. They probably haven't even realized I'm gone yet."

"I doubt that," Nadia said gently. "What is it you're trying to avoid telling them?"

Greta blinked.

Nadia shook her head. "I'm the most disinterested of observers, my dear. I don't know you. You don't know me. Whatever you tell me I can take at face value since I have no idea who's who. Take advantage of my willingness to listen. You don't get chances like this often."

Greta licked her lips. *Well, why not?* "My marriage broke up. And my brother was supposed to get married, but then his fiancée left him at the altar. Sort of. And I can't bring myself to tell my mom that my husband walked out too."

She breathed deep. *There now, that wasn't so bad, was it?* Actually, it was. Definitely.

Nadia frowned. "Why wouldn't your mother be sympathetic to you?"

Greta pushed her fingers through her hair, probably leaving it standing in spikes. "I'm sure she'd be sympathetic. Eventually. But I have this...reputation. I'm always doing things wrong. I keep rushing into things without stopping to think about it. And this might look like one more thing I've screwed up."

"Actually, dear, I think that's something of a misstatement. It usually takes two to break up a marriage." Nadia picked up another muffin crumb.

"Well, maybe. But I still think a lot of people will figure it was mostly my fault, given my track record."

"Bullshit," Nadia said cheerfully. "Anyone who'd think that isn't worth worrying about. What happened?"

Greta took a deep breath, ready to tell her, politely, to butt out. Nadia stared back at her, smiling slightly. *Take advantage of my willingness to listen. You don't get chances like this often.* True enough. Her mother probably wouldn't be quite as relaxed about it.

"My ex-husband, Ryan, is a bond trader. In Boston," she began slowly. "He had this secretary, Dorothy. She was really good at her job. Very efficient. Very professional."

In fact, Dorothy always looked like she planned on moving up to the executive suite within the next fifteen minutes. Her ash-blonde hair hung just below her jaw in a smooth line. Her brown eyes were always made up flawlessly with just the right amount of taupe shadow and dark brown mascara. Even her lipstick was a perfectly modulated shade of pink. Greta herself could never quite pull off that kind of organization, so she had always been suitably impressed.

Nadia picked up her coffee cup. "And?"

"And one day she called me and said Ryan wanted me to meet him for lunch."

One of Nadia's dark brows arched up. "Was this unusual?"

"Sort of. He'd never done it before. And he'd seemed a little preoccupied before then, so I was kind of surprised. But I figured maybe he wanted to make it up to me for being preoccupied."

"Right." Nadia's eyebrow stayed up. "Go on."

"Well, when I got to the restaurant, Ryan was there but he seemed sort of surprised to see me. Shocked, in fact."

"He hadn't asked his secretary to call?"

Greta shook her head. "When I mentioned Dorothy's name he actually turned a little pale." Which should have been the tip-off, of course, but Greta had still been living in her nice little bungalow in the Land of Denial.

Nadia grimaced. "Let me guess—Dorothy herself soon appeared."

Greta nodded. "She did. She sat down next to Ryan and told me to take a seat too." Greta had actually been too shocked to do anything else at that point, and Ryan had looked almost as shocked as she was.

"What did she say?"

"She said they were in love—she and Ryan, that is. She said it was time for everybody to move on. And for me to move out."

"Did your husband say anything at that point?"

Greta shook her head. "He looked sort of stunned."

"Meaning he hadn't realized what his secretary was up to."

"Probably not. But he didn't contradict her either."

Nadia gave her a dry smile. "Some men find it easier to let strong women take the lead. Perhaps your husband was that kind of man."

Greta sighed. "Maybe."

"So what happened next?"

Greta shrugged. "He moved out. We got a divorce. I put my stuff in storage." And she'd come back to Promise Harbor for a quick reconnaissance that had turned out to be the Wedding That Wasn't.

"Yes, I get that. What I actually meant, though, was what did you do at the time. In the restaurant. Did you walk out meekly or did you tell your husband what you thought of him?"

Greta blew out a breath. "Well, neither actually. I mean, the waiter showed up and asked if he should set another place at the table. So I told him no, and then I dumped my glass of water into Ryan's lap and left." She shrugged again. "Not much of a gesture but it felt good at the time."

Nadia's lips spread up in another dry smile. "I'm sure it did." She pushed herself to her feet, dusting the crumbs from her fingers. "Well, this has been delightful, but I really must get started on my creams. I'm doing tea rose today, if you're interested."

Greta nodded. "I might be at that."

"Good enough." Nadia gathered her caftan around her, pausing as she reached the door. "I'll mull all of this over and see if I have any advice to give you. And I do hope you'll call your mother. She must be worried. And you're certainly welcome to stay as long as you wish." She gave Greta a warm smile, then sailed through the swinging door, presumably to change into her gypsy outfit.

Greta put the last pan in the drainer, sighing. She would call her mother. Soon. She honestly would. Just not right now.

# Chapter Six

Sophie Brewster woke up angry, although it took her a moment to remember just what she was angry about. But once she remembered, the anger escalated.

Josh. Allie. Gavin. The mind reeled. Didn't anyone know how to behave anymore? If Gavin was so bent on stopping the wedding, why couldn't he have called Allie before the ceremony? Sophie refused to believe he didn't have enough bars on his cell phone. No matter where he was, if he couldn't phone, he could have used email. Or Spacebook or MyFace. Or whatever it was they did.

He didn't have to show up at the wedding Sophie had spent months putting together. And, of course, Allie hadn't had to go off with him. She really hadn't.

After a shower, which did nothing to cool her off, and some minimal makeup, Sophie headed down to the kitchen to make breakfast for Greta and herself. Being angry was no excuse not to provide food. And she had a feeling she'd soon have more visitors to contend with, some of whom might possibly want coffee. Not that she'd really want to give them any. She swore if anybody brought her a casserole, she'd throw it in the street.

She paused, taking a quick mental survey of her mood. Angry, yes. Sad? Down? Ready to sink back into darkness again? She blew out a long breath, then shook her head. Nope.

Angry was it.

Now that it was morning she also wanted to talk to Greta. Because she was also somewhat miffed at her daughter, although not as miffed as she was at her son and his erstwhile fiancée. Greta really should have come back home after the ceremony to help deal with the fallout. She should have stood shoulder to shoulder with her mother as the town gossips descended, talons bared.

Her first responsibility, after all, was to her family. But then responsibility had never been Greta's strong point. Nor had common sense. Greta seemed to spend her life rushing from one disaster to the next.

As it was, Sophie's only support had been Owen, Allie's father, who'd stayed with her through the worst of the visitors and then taken her to dinner two towns over, where none of the wedding guests had been around.

In fact, if it hadn't been for Owen... Sophie sighed. At least she and Owen shared a common disaster, although they'd both been looking forward to sharing a married son and daughter. And it certainly wasn't Owen's fault that Allie had panicked. With any luck, the girl would come to her senses and come back to Promise Harbor.

Assuming, of course, that Josh would take her back. Sophie wasn't at all sure about that one. And to tell the truth, she wasn't sure he should. Not after that wedding disaster.

She turned on the coffee, then stepped back out into the hall again. "Greta," she called. "Breakfast."

She had half a mind to let Greta do the cooking to make up for her absence yesterday. Let her put that fancy culinary school degree to work for once. Instead of wasting it as Ryan McBain's wife. Sophie doubted Ryan and Greta ever ate at home, given all the social events Ryan attended as part of his job. And Ryan hadn't seemed as interested in Greta's skills in the kitchen as the rest of the family had been.

His loss. Greta really was a wonderful cook. Not that Sophie had ever admitted it openly before, given that culinary school had been another of Greta's impulsive decisions.

"Greta," she called again, louder this time. She glanced at the clock. Eight thirty. Surely the girl couldn't have been out late enough last night to justify sleeping in. Particularly not on a day that gave every indication of being just as annoying as yesterday had been. She turned back to stomp up the stairs. Might as well vent some of her frustration on her daughter before she had to pull herself together to greet the nosy neighbors.

She knocked briskly on Greta's bedroom door. "Greta, time to get up," she called. Without waiting for an answer, she twisted the knob and leaned into the bedroom.

The empty bedroom. Greta's bed was still neatly made, no evidence that she'd slept in it at all last night. Sophie stepped to the door of the guest bathroom, although she really had no hope Greta was in there.

She stood in the doorway for a moment, gritting her teeth. Just like Greta. When faced with a nasty situation, take off. Sophie tried to think who among Greta's friends might be in town, who she might be staying with.

She sighed. She really hadn't been paying much attention to Greta over the past few days, what with the wedding to plan and then the disaster to cope with. She had no idea what her daughter might do or where she might go, but maybe Bernice could help.

Calling Bernice on the landline meant Sophie had to spend fifteen minutes talking to Bernice's mother, who happened to be Allie's aunt. At least she was apologetic about her niece's behavior. But then Owen had been apologetic too. More than apologetic. He'd been heartbroken. As had Sophie, of course. They'd both been so happy at the thought of having Allie and Josh together. She took a deep breath. No more dwelling on the whole might-have-been part of things.

When she finally came to the phone, Bernice sounded sleepy. "No, ma'am," she mumbled. "I haven't seen Greta since she left the inn yesterday."

Sophie frowned. Greta was at the inn? "When was that?"

"Sometime in the afternoon. She went to the reception for a while and then she checked the dressing room where I was looking after Allie's things." Bernice paused. Apparently she was a little embarrassed about mentioning Allie's name.

Sophie gripped the phone more tightly. "Did she say where she was going then?"

"No, ma'am. I thought she was going back to your house."

A fair assumption. Unfortunately, wrong. "If you see her, would you ask her to call me, please?"

"Yes, ma'am, I'll do that." Bernice yawned again as Sophie hung up.

She headed back downstairs, ignoring the faint niggle of unease that made her shoulders feel tense. In the kitchen, she opened her cell phone again, checking the voice mail. Nothing. No messages. And there hadn't been any messages on the landline either.

"You'd think she'd at least call," she muttered.

*You didn't call her.* Sophie blew out a breath. No, she hadn't, but why should she? Greta was supposed to be here at home. She dialed her daughter's number now, only to be transferred to her voice mail. "Greta, where are you?" Sophie snapped. "You're supposed to be here. Call me as soon as you get this."

She stood for a moment, frowning at the sunlight filling her backyard. The child wouldn't have gone back to Boston, would she? Without changing clothes? Without saying good-bye? Leaving all her things in her room? Surely she'd know better than that. Her hand hovered over the phone for a moment, and then she pulled up her address book. She must have Ryan's work number somewhere. Greta claimed he hadn't been able to get away from the office for the wedding, but surely he could take a few moments to talk to Sophie.

Of course, getting Ryan on the phone once she'd found the number wasn't as easy as she might have hoped. By the time his secretary finally deigned to ring his office, Sophie was doing deep breathing exercises to keep from yelling.

When Ryan finally came onto the line, he sounded oddly tentative. "Yes?"

"Ryan, dear, it's Sophie. I'm so sorry to bother you at work, but I wondered if Greta had gotten back to Boston yet. Have you spoken with her today by any chance?"

There was a very long pause before he spoke again, long enough so that the niggle of unease at the back of Sophie's mind began to move toward full-blown anxiety. "I haven't spoken with Greta in over a week," he said slowly. "Not since the final decree was awarded."

Sophie gripped the edge of the counter in nerveless fingers. "Decree? What decree? What are you talking about?"

This time there was a very, very long pause before she heard Ryan sigh. "She didn't tell you, did she? I was afraid she might do something like that."

"Tell me what?" But of course she already knew.

"We're divorced, Sophie. We have been for about a week now. We were separated for a few months before that."

"Oh." Sophie closed her eyes, leaning against the counter. *Oh, Greta. Oh, damn it.* "No, she didn't mention it. Well, I'm sorry I bothered you."

"Wait," he said sharply. "Why are you calling about Greta now? What happened?"

"She didn't come home last night. I thought perhaps she'd decided to head back to Boston instead," Sophie said stiffly. "It's nothing for you to be concerned about."

"Nothing?" He sounded slightly annoyed.

"No. It's not your concern. Don't worry about it. Thank you for your time." She disconnected quickly, then leaned harder against the counter, trying to catch her breath.

Her mind was racing in a hundred different directions. Normally, she'd call Josh and ask for his advice. But she'd already called him three times since yesterday, trying to convince him to go after Allie. She had a feeling he wouldn't be up for a conversation with her now, even if it was on a different subject.

She glanced down at the phone again. One of the little icon things had a red number in the top corner. She wasn't sure what it meant since she never did anything with the phone except take calls and voice mail. She pressed it gingerly.

A screen popped up. Text message. All right, she knew about that. She stared at the green bubble in the upper corner with Greta's name at the top. *I'm all right. Don't worry.*

Suddenly, her heart was thumping so hard she was afraid she might have palpitations. *Don't worry.* To Sophie, that seemed to be the signal to be very worried indeed.

Greta tried to ignore her phone sitting on the bedside table.

*Don't want to run down the battery.* Yeah, right. Maybe she'd just check for messages. Sighing, she turned it on again.

A blinking icon showed she had a text message. She clicked on it—Josh.

*Where are U? What's up?* Greta gritted her teeth. Hell. *I'm fine* she texted quickly, hoping against hope he'd leave it at that. Maybe he was just checking on her whereabouts in a general way.

Vain hope. The text icon blinked accusingly. *Since when are you divorced? Why didn't you tell Mom?*

Greta closed her eyes. Obviously, this had moved beyond the texting stage. She punched in Josh's number and waited for him to pick up. "Greta?" he snapped. "What the hell is going on?"

"Well, hello to you too." She gathered her hand into a fist in her lap, staring resolutely at the floor. "I'm assuming you talked to Mom and she told you I was taking a break from Promise Harbor. I gather she also told you that Ryan and I broke up, as in divorced."

"You're fucking kidding me," he said.

"No, actually, I'm not. We separated a few months ago. The divorce was final a few days before I came to the harbor. I really meant to tell you and Mom about it. But then things got all...complicated."

"What happened, Greta?" At least he no longer sounded pissed.

"Long story short—he cheated and I threw him out. Do you want more details than that?"

"Seriously? I can't believe this. Why didn't you say anything?"

She closed her eyes. This conversation had all been so

much easier in her mind. "I couldn't think of how to explain it. And I knew Mom would be upset. I was going to tell her when I got home, but then she was so happy about the wedding and everything..."

The wedding probably wasn't the most politic thing to bring up right then, but maybe he was tired of people tiptoeing around the subject. She swallowed hard. "I should have told you both, I know. I was just sort of scared, I guess."

"Yeah. Yeah, I get it. Hell, Greta." He sighed. "I thought you were there to look after Mom."

"Look after Mom? Why would Mom need to be looked after?" Her mother had always struck her as a kind of force of nature. The only time she'd ever seemed less than totally in charge had been after her father had died. Of course, that had been a pretty dark period for everybody.

"Why?" Josh sounded slightly confused for once. "Because of the wedding being off. I'm sure she's upset."

Of course, Josh would be the one to think about other people before he thought about himself. Unlike his little sister. But she didn't think he was right about this particular crisis. "She's not upset, Josh. She's pissed. I saw her at that church. Trust me, the biggest thing we need to worry about with Mom right now is that she'll tell off one of the town gossips or kick Bernice in the rear end. She's not going to crumble under this. She's stronger than you think."

He sighed again. "Yeah, you're probably right. Where are you, anyway?"

"I'm staying at a hotel down the road," she said carefully. "They needed a cook and I needed a couple of days off." *Decision-free zone, bro.*

"Goddammit, Greta," he snapped. "Do I have to come and hunt you down too?"

"No, you do not. I'll be back at the harbor by the end of the week." She wondered if he could tell she was gritting her teeth. "And I'll face up to whatever I have coming from Mom."

"Fine. I won't. But..." His tone softened. "Are you really okay? Are you sure you don't want me to come and get you? Or head over to Boston and kick Ryan's ass for you?"

Greta shook her head. "Tempting as that might once have been, no. I'm fine, bro. Honest. How about you?"

"Okay. Yeah, I'm okay too."

She frowned slightly. Had anybody even checked to see if Josh was actually okay, rather than just saying he was? "Are you? I mean, really?"

"Really," he said.

"What are you... I mean, do you have any ideas about what you're going to do?" *Are you having any better luck in figuring out that whole future-plans thing than I am?*

"I don't know. I really don't, but...whatever." He paused. "Seriously, if you need anything, call me."

"I will. Thanks, bro."

She sat staring at the phone in her hand, then sighed. *One down.*

At eleven, Greta took another cruise through the Dubrovniks' pantry. It still seemed sparse at best, and some of the food was stuff she wouldn't dream of serving. As Nadia had said, she seemed to have a preference for canned pasta.

Still, Greta found a couple of cans of tomato soup. And she knew there was American cheese in the refrigerator. She'd make grilled cheese sandwiches and soup, then bring Hank a Thermos, assuming that there was one hiding somewhere in the multitude of kitchen cabinets.

Hyacinth wandered in at eleven thirty, carrying what

looked like a jelly jar full of dirt. Alice arrived just behind her, narrowing her eyes. "What's in there?"

Hyacinth blinked, then shrugged. "Just a couple of beetles. I need to check my field guide to see what they are."

"They don't belong in the kitchen," Alice said severely.

"They're in a jar," Hyacinth explained. "They can't do anything."

"I don't want to have them around in the room while I'm eating. Take them out on the back porch."

Hyacinth's brow furrowed. "Grandma," she muttered in a long-suffering voice.

"Hyacinth." Alice folded her arms. "Outside."

The child sighed, then headed for the back door.

Greta half turned from the stove. "Do you want your food here or in the dining room?"

"Here is fine." Alice frowned slightly. "Usually we just make our own lunch. I never expected Nadia to cook it."

Greta shrugged. "Soup and grilled cheese won't need much fixing."

"And you're going to check on the absent-minded professor?"

She shrugged again. "Well, somebody needs to make sure he hasn't killed himself." The thought of Hank actually having a fatal accident this time around suddenly made her feel a little nauseated, but she fought it down.

"Agreed." Alice served herself a bowl of soup and took a seat at the table as Greta flipped a golden cheese sandwich off the grill. "So you're running away from a bad divorce?"

Greta sighed. Probably too much to ask for Nadia to keep things to herself. "It wasn't all that bad. It's not the divorce I'm avoiding—it's my mother."

"Your mother liked your husband?"

"Sort of, I guess. Mostly my mom likes to have everything settled. Me married. Josh married. Everybody taken care of. I really intended to tell her about my husband and me, except then my brother's fiancée ran off with her former boyfriend on the day of the wedding, and I figured Mom had enough to deal with." This was, at best, a very lame excuse, given that she could have told her mother about the divorce several months ago, or at least about the separation. But Alice seemed willing to let her get by with it.

The back door opened again and Hyacinth returned. "I let them go."

Alice frowned. "I thought you were going to look them up in your field guide."

"I'll remember them." Hyacinth turned toward the plate of grilled cheese sandwiches. "Those look good."

Greta narrowed her eyes. "You might want to wash your hands first."

"No *might* about it." Alice gave her a severe look. "Hands, Hyacinth. Before you touch anything."

"Yes'm." She stepped to the sink, glancing at Greta. "Are you cooking now?"

Greta nodded. "For a while."

"Good. Aunt Nadia could use the rest."

Alice snorted, but Hyacinth didn't look like she paid much attention to her grandmother's attitude. She piled a cheese sandwich on her plate while Greta ladled soup into a bowl for her.

"About your mother," Alice began.

"I texted her," Greta said hurriedly. "And I called my brother. The family knows I'm okay."

Alice took a bite of grilled cheese. "Telling her where you are might be a nice touch."

Telling her mother or Josh where she was could be seen as an invitation for her mother to arrive within the hour, something Greta had no intention of initiating. Not until she was ready to get back into decision mode. "I'll call her later." *Later* being a very relative term.

After Alice and Hyacinth had finished and Nadia had dismissed lunch with a wave of the hand ("Getting ready to harvest some sage, dear, no time"), Greta made a couple of non-grilled cheese sandwiches and filled an ancient Thermos with the last of the tomato soup.

She was pretty sure she could find the dig again. Sure enough, at any rate, that she'd declined Hyacinth's offer to serve as a guide—which, of course, earned her a sardonic smile from Alice.

*All right. Okay. He's hot.* But she wasn't necessarily looking to hook up with anybody right now. Not so soon after Ryan. According to all the self-help books she'd read, you were supposed to let yourself cool off first, kind of like radioactive material.

Of course, she'd never been great at accepting advice. Witness the current shambles of her life. If she'd only listened a little more carefully to the advice her mother had given her when Ryan proposed, she might not be hiding out in Tompkins Corners right now.

She identified the parking area next to the dig by Hank's truck and the *Danger* signs. The forest was surprisingly dense, even on the narrow trail leading from the parking lot. She hadn't remembered it being that bad, but then she'd had her mind on other things the first time she'd taken the trail. She wondered how Hank had found the place to begin with, assuming, of course, that he'd been the one to find it.

She stepped through the space between a couple of maples and arrived at the clearing again, but this time she could see Hank's head and shoulders above the top edge of the excavation. "Hey," she called.

He stopped doing whatever it was he was doing and gave her a smile. "Hey."

Quite a smile, really. He looked a little like some kind of Norse god, standing there in the clearing, his face bathed in sunlight that caught the shimmer of gold in his hair and his eyebrows.

*Oh my.* She wondered fleetingly if she was up to this. But then, why not at least give it a try? She couldn't be hurt any worse than she already had been, right?

*Right.*

"I brought you a sandwich. Also some soup." She lifted the bag she was carrying, as if he needed to see the proof.

"Great. I was ready for a break." He limped toward the ladder and she had a sudden memory of boosting him up the rungs, her hands fastened tight to his ass. *Ah, good times, good times.*

Once he stepped onto the top rung, she got a good look at the total Hank—broad shoulders, triangle of tanned skin at the top of his shirt, jeans that fit very well indeed. And running shoes.

Who knew running shoes could look that good?

"Come on over here. We can use the table for lunch." He picked up a somewhat grubby-looking towel from the battered camp table where he had his gear. Like the coffee table in his apartment, the camp table was covered with rocks, which he pushed to the side to make room.

"What are all these rocks you've got here and back at the hotel?" she asked as she lifted the Thermos and sandwiches out of the bag. "I assume they're important."

He shrugged. "Possible artifacts. I brought them up here where I could look at them more closely. And I've got a couple of arrowheads." He pointed at a pair of what looked to be smaller, more chipped rocks.

"Oh. So I gather your intern didn't show up." She handed him a sandwich.

"Nope. His ass is grass. Smart kid, but he's got to learn this isn't like cutting class." Hank took a large bite of sandwich, then gave her a smile. "Very nice. Cheddar?"

She nodded. "And American cheese. From the general store. One of the few things in there I could use."

"Yeah. Alice just stocks the basics." His gaze flicked to her general store-issue T-shirt and jeans, then quickly away. *No, Professor, I'm still not wearing a bra.*

"Right. I scavenged enough to make breakfast and lunch, but I'm going to hit the grocery in Merton before I head back. Otherwise, we'll be stuck with mac and cheese."

One sandy eyebrow arched up. "Alice is okay with you shopping at a competitor?"

She shrugged. "I figure as long as I'm paying for it, Alice doesn't have a lot of say in the matter."

"You're paying for it." He put his sandwich down. "I thought you were strapped. I mean...well, the free room in exchange for cooking and all."

"Just because Alice doesn't take credit cards, that doesn't mean other people don't." She gave him her brightest phony smile. "So what are you in the mood for in terms of supper? Me, I'm thinking chicken."

He still made no move to pick up his sandwich. "What's going on, Greta? I can accept a moderate level of crazy, maybe the zany level. But at a certain point, I like answers. And you don't strike me as somebody who just does things on a whim."

She spent a moment carefully unwrapping her sandwich, then glanced up again. He was still watching her. "Okay, look. It actually is a whim, sort of—I mean staying with the Dubrovniks and all. But it's based on something real. I just need a few days off right now. Someplace to think without having to face up to...a lot of stuff. Sort of a decision-free zone. Alice and Nadia both know about it, and they're okay with it." *Well, sort of.* She felt a little like crossing her fingers.

"So how long do you need to think things over?"

"Maybe a week. I figure give it a week, and then I'll head back where I came from."

"Which is?"

"Which is something I don't really want to get into right now, thank you very much." She gave him another weak smile. "Would you like some soup?"

"Sure." He took the cup from her fingers, his gaze never leaving her face. "Will you at least tell me how you came to be wandering around the woods in a hoopskirt?"

"I was a bridesmaid at a wedding that didn't happen. My brother's fiancée ran away with another man. I was taking a walk in the woods and then I found this guy in a hole. Enough background?" She picked up her own sandwich. "How did you happen to be in that hole anyway?"

"Stupidity. I decided to go on digging without my intern. Part of the wall collapsed on my foot."

"But you're digging today without your intern," she pointed out. "What's to keep that from happening again?"

"Nothing. But at least this time you'll come rescue me." He gave her a smile that made a quick chill run up her backbone. Heady stuff.

"I suppose I could do that. If I'm not busy cooking." Her smile slid into a version that felt a little more sincere. "Do you need me to come and get you this afternoon? Will you be all right driving?"

"Won't know until I try, I guess. But I can always call you if I need help." He patted his pants pocket. "This time I remembered to keep my phone with me. What's your number?"

"Oh." She blinked. "I don't have my cell phone turned on right now. I didn't bring the charger along with me, and I didn't want it to go dead while I was staying at Tompkins Corners. If you need a ride, could you call the Dubrovniks and have them give me a message?"

"Yeah, sure." He narrowed his eyes. "Is this some kind of sneaky way to keep from giving me your phone number?"

She shook her head. "I will gladly give you my phone number. I just may not answer when you call."

"Okay, fair enough." He gave her one of those spine-tickling smiles again. "I'm guessing this is going to be one interesting week."

"It could be, Professor." She gave him a sort of dazzling smile of her own. "It very well could be."

# Chapter Seven

Greta stood in the kitchen, flouring chicken parts and humming. She hadn't had a chance to do any real cooking for weeks, months in fact. Well, years if she was being honest. Not since she'd gotten married, anyway. She'd tried cooking a couple of meals for herself after Ryan had left, but she just couldn't get excited over cooking for one. Eventually, she'd started grabbing meals from the grocery, lousy though most of them were.

And she'd barely cooked at all while she'd been married to Ryan. His family seemed to find her cooking sort of embarrassing, like having a wife who was a former stripper or something. *Oh baby, yeah, let me see you fry that bacon.*

Of course, she'd had plenty to do as Ryan's wife even without cooking. Sometimes it had seemed like she'd volunteered for every worthy cause in Boston. And in the evenings, Ryan always had places for them to go and things to do. Places to be seen mostly. She couldn't have held a restaurant job after they'd gotten married, even if his parents hadn't been dead set against it. She wouldn't have had the time.

After she and Ryan had separated, she'd taken a part-time job at a friend's bakery. It had given her a small salary to pay the bills without Ryan's support, but it wasn't like pulling together a whole meal. Her friend was still willing to give her the same baking job, maybe full-time, assuming she returned to Boston after her Promise Harbor adventure.

Assuming she returned to Boston. Another decision to avoid thinking about for the next week. *Decision-free zone.*

She sighed, pouring a puddle of olive oil into a large, nicely seasoned cast-iron skillet. She had to hand it to Nadia, or whoever had originally set the kitchen up. The equipment was first rate even if it hadn't seen much use lately.

"What are you cooking?"

Greta managed not to jump. The voice was coming from somewhere in the neighborhood of her right hip. "Hyacinth?"

The child climbed up onto one of the kitchen chairs beside her. "You're doing chicken?"

She nodded. "Chicken Marengo."

Hyacinth regarded her suspiciously. "It sounds like it has hot stuff in it. I don't like hot stuff."

"No hot stuff," Greta said firmly. "It's French. The story behind the recipe is that Napoleon's cook created the dish to celebrate their victory in the Battle of Marengo. But he didn't have much in the way of ingredients because they were out in the country. He ended up with chicken and some vegetables and crayfish. Today cooks usually skip the crayfish. Or I do anyway."

Hyacinth opened her mouth to say something, then apparently thought better of it. "What's a crayfish?"

"It's a kind of freshwater shellfish. They look like little lobsters."

"Where do you get them?"

Greta frowned. "Most of them are grown down South, I think. Louisiana is famous for crayfish. They call them crawfish, though."

"Not here?"

She shook her head. "Too cold. They like warm weather."

Hyacinth sighed. "Darn. I thought maybe I could find one in the creek."

"Probably not." She placed the chicken in the hot oil. "You like collecting animals?"

"I just look at them," Hyacinth said quickly. "I always let them go. After I find out what they are."

Greta nodded absently, prodding the chicken with her tongs. "Good."

"Are you in love with Professor Mitchell?"

Somehow Greta managed not to drop the tongs as she turned around quickly. "No. Whatever gave you that idea?"

"I guess the way Aunt Nadia's humming. She gets happy when she thinks people are in love."

Greta huffed out a breath, then started slicing onions to give herself something to do. "Well, I'm sure she doesn't think Professor Mitchell and I are in love. We just met yesterday. It takes a lot longer than that to fall in love, believe me."

Hyacinth nodded solemnly. "Probably."

"Absolutely. Don't ever let anybody tell you that you can fall in love at first sight. That only happens in fairy tales." She felt an uncomfortable tightness in her chest. No matter what her mother thought, she hadn't fallen in love with Ryan overnight. They'd gone out several times before she'd even decided she was interested in him. Hell, she hadn't even slept with him until they'd been dating for a few weeks. Nothing precipitant about that relationship, no sirree, even if she had married him three months after she'd met him.

Had he ever sent shivers down her spine, even slightly?

Greta frowned again. He must have. At least a few times.

"How would you know if you were in love?" Hyacinth reached for a piece of green pepper.

"It just feels...different." Greta shrugged, moving on to the mushrooms. "You know when it happens, but it's not something I can really describe."

"I bet a scientist could. Scientists have to be able to describe things. Maybe Professor Mitchell could."

Greta gritted her teeth. *Don't you dare ask him if he's in love with me.* She began flipping chicken with grim determination. "Would you rather have rice or noodles with your chicken?"

"Rice please. But I won't eat the chicken."

"You won't?" Greta paused with her tongs in midair. "Why's that?"

"Because I don't like to eat animals," Hyacinth explained carefully. "I haven't decided yet about fish. I have to think about it."

Greta glanced toward the pile of vegetables that she'd been ready to dump into the skillet. "How do you feel about having things cooked with meat? Would you rather I cooked the veggies separately?"

Hyacinth's forehead furrowed as she worked it through. "I don't know. Aunt Nadia just took out the meat before she put the food on my plate. But maybe not cooking them together would be a good idea."

Greta sighed, staring down at the chopped vegetables on the cutting board. She really wanted to use that fond in bottom of the pan, and she really liked the flavor of chicken and vegetables braised together. On the other hand, the child had a right to her principles. "How about this. I'll cook you a separate dish of rice and vegetables, maybe throw in a little spice to give it a kick. Would that be okay?"

Hyacinth frowned again. Then she gave her one of those beatific smiles. "I think that would be okay, thank you very much. But no spice, please, because I don't like hot stuff."

"Right. I remember. So I'll fix your dinner separate from everybody else's, but you'll get mostly what they get—just without the meat."

"Super." Hyacinth climbed down from her chair. "Would you like to see Carolina?"

Greta blinked. "North or South? Actually, I've already seen South Carolina. Or anyway, I've seen Charleston." Good restaurants there, as she recalled.

"It's not a place," Hyacinth said indignantly. "Carolina is an animal. I named her Carolina."

"Oh." Greta started warming oil in another skillet for Hyacinth's vegetables. "Maybe later then. I'm in the middle of cooking right now, and I can't leave the kitchen."

"Okay."

Hyacinth headed for the back door just as Alice entered from the front desk. "Did you clean up the back stoop, Hyacinth? I don't want mud and leaves out there."

"Yes ma'am." Hyacinth sighed, heading out the back door. "I'll clean it up now."

"And no worms," Alice called after her. "Or other bugs."

Hyacinth paused in the doorway. "Worms aren't bugs. They're annelids."

"Hairsplitting," Alice snapped. "Nothing invertebrate on the back steps."

"Yes, Grandma." Hyacinth sighed again, clearly feeling abused, and closed the back door behind her.

Alice narrowed her eyes as she checked the stove. "What's for dinner?"

"Chicken Marengo." Greta made a quick decision not to go through the Napoleon story again. She had a feeling Alice wouldn't be charmed.

Alice added a furrowed brow to the narrowed eyes. "I don't recall that we had any chicken sitting around here."

"We didn't." Greta shrugged. "This came from Merton."

Now Alice was openly scowling. "I didn't say you could buy from someplace else."

"I didn't ask." Greta measured rice into a pan. "Don't worry. I'm not charging you."

Alice sat down at the table, folding her arms across her chest. "I can't say I'm happy with that alternative either."

"Why not? We all get fed, and you're not paying extra. Works for me."

She shook her head. "I can pay for my own food, missy. I've been doing it for a good long time. Granted, you're one hell of a cook. But I don't want you buying food from somebody else. If you're cooking for us, I provide the food."

Greta poured wine over the chicken and vegetables in one pan, then gave a stir to Hyacinth's mixture in the other. "The problem with that is, you don't have a lot of food available. All I found in the pantry was cans. And all I found in the general store was frozen hamburger patties and processed chicken nuggets. I am one hell of a cook, Alice, that's the truth. But even I can't do much with that."

Alice huffed out a breath. "Don't have much call for fresh meat around here. People go to Promise Harbor or Merton to buy fresh. They come here to pick up stuff like salt or flour that they've run out of. If I started stocking vegetables and meat, I'd go broke."

Greta frowned. "How did you deal with grocery shopping before I showed up?"

"Nadia headed off to Costco every six weeks or so and brought back what she needed. Mostly cans."

"Well, there you are." Greta sighed. "Like I said, I don't do cans."

Alice scowled, leaning back in her chair. "How many of those muffins did you make this morning?"

"A dozen. Enough for everybody to have two with a couple left over." Except, of course, nothing was left over now.

"Suppose you made two dozen tomorrow? I can sell them in the store. Whatever we make goes to buy whatever you want to cook."

Greta folded her arms. "Wouldn't it be easier to just give me some money for groceries?"

"It would." Alice nodded. "But we'll do it this way instead. Doing it my way, you earn your keep. Agreed?"

"Why not? It's your money either way."

"It is." Alice nodded again. "It is indeed."


Hank limped up the walk to the rear entrance of Casa Dubrovnik, having left his truck under what passed for a carport at the hotel. He had high hopes for dinner, but he figured he needed to get cleaned up first, having spent the day getting increasingly dusty at the dig. Still, if he entered through the kitchen, he might get a quick glimpse of Greta before he went upstairs. He hoped she hadn't bought more clothes when she'd bought food. Or at any rate, he hoped she hadn't bought more underwear.

*And when exactly did you turn into a sexist pig, Professor Mitchell?* Probably when he'd seen Greta Brewster hovering at the edge of the dig in her hoopskirt and sneakers.

Stepping inside the kitchen door, he felt as if he'd been hit by a sensual carpet bombing. Delectable smells assaulted him. The sound of Greta's laughter mingled with Hyacinth's. Platters and bowls heavy with glistening vegetables were being served up on the counter. Suddenly, his mouth was watering so much he was afraid to talk.

At that moment, Greta turned and saw him. Her reddish-brown hair was damp from sweat and steam, her face slightly pink from the heat. She should have looked lousy. She didn't. Her lips parted in a slow smile, full of promise.

All of a sudden, he had a feeling sitting down for dinner was going to be difficult.

"Good evening." Greta arched an eyebrow. "Dinner in five minutes. If you have any freshening up to do, I suggest you do it now."

He nodded. "Right. I'll be back." He limped toward the stairs, wondering if he had time for a fast cold shower.

Dinner lasted about twice as long as it had in the past, mainly because for once nobody was trying to eat so quickly they wouldn't taste the food. Hank managed to partially solve what he thought of as the Greta Problem by rationing the number of times he looked at her during the meal. Once every twenty bites seemed fair. And that way nobody could accuse him of being obsessed with the cook.

Nobody would accuse him of that anyway, of course, because he wasn't. Absolutely was not.

Greta refilled his glass with iced tea, and he felt as if the lower half of his body had turned to granite. He was careful not to look at her after she'd set the glass in front of him. He knew she'd be smiling. When he finally looked up, she'd walked back to the counter again.

She pulled down what looked like an old fruitcake tin from the cupboard. "I didn't have time to do much for dessert. Just cookies. Maybe I'll be able to do something more elaborate tomorrow."

Nadia touched her napkin decorously to her lips. "I'm sure a cookie is all I can manage, dear. My compliments on a wonderful dinner."

The plate of oatmeal raisin cookies she set out on the table disappeared with astonishing speed. Hank managed not to gobble his down, but given the intoxicating tastes of butter and brown sugar that laced through the oatmeal, it was a near thing.

"Would you like me to help with the dishes?" Hyacinth carried a pile of plates to the sink. "I'm good at it."

"That would be great. Thanks."

"Actually, Hyacinth dear, we have other things to do." Nadia rose to her full five foot two or so, augmented at the moment by pink satin mules beneath the usual swirling skirt. "Come with me?"

Hyacinth narrowed her eyes. "What other things?"

"Things." Nadia gripped Hyacinth's hand, drawing her briskly toward the door to the dining room. "I'm sure Hank can help with the dishes."

Hank blinked. He'd never washed a dish in Casa Dubrovnik before.

Alice pushed herself to her feet, dropping her napkin next to her plate. "Can you stand up long enough to dry some dishes, Mitchell?"

He shrugged. "Sure."

"Then you might as well go along with my sister's rather heavy-handed attempts at matchmaking. Otherwise, Greta here will be washing dishes by herself." She turned and stalked after Nadia and Hyacinth.

Greta shook her head. "Was that what Nadia was doing? I must be out of practice. I missed it entirely."

"I'm not sure there's any way to practice for Nadia." Hank carried the last stack of plates to the counter. "Great dinner, by the way. How did Alice react when she found out you'd bought your own food?"

"In her own unique way," Greta said dryly. "We're good for now."

He followed her to the sink, where she was rinsing the dishes before stacking them on the side. "How do we work this?"

"I wash and rinse, you dry. Classic division of labor. Towels are over there." She gestured toward a wooden drying rack near the stove.

Hank grabbed the nearest towel and stepped back next to her. "Bring it on."

As he stacked dried dishes on the counter, he considered the problem of how he might be able to get Greta out of the house. Maybe go for a walk—or in his case a limp—in the Dubrovniks' surprisingly pleasant garden. There was a full moon tonight. The June temperatures were warm but not yet hot. Perfect night for a getting-to-know-you-better kind of thing.

Before coming down to dinner, he hadn't figured on making any moves in her direction. But that was before he'd spent some time in the slightly steamy kitchen, watching her step back and forth in front of the sink, her T-shirt alternately clinging to and dropping away from her body. She'd pushed her short hair behind her ears, and for some reason she had a tiny bit of detergent foam on the tip of her nose.

He'd never wanted to touch a woman more in his life.

*Just put the dishes away, jerkwad.*

"So what do you think of Hyacinth?" Greta reached for a dish, drawing the T-shirt across her breasts long enough to show a brief outline of nipple.

*Sweet lord.* "She's a nice kid. Why?"

"I'm trying to figure out if she's just got the usual kid fascination with animals or if she's actually thinking more like a budding scientist."

He frowned. A welcome diversion from the warm bundle of temptation standing next to him. "She's got a big thing about science. Asks a lot of questions. Has a lot of field guides to local fauna. I'd say she's serious. Or as serious as the average nine-year-old can be, anyway."

"I don't think of her as average." Greta reached for another plate, spiking his temperature by a couple of degrees. "She seems unique."

"I guess she is. I haven't spent a lot of time around kids before. I like her."

"I do too." She gave him another slow smile.

*Down, boy.* He picked up the last two glasses and stowed them in the overhead cabinets as a way to keep from drooling over that smile. "Want to go for a walk?"

"Sure." She spread her dishrag across the sink divider. "How far can you walk without wincing?"

"Not that far. I was thinking once around the garden."

"You're on. I need to get some rose geranium leaves out there anyway." She pushed the back door open, holding it for him. "Why don't you lean on me? That way you won't have as much weight on your foot."

*Oh lordy yes, why don't I do that?* He put his hand on her shoulder, feeling warm skin and damp T-shirt against his palm. "Thanks."

The balmy night air was scented with lavender and something vaguely lemony. He'd never been able to figure out why someone as talented in the garden as Nadia undoubtedly was couldn't find more effective ways to turn that produce into something edible.

"Just a minute. The rose geranium plants are over here." She stepped carefully between the plants at the side, leaning down to snap off some leaves that she put in her pocket.

"Dare I ask..."

"I'm going to do a rose geranium cake for dessert tomorrow. And the butter and sugar need to infuse overnight."

"Oh." He had no idea what to say to that. He wasn't even sure what *infuse* meant in this context.

Greta stepped back beside him, lifting his hand back to her shoulder and moving slowly forward.

"Nice night," she murmured. "Look at that moon."

The moon had just begun to rise, impossibly large and golden, low on the horizon. He stood for a moment, feeling himself relax. "When you see it looking like that, you realize why people felt like worshipping it."

"Did the people in your village worship the moon?" She walked forward again, letting him lean against her. "That sounds interesting."

"I don't know anything about the people in my village." He took a breath. "To tell you the truth, I don't even know for sure that it's a village. These walls are all over New England. Some of them came from native people, but a lot of them were just root cellars."

"Not Celtic worship sites?"

He grimaced. "No, that's just romantic crap." He glanced down and saw her grin. "Okay." He sighed. "Got me."

She shook her head. "If you don't know for sure that it's a village, why are you working on it?"

"Because it might be. It's a kind of puzzle. I should have some idea of what I've got by the end of the summer. Then I can spend the winter analyzing what I've found. Right now I'd say the odds on it being a Wampanoag settlement are pretty good."

"And the Wampanoags were..."

"The principal Native American group living in this area."

"That's cool." She smiled up at him. "Spending your time solving a puzzle that's maybe several thousand years old. That's very cool."

Her eyes were dark in the moonlight, her lips curving up as she smiled. He smelled lemon and lavender again, and something like roses but not exactly. Suddenly he felt a little dizzy.

If he'd thought too much about what he was going to do next, he'd never have been able to go through with it, but irresistible impulse took over. He lowered his mouth to hers, running his tongue tentatively along the line of her lips until she opened for him, then giving himself time to taste and savor. There was a hint of sweetness mixing with the scent of rose geranium and mint, sending his head swimming. She made a sound low in her throat, a faint hum of pleasure, and then her hands looped around his neck, pulling her body against his.

Soft breasts pressed against his chest, and he touched warm skin as he slid his hands down her sides to rest finally on the jut of her hipbones. She seemed right at home in a garden full of sweetness.

After another moment reveling in the taste of her, he raised his head again, trying to think of something unfoolish to say. *So who are you exactly, and what the hell are you doing here in my arms?*

"Maybe we should go in," Greta murmured. "I need to put together some cinnamon rolls for tomorrow morning. And I've got to do the butter and sugar for the cake."

He sighed. "Okay."

If she was true to her word, they had the rest of the week for more conversation. He figured sometime during those six days, he'd find out all he needed to know about Greta Brewster. And maybe a bit more.

# Chapter Eight

"I don't understand."

Sophie gritted her teeth to keep from growling with frustration. She knew Owen wasn't trying to be difficult. Ever since his accident and the brain damage, it took him a little longer to put ideas together. It wasn't that he couldn't understand. It just took some time. And patience.

And the most important thing was that he was here. He'd come over from the greenhouse as soon as she'd called him first thing in the morning after she'd spent a night worrying. Which was more than she could say for either of her children, who still weren't answering their respective phones.

Owen Ralston was nothing if not dependable. Too bad his daughter Allie didn't share that trait.

She'd tried to send Greta her own text message, but had given up in disgust after five minutes of typos. How did they expect you to fit your fingers on those tiny keys? And that screen was much too small for the message Sophie wanted to send.

It was at times like these that she missed her friend Lily so much it was almost painful. But Owen had been such a help yesterday when the town gossips had descended en masse. When she'd been almost at the end of her rope, he'd taken her hand in his and given her a smile that somehow made her shoulders relax a little. If anyone could help her work her way through this problem with Greta, she thought Owen was the one most likely.

She took a steadying breath and began to explain the facts again. "Greta drove off right after the wedding without telling anyone. She left all her things here. The only word I've had from her is a two-sentence text message: 'I'm all right. Don't worry'." Her lips began to tremble "I'm really afraid she's been kidnapped."

Owen nodded slowly. "Okay, so why?"

Sophie sank onto the couch beside him. "Because... I guess because I haven't heard anything else from her. And then I called her husband. Her *ex*-husband." She paused trying to put her thoughts together.

"*Ex*-husband?" Owen raised a questioning eyebrow.

Sophie rubbed a hand across her eyes. "She didn't tell me, Owen. She didn't even hint about it. He said they'd been separated for months, but she never mentioned it. Why wouldn't she even hint?"

"You were busy. Maybe she was afraid."

"Afraid of what?"

He shrugged. "Bothering you maybe."

Sophie managed not to let her expression slide to a grimace. She *had* been busy. She'd been working so hard to get Josh and Allie married and settled in Promise Harbor. She fumbled for her handkerchief, pressing it to her lips.

"Sophie, I'm sorry." Owen turned toward her, resting a hand on her shoulder. "Please don't."

She took a shuddering breath, shaking her head. "I'm all right. I really am. And you've got a point—she probably didn't want to bring it up in the middle of the wedding preparations.

But why didn't she tell me afterward? Why did she just take off like that? It's not like her."

Actually, of course, that was a screaming fib. It was just like Greta to do something like this. To run away rather than facing up to something that would make other people unhappy with her. She'd never been able to take criticism, even when she deserved it. Maybe especially when she deserved it.

"She's still afraid," he said gently. "Afraid of what you'd think."

Sophie sighed. "I might have been upset. I am upset, in fact." She stood up, pacing toward the windows on the far side of the room. "I can think of a half-dozen examples right off the bat—things she jumped into without thinking. She painted her bedroom black without asking. She took my car and then got stranded on the cape. She dropped off the tennis team so that she could work at the Bistro. And then the job only lasted a month. She was supposed to graduate from college and she dropped out to go to cooking school. Cooking school, for heaven's sake!"

"She finished cooking school," Owen said slowly. "And she's good."

"Yes she is, but what did she do with it? She got married and never cooked at all. And now this marriage she rushed into falls apart. She doesn't think things through, Owen. She just doesn't." Sophie pressed her knuckles against her lips. It probably wasn't fair to charge that last disaster to Greta just yet. It might not have been her fault. And maybe she'd been right to think Sophie wouldn't have been all that supportive.

Owen apparently agreed. "Two people in the marriage, Sophie," he said quietly. "Maybe it wasn't her fault. Not all of it, anyway."

Sophie gritted her teeth. Somehow the fact that he was

right made it worse. Greta should have been willing to give her a chance, damn it! "Then why didn't she stick around to tell me her side of it? Why did she take off like that?"

"She's afraid you'll be angry with her." He shrugged. "Maybe."

"I would have understood," she said softly. "I would have, Owen. She's my child."

"Of course you would. She knows that." He nodded, coming to stand beside her. "She'll be back."

Sophie took a deep breath, trying to fight down the panic she felt building again. "But what if she's hurt? What if she had an accident? What if she hit her head and she doesn't remember who she is? Owen, what's happened to her?"

He put his hand on her shoulder, turning her slightly so that she could look at him. "Maybe you should talk to the police. Hayley Stone works there. Remember Hayley Stone?"

*Remember?* Sophie grimaced. Oh yes. How could she forget? Hayley Stone had been one of the thorns in her side during Hayley's years as a Promise Harbor High School student. The girl had never made it to the criminal level, but she certainly fit into the wild crowd. And Sophie was pretty sure Hayley had been friends with Gavin Montgomery. The same Gavin Montgomery who'd broken up her son's wedding and absconded with his fiancée. She wasn't at all sure she could talk to Hayley Stone without snarling.

"I don't think..." she began.

"She's good at her job," Owen cut in. "Allie trusted her."

Which might or might not be much of a recommendation. Sophie wasn't feeling too charitable toward Allie either just then.

But she did feel charitable toward Owen. More than

charitable, in fact. "All right. If you think it's a good idea, I'll go ahead and call her."

He nodded. "Maybe she could come by and talk later."

"Maybe." But Sophie found herself hoping once again that Greta would come to her senses and give her a call before she had to talk to the Promise Harbor Police Department.

Greta made two and a half dozen cinnamon rolls, give or take, letting them rise overnight and then baking them first thing in the morning. Hank ate three and looked as if he was considering three more. Hyacinth had two and said she'd decided she couldn't do without butter so she wasn't going vegan after all. Alice and Nadia each had one with coffee.

Alice gave her a tight smile. "Any way we can wrap those up individually?"

Greta shrugged. "Sure, I guess. Assuming plastic wrap is okay."

"Plastic wrap is fine."

Nadia, perhaps anticipating what was to come, had already made her exit, and Hank was long gone to the dig. Hyacinth and Greta wrapped the remaining rolls and took them to the store.

As stores went, it reminded Greta of a cross between a 7-Eleven and one of those general stores in western movies. Long shelves stretched from one end of the room to the other, holding canned goods and bags of flour, along with cartons of motor oil and WD-40.

It was hard to see the shelves at the moment, however, given that at least ten men in Carhartts and baseball caps were crowded around the front counter, where Alice had installed an ancient coffee urn.

Ten pairs of hungry eyes watched Greta and Hyacinth approach with their plates of rolls.

"How did they know about the buns?" Greta muttered.

Alice shrugged. "Turned on the exhaust fans while you were baking. Whole town's been smelling them for an hour."

"Devious."

"Inspired."

Alice propped a sign next to the plate: *Cinnamon buns, $3.00.*

Greta blinked. "You're kidding."

Alice shrugged. "They'd sell 'em for twice that at Starbucks."

"This isn't Starbucks."

"Trust me. They'll still move."

And they did, or at least they were being grabbed up quickly when Greta headed back toward the kitchen.

She was still cleaning up from breakfast when Nadia came back, carrying a bag of lavender buds and flowers. "Good morning, dear," she trilled. "Don't mind me. I'm just going to put these flowers out to dry and then make some more essential oil."

Greta leaned back against the counter, watching Nadia lay out a double layer of paper towels. "I saw the hand creams in the general store. Do you sell many?"

"Enough." Nadia shrugged. "Tourists love to buy locally made things. Of course, we don't get too many tourists, but there are always some people looking for undiscovered jewels. I like to think I can provide a moonstone or two."

"Do you have any problems with shelf life? Natural stuff

isn't all that stable, is it?"

Nadia shrugged again. "I use grapefruit-seed oil to stabilize it. And it's only small jars. It may not last as long as Jergens lotion, but it lasts long enough for people to enjoy it."

"Oh." Greta went on with what she'd been doing, which was to get a start on her cake. "I helped myself to some of your rose geranium leaves last night. I hope you don't mind."

Nadia narrowed her eyes, running a sprig of lavender between her finger and thumb to pop off the buds. "For what purpose?"

"Cake. I needed to infuse the butter and the sugar last night." She lifted the leaf-wrapped stick of butter out of the refrigerator. "The sugar's on the counter."

Nadia looked intrigued. "So you don't actually put the leaves in the cake?"

Greta shook her head. "God, no—you'd probably end up with a cake that tasted like spinach. It's the fragrance you want, not the taste. You put some around the bottom of the pan too, but you peel them off before you frost the cake."

"Hmm."

They worked side by side for a few minutes, Greta buttering the pans and laying out the rose geranium leaves, Nadia deflowering stalks of lavender, then smoothing the pile of buds onto the paper toweling. She smiled. "So I've been thinking about your divorce, dear, and I have a few observations. We're about a third of the way through the week, you know. This may be the best chance to discuss it. Also, I have a few questions."

Greta stiffened, running her buttered fingers across the pan. *Trust Nadia.* "I already explained what happened."

Nadia nodded. "You did. But you didn't really talk about what happened afterward. And why you haven't yet told your mother. I understand that you had both the divorce and then your brother's wedding problems to deal with. That must have been painful."

Greta blew out a breath, pulling the mixing bowls out of the cabinet. "I don't know what more to say about it. The wedding foofaraw plus the divorce just sort of...freaked me out. I wanted some time to think."

Nadia nodded again. "Quite understandable. But you've had a couple of days now. And you still need to talk to your mother."

Greta set the bowls out on the counter, carefully not looking at Nadia. "I will. Eventually. I mean, it's really not such a big deal. People get divorced all the time."

Nadia frowned, adding more flowers to the pile. "Divorces would most probably qualify for what most people think of as a big deal. And your mother may very well share that opinion, particularly when the divorce in question involves her daughter."

Greta paused for a long moment, staring down at the pile of rose geranium leaves. "I know. That's one of the reasons I haven't told her yet. I just couldn't think what to say to her after the whole mess with Josh's wedding. She's going to see me and Ryan as another example of my tendency to screw things up."

"I'm not sure I follow your reasoning here." Nadia raised an eyebrow. "Your husband was the one who had an affair, not you. How does that become your failure?"

Greta shrugged. "My mother thought I rushed into the whole thing. Marrying Ryan, that is. She didn't believe I thought it through."

"Was she right?"

"Maybe." Greta turned to the bowl of dry ingredients. She

picked up her whisk, trying not to be too energetic about mixing them but still managing to send up a small cloud of dust. Probably not the best thing to be doing while she was thinking about Ryan and Dorothy. "I guess I didn't know him as well as I thought I did when we got married. I didn't realize he was the kind of man who'd have an affair with his secretary, that's for sure. I mean, it's such a cliché. Then again, Ryan's a busy man and his secretary was right there."

Nadia sighed. "Did he actually ask for a divorce at that infamous lunch?"

Greta shook her head. "He looked really surprised when I walked in. So I sat down and said something innocuous like Dorothy had called me. And then he started looking sort of sick."

Nadia blew out a breath. "I see. She hadn't told him what she was up to."

Greta nodded. "That's what I think. She was doing an end run. Maybe Ryan was taking too long to end the marriage and she decided to take matters into her own hands." She managed not to grit her teeth. *If I'd taken the time to know him better, could I have seen that coming?*

"I'm assuming that your husband hadn't mentioned this great love affair before this," Nadia said dryly.

"No." Greta gave her a sour smile. "My guess is he hadn't thought of it in quite the same way she had. Anyway, after I dumped the water in his lap, I got up and went home. And then I called a woman I knew from the harbor who was a lawyer in Boston, and she put me on to the guy who represented me in the divorce. It actually doesn't take too long to get one in this state, as it turns out. We were separated for a few months and then it was over." Yet another quick decision and follow-through. Although this one hadn't been quite as catastrophic.

"Did you ever talk to your husband about the entire affair?"

"You mean the lunch date or Dorothy?"

Nadia shrugged. "Both. Either."

Greta shook her head. "At first, I was too mad to talk to him. Then it just seemed pointless. I wasn't going to take him back no matter what he had to say. And really, I don't think he wanted me to take him back anyway. I think he was ready for the marriage to be over. Both of us were."

Nadia began blotting the blossoms with another piece of paper towel. "Why?"

"I don't think we had much left," Greta said slowly as she unwrapped the leaves from the butter. "Maybe we never had much to begin with. I think I married him because it seemed like a good idea. And then it wasn't." Like the purple hair. Like dropping off the tennis team.

"Because of the secretary?"

Greta closed her eyes. "Because we didn't really love each other. Because he married me to get a wife, and I married him to get a husband."

"Why did you think you needed one?" Nadia's voice was neutral, but her dark eyes had a suspiciously hard shine.

Greta stared down at the butter and sugar in her mixing bowl. "My parents had been married for twenty-five years when my father died. My mom's best friend Lily died last year, and she was married for over thirty. People in the harbor get married and stay married. I guess I thought I needed to do that too." *And I never stopped to wonder why I thought so.*

"Because your mother wanted you to?"

"Maybe. She never said anything one way or the other, but I think she thought I needed to settle down. And I really messed up with college and all—I mean, I started college and then I dropped out and went to culinary school. She probably thought I was beyond help." Greta started beating the sugar into the butter, stirring maybe a little more vigorously than she needed to. She really hadn't proved her mother wrong, had she?

"Did you finish culinary school?"

"Oh yeah. I really enjoyed it too."

"But that didn't please your mother?"

"Not so much. She calls it cooking school."

"So you got married to make up for not finishing college?" Now both Nadia's brows were elevated.

Greta sighed. "I don't know. Maybe. It seemed like a good idea at the time. But now I've messed up again. Mom's going to be very unhappy with me." She probably already was, in fact.

"How precisely did you mess up, dear?" Nadia said briskly as she moved the paper towels to the back of the counter. "Your husband had an affair with his secretary and got caught. I fail to see how that was any of your doing."

"Well..." Greta began and then stopped. When you put it like that, it did sound a little weird.

"And please don't tell me that if you'd been a better wife, he'd never have slept with her." Nadia dusted her hands. "Men who sleep with their secretaries don't need any particular excuse."

Greta sighed, pouring sugar into one of the bowls. "You could be right."

"I am definitely right. Does your ex-husband plan to marry this woman?"

Greta shook her head. "I have no idea, but I haven't heard anything about an engagement."

"Then my guess is she's not really the love of his life, no matter what she thought about it herself. He didn't leave you because he loved her."

"No, I'll grant you that. I'm pretty sure he didn't love his secretary." Of course, Greta wasn't sure he'd ever loved her either. Not even when he'd asked her to marry him.

"What other excuse might you come up with to assume this situation is all your fault? Perhaps that you aren't attractive enough. But I assume you're much too smart to fall for that one." Nadia leaned back against the counter, folding her arms across her ample bosom.

Greta paused, then shook her head. "No, I look okay. Maybe not as good as Ryan would have liked—I mean, nobody would ever mistake me for a supermodel—but definitely okay. When I take care of myself." Had she taken care of herself? Had she made enough effort to make herself presentable for Ryan? She really didn't know for sure. But she thought she had. And she was beginning to think that wasn't really an issue.

On the other hand, she'd rushed into a marriage with a man who didn't love her against her mother's advice. That particular issue still loomed large.

Greta squinted at Nadia's lavender flowers. "How long do they have to sit there?"

"A few hours. The scent intensifies as the flowers dry."

"And then what?"

Nadia shrugged. "And then I pack them into jars and fill the jars with olive oil. What are you going to do now?"

Greta glanced down at the collection of bowls on the counter. "I need to mix up some milk and water and vanilla. Then I beat some egg whites into the butter and sugar. Then I put it all together, mix it up, and bake it in the pan with the rose geranium leaves."

"Fascinating," Nadia said dryly. "What I meant was what

are you going to do about telling your mother?"

"Oh." Greta shrugged. "Well. I need to do that, I guess."
*Guts up, Greta.*

Nadia nodded. "I would recommend that you do it sooner
rather than later."

Greta closed her eyes. "I know. I will."

"Would you like to use my phone?" Nadia gave her a bright
smile.

Greta shook her head. "I'll use my own."

"Do it now."

"I'm in the middle of something." Greta narrowed her eyes.

"Nothing that can't wait a few minutes. You need to face
this, dear. And you need to do it now."

"All right, all right," Greta grumbled. It didn't help anything
that Nadia was absolutely right.

Her phone was upstairs in her room. Maybe someone
would waylay her on the stairs before she found it.

Unfortunately, all the potential waylayers seemed to have
moved on to other things. She reached her room without seeing
anything or anyone unexpected. Her phone sat where she'd left
it on the nightstand. She picked it up, turning it on for the first
time in two days.

The first thing she saw was the voice mail icon. She'd
ignored it when she'd called Josh. Now she clicked on the icon
and looked at the list. Four messages were from her mother.
One was from a number in Texas that she assumed wanted to
sell her something.

One was from Ryan.

She blinked. Why would Ryan want to talk to her? He'd
managed to say little enough during the entire divorce debacle.
Why would he want to talk now that it was over?

She took a deep breath and clicked on the first of her mother's messages.

"Greta," her mother's voice snapped in her ear. "Where are you? Why did you leave without telling me? Call me as soon as you get this."

The second was more of the same, although her mother's voice sounded slightly more anxious. Greta felt a brief pang of guilt. *Of course she's anxious. Did you expect her not to notice? You know this counts as another screwup, right?*

She flipped through the last two, listening to her mother's voice rise. It was message four that made her clutch the phone so tightly her fingers hurt. "Oh Greta, why didn't you tell me? What on earth happened? You've been separated and divorced and you didn't even mention it? What were you thinking?"

Greta licked her lips. What had she been thinking exactly? That time would stand still until she got around to explaining everything to her mother? That her mother wouldn't call her ex-husband when she didn't realize he was an ex? She closed her eyes for a moment. *Definitely another screwup, Greta.*

She took a deep breath, then clicked on Ryan's message. "Greta." Her ex-husband sounded faintly annoyed. "Where are you? Your mother is trying to reach you." There was a long pause and she thought the message was over. Then she heard Ryan's voice again. "Are you all right?" He sounded concerned. More concerned than he'd sounded when they got the final decree.

*Well, crap.* Her mother was furious, and her ex-husband was annoyed. What was she supposed to do now?

Call them, of course. Except she had a cake to finish. *Decision-free zone.*

# Chapter Nine

Sophie had to admit it—Hayley Stone really had changed. Or at least she'd changed her outfit. Her red top and black slacks were a lot more serious than the outfits she used to wear, most of which featured safety pins in picturesque formations. Of course, the fact that Hayley had let her hair go back to its natural blonde rather than the jet black she'd worn in high school, added to the fact that her eyes no longer looked like they'd been outlined in crayon, definitely helped.

Hayley rested her notebook on her knee, listening carefully—and patiently—as Sophie filled in the details, with Owen supplying the occasional bit of support. Sophie had to hand it to her. Not everyone was so patient with Owen. She began to feel a lot more sympathetic toward Hayley than she had when she'd first arrived.

They finally finished explaining everything, and Hayley glanced down at her notes, pushing a strand of blonde hair behind her ear. "Let me see if I've got this right," she said carefully. "Greta drove off after the wedding." She paused briefly, keeping her gaze resolutely on her notebook, and her face flushed.

*The wedding. The disaster. Right. Carry on, Officer.*

"She sent you a text that said 'I'm all right, don't worry'. And you haven't heard from her since. Is that the gist of it?"

She raised her gray eyes again, glancing first at Sophie and then at Owen.

"Yes," Owen said.

Hayley's forehead furrowed in a frown. *Crap.* "I'm sorry, but I don't see anything here I can act on. There's really no evidence of foul play. Is there any particular reason you're concerned aside from not hearing more from her?"

"She left all her things here," Sophie said in a rush. "She left wearing that ridiculous bridesmaid outfit, with nothing else except her purse."

Hayley nodded. "I can see how that would be worrying. But..." She paused again.

"But?" Sophie prompted stonily.

"But Greta was always sort of...impulsive. As I recall. Couldn't it be that she just decided to go visit someone? Or take a couple of days to decompress?" Hayley gave her a guarded smile.

Sophie gritted her teeth. Of course, that's what everybody in town would think. Greta the flake. Takes off and leaves her mother to worry without even thinking about it. Which was pretty much what had happened, after all.

"She just got divorced," Owen blurted. "She didn't tell Sophie."

Sophie closed her eyes for a moment. She hadn't really intended to tell anyone about the divorce. Not until she'd had a chance to talk to Greta about it first. She didn't especially want the news to spread around Promise Harbor before she had all the details.

Hayley nodded slowly. "Well, that could be a reason for her to want to take some time off to think, couldn't it?" She gave Sophie another faint, sympathetic smile. "I mean, if I were to come up with a reason for her to take off, having her marriage break up would be a good one."

Sophie blew out a breath. She really hated being pitied by a former student. Particularly one who was friends with Gavin Montgomery, the wedding-wrecking snake. "That's true, but she could also have had an accident. Or worse. I just want to make sure she's all right." Much to her annoyance, her voice wobbled on the last two words. Lord, she hated that sympathetic look in Hayley's eyes.

"I understand. Has Greta's ex-husband heard from her?"

Sophie blew out a breath. "I don't think so."

"Is there any reason to believe it was a bad breakup?"

A drip of ice coursed down Sophie's backbone. *Ryan? Ridiculous!* "If you're implying that he could be involved in her disappearance—"

"I'm just trying to cover all the bases, Mrs. Brewster. If you'll give me his name and number, I can give him a call and see if there are any other places Greta might have gone that he knows of."

"Of course," Sophie said stiffly. She dug Ryan's number out of her cell phone address book. She'd have to delete it now.

"In the meantime I'll check the accident reports and do a little calling around to make sure no unidentified accident victims have shown up at any of the hospitals in the area." She gave Sophie another of those reassuring smiles. "For what it's worth, we probably would have heard about anything like that by now. The fact that we haven't is really good news."

*Oh yeah, really good news.* Sophie managed not to snarl.

"That's good," Owen said quickly. "That's great. Thank you."

"I'll let you know what I find out." Hayley pushed herself to her feet. "If you should hear anything from Greta..."

"I'll certainly call you." Sophie gave her a tight-lipped smile. "Thanks."

She watched Hayley stride back to her truck, parked in the driveway where all the neighbors could see it and probably call one another ASAP. *Something else going on with the Brewsters. Hayley Stone stopping by.*

Why couldn't Greta have gone into something steady like the Promise Harbor Police Department? Instead of rushing off to cooking school and then rushing off to marry Ryan McBain? Why did Greta keep rushing off, period?

"Sophie." Owen stepped next to her, his hand on her shoulder. "She's all right. Like Hayley said, she probably took off to think."

Sophie closed her eyes and counted to ten. She wasn't sure if the fact her daughter had absconded without a thought about telling her mother what she was doing was much of a comfort. And now that Hayley knew, she had no doubt the rest of the town would find out soon enough. Mabel Standish, the police dispatcher, was a human public address system.

*Poor Sophie. First her son loses his bride, then her daughter loses her husband and runs away. What's wrong with that family anyway?*

Sophie felt a brief pinch of guilt. *What would you have done if Greta had told you she wanted to leave?* Probably ordered her to stay. And talk to the neighbors and the gossips and everybody else in town. Just like she'd tried to order Josh to go after Allie and save the wedding. And she wasn't sure he'd listened to her either, given that he also didn't seem to be around town right now. According to one of the men at the fire station, he'd taken off with his former girlfriend, Devon.

*None of this is their fault. Both of them just got caught up*

118

*in...events.*

Her chest felt tight suddenly. "Nothing," she muttered. "There is nothing wrong with my children. They're both perfect!"

"Sophie?" Owen sounded concerned.

"My children are perfect," she said flatly. "They are absolutely wonderful. And I won't let anybody say anything different." *Not even me.*

"Okay." Owen had moved from concerned to wary.

"I'm just..." She blew out a breath. "I've been so concerned about what everybody would think, I forgot about what *I* think. And I think my children are wonderful."

"They are. Allie too." He shrugged. "Sorry, Sophie."

Sophie sighed. "It's not your fault they didn't want to get married, and it's not my fault either. It's just something that happened." She sighed again, harder this time. "Of course, now we're stuck with the fallout while the children get to run away. Lucky them."

Owen frowned. "Why?"

Sophie shook her head. Sometimes Owen had trouble following the line of a conversation. Maybe she should backtrack. "Well, I mean, we're here and they're gone..."

"No." Owen smiled slowly. "Why stick around while they run away? Can't we run away too?"

Sophie blinked. He couldn't possibly mean... "What do you mean?"

"New resort I heard about—Greenbush Island. Nice place. We could spend a few days there. Get a massage, play some golf. We get back, and everything's blown over."

*Oh my.* "I couldn't. Really. Not now. There's so much..."

"Stuff you have to do?" Owen's eyebrows went up. "Do you want to do it?"

A moment of silence stretched between them.

"Let me think about it," she said softly. "It might work."

Owen gave her another slow smile that made him almost handsome. "There you go."

Greta sat on her bed, staring down at her phone. She knew what she needed to do. Why was it so hard to do it?

She took a deep breath and then punched in the numbers for her mother's cell phone. With luck, she'd have enough charge left in her own phone for this conversation. With even more luck, she'd only have enough to last through the first few set of reproaches her mother would give.

*Please, Mom, just get it over with.*

The phone rang three times and then cut to voice mail. *Thank you, Jesus!* She wasn't sure why her mother wouldn't be answering her phone, but she wasn't going to look a gift horse in the mouth. "Hi Mom," she said cheerily. "Just wanted to let you know I'm staying at a hotel up the road for a couple of days. They needed a cook. Don't worry, please. I'll be home by the end of the week. Promise."

She turned the phone off quickly. Save the charge. *Right, Greta, that's why you're not giving her a chance to call back.*

"Greta?"

She glanced up. Hyacinth stood in the hallway, peering timidly into her room.

"Hi, Hyacinth." She tossed the phone onto her bed, pushing herself to her feet. "What can I do for you?"

"Would you like to meet Carolina now?"

Greta frowned, glancing at the clock next to the bed. "Well, I've got a cake in the oven, but I've got a little time to spare. Will it take more than ten minutes or so?"

Hyacinth shook her head.

"Okay, then, let's go. I'd love to meet Carolina." Whoever or whatever she might be.

Hyacinth bounced down the stairs in front of her, humming. Greta felt a little like humming herself. Leaving her mother a message had taken a huge load off her mind. For a moment, Ryan's hushed *Are you all right?* floated through her memory, but she ignored it. Her mother's feelings were worth being concerned about. Ryan's definitely weren't. Let him worry.

Hyacinth threw open the back door and started down the path toward the garden shed. Greta had to increase her speed a little to keep up. At the door to the shed, Hyacinth paused briefly. "Just a sec. I've got some food to give her." She ducked back toward the side of the shed, emerging with a plastic bag full of lettuce leaves. "It's just the outer leaves," she said quickly. "We don't eat them anyway."

"Right." So Carolina was an animal that ate vegetables. Greta's jaw tensed. *Please don't let it be something really disgusting.*

Hyacinth opened the shed door and stepped inside.

At first the contrast of darkness with dazzling sunshine made it difficult to see, but once Greta's eyes became accustomed to the dimness, she noticed a collection of garden tools leaning against the walls, a half bag of fertilizer at the side, some plastic pots in the corner.

And a large glass aquarium at the back of the room closest to one of the small windows. Sunshine from the window poured onto the contents of the aquarium—a shadowy accumulation of castle spires and gravel. And one medium-sized turtle.

Greta stepped closer, squinting so that she could see better. The turtle was about six inches long. It raised its head as Hyacinth stepped near, showing its yellow-splotched black throat. Its black shell formed a high dome behind its head, the yellow splotched scales echoing the splotches on its feet and neck.

Greta blew out a breath. "A box turtle."

Hyacinth nodded enthusiastically. "An Eastern box turtle. *Terrapene carolina.* That's why I named it Carolina. Isn't it pretty?"

Greta knelt down for a better look. *Pretty* wasn't exactly the word she'd have used. "It's a nice-looking turtle. How long have you had it?"

"I just found her day before yesterday." Hyacinth knelt beside her.

"I thought you said you didn't keep animals after you'd identified them." Greta glanced back.

Hyacinth licked her lips. Greta had a feeling she was blushing, although it was hard to tell in the darkness of the shed.

"I caught a turtle once when I was little," Greta said slowly. "My dad let me keep it for a couple of days, but then he told me to set it free. He said it would get sick and die if I kept it." Also, of course, he wasn't crazy about having it in the downstairs bathroom. But it had still been a legitimate point.

"It's endangered," Hyacinth said quickly. "I can't let it go. It might get hurt."

Greta blinked. She didn't know much about endangered species, but she was pretty sure you weren't supposed to keep them in aquariums in your garden shed. "But my dad was right—I think turtles need to be free. I mean, being in an aquarium can't be the right kind of life for an animal like this. Plus it really isn't good for her."

Hyacinth stuck out her lower lip. Suddenly she looked very much like a nine-year-old and a little like her grandmother. "If I turn her loose, she might get run over by a car. Or a farmer might mow her nest. There are all those dangers out there, things that could kill her. I'm keeping this one safe."

Greta nodded slowly. "I can see that. But she probably won't do well in the aquarium either. You wouldn't want to do anything that would hurt her, would you?" She didn't like to think about how Hyacinth might react if the turtle died, which it was quite likely to do if Greta was any judge. Bad enough if a pet died on its own. Even worse if it died because the child had done something wrong.

Hyacinth looked away. "I know how to take care of her. I looked it up on Grandma's computer. I won't do anything to hurt Carolina."

Greta chewed on her lip. "Sure, but…"

"What about your cake?" Hyacinth said quickly. "Isn't it almost done?"

Greta pushed herself to her feet. "Probably. Thank you for showing me Carolina."

Hyacinth nodded. "You're welcome," she muttered, focusing on Greta's toes.

"Would you like to help me frost the cake?" Greta asked a little desperately.

"Maybe later."

Greta sighed, turning toward the door of the shed. Obviously, Hyacinth wasn't open to suggestions about her pet. Still…

As she walked back toward the house, Greta wondered how much Hank knew about turtles. Hyacinth might not listen to her, but maybe she'd be more open to the Voice of Science.

Dealing with a heartbroken child and a dead turtle didn't rank high on her list of favorite things.

Hank pulled his truck into the carport a little earlier than usual. Part of the reason he'd left before the usual time was his foot, of course, which still bothered him, although not as much as it had before.

The other part of it—maybe the larger part—was Greta. That kiss in the moonlight had skipped around his mind most of the night, showing up in a couple of dreams that had left him hard and aching in the morning.

Sort of like high school. Not exactly an experience he wanted to revisit.

Still, he wanted to spend more time with her. Maybe taste those lips more fully. Maybe find out whatever secret she was trying to hide. She was a fascinating combination, Greta Brewster. Practical and fantastic. Sneakers and *Gone With the Wind* dresses. He wasn't sure he'd ever run into anyone quite like her before. He certainly didn't know any archaeologists who ran around in hoopskirts—no sane ones, anyway.

He stepped inside the kitchen door, pausing to appreciate the smells. Pastry, with an added sort of flowery scent.

Greta looked up from the stove, where she was working on something. "Hi."

"Hi. Smells good." Smelled fantastic, if he was really honest. "What is it?"

"Probably my cake." Greta frowned down at the pan in front of her. "Let me get this gratin to the stage where it can fend for itself, and then I can talk."

He leaned against the counter, watching her arrange the

potato slices in a fan around the pan.

"How did you slice them so thin?"

She shrugged. "They're not as thin as they should be. I didn't have a mandolin. I sort of improvised with a knife."

He stared at the spiral of slices that looked paper thin. "And you didn't slice off a finger in the process?"

Greta gave him a dry look. "Slicing off parts of your body while you were cooking was frowned upon in culinary school."

"Right. Still impressive, though."

She gave him a quick smile. "Thanks. I love being impressive."

*Oh, babe, trust me—you've got impressive down.*

He glanced around the room. "Where's everybody else? I thought you usually had an entourage in the kitchen. Yesterday, Hyacinth looked like she was training for the Iron Chef."

Greta gave her potatoes a pat. "Hyacinth's sort of mad at me right now."

"I don't think I've ever seen Hyacinth mad. What's up?"

"How much do you know about turtles?"

He shook his head. "And now for something completely different? I had a few turtles when I was kid. That's about it."

"Hyacinth showed me her turtle. Has she showed it to you?" She folded her arms across her chest.

He shook his head again. The turns in this conversation could give a man whiplash. "Nope. Is it something I should see?"

"I don't know. She's got it in an aquarium out in the shed. I probably wasn't as enthusiastic as I should have been. I mean, I don't think wild turtles are good candidates for house pets."

"Nope." He shrugged. "It should be okay if she doesn't keep it more than a couple of days."

"She says it's endangered. Aren't you supposed to leave endangered species alone?"

Hank pushed himself upright again. "Strictly alone. That's the kind of thing that can get you in trouble with all kinds of people, including the Feds. What does she want to do with it?"

"She wants to keep it. She's feeding it lettuce." Greta picked up a spatula, pushing the potatoes down flat in the casserole dish. "Is that what you're supposed to feed turtles?"

"Some turtles, yeah. Some turtles eat insects. Hell, some turtles eat meat along with their veggies. She can't just feed it lettuce, even if she plans on letting it go eventually. And if it's really endangered, she shouldn't be keeping it at all. Where is she?" He started toward the dining room door.

Greta frowned. "I haven't seen her since earlier this afternoon. Come to think of it, I haven't seen any of the Dubrovniks since I took my cake out of the oven. Nadia was here then, but she left. You'd think Alice would at least be around."

"I'll see if I can find them." He pushed open the door to the dining room. The empty dining room. Also the empty lobby. He stepped toward the front door, only to see a *Closed* sign, with another on the door of the general store.

"Curiouser and curiouser," he muttered, heading up the stairs. Alice usually closed the store around six, but she left the light on in case anyone wanted an emergency can of beans.

A note was thumbtacked to his door.

*Gone to Promise Harbor for dinner and a movie,* Nadia had written in her dramatic script. *I suggest a picnic.*

Hank unpinned the note, heading back down the stairs

toward the kitchen. Greta glanced up as he came back through the swinging door. "What's up?"

"Apparently, we're on our own for dinner." He handed her the note.

She frowned, reading it over. "Well, hell. I'm not taking potatoes gratin on a picnic, even assuming I could get it baked in time."

"Can you put it in the refrigerator?"

She shrugged. "Sure. I guess we could have it for dinner tomorrow night."

"And do we have anything we could take on a picnic?"

"Ham sandwiches." Her forehead furrowed in thought. "There are some chips in the pantry, although I don't know how fresh they are. And I got some tomatoes and carrots at Merton yesterday. And, of course, there's rose geranium cake. I don't know what we have to drink, though."

"Do you have any objections to beer?"

She shook her head.

"Then we've got it covered. Sounds like a plan to me."

Greta gave him one of those slow smiles that made his blood pressure spike. "I'm all in favor of plans."

"Good. You grab the food, I'll grab the beer, and we'll be on our way."

She raised an eyebrow. "On our way where?"

"Leave that to me." He took a deep breath as he headed for his room and the six-pack of Samuel Adams he had tucked in his minirefrigerator. *Thank you, good old interfering Nadia.*

# Chapter Ten

By the time Hank had maneuvered his truck down the dirt road leading from the sign for Tompkins Lake, Greta had given up trying to figure out what exactly was going on. Nadia hadn't said anything about taking Hyacinth and Alice to the movies while she'd watched Greta take the rose geranium cake out of the oven. Nor had she said anything while Greta spread the cake with fragrant pink frosting. Greta had even talked about her plans for dinner, and Nadia hadn't said a word. Maybe because she was plotting.

Clearly the whole movie thing was a last-minute decision. But Greta wasn't at all sure why Nadia had decided to do what she did or how Greta herself was supposed to feel about it. Nadia was the only one at Casa Dubrovnik who knew all the details of Greta's marriage disaster. It didn't make any sense that her first reaction would be to send Greta out on a date with Hank when she was still decompressing from the divorce bends.

*A date? Is that what this is?*

Well, sort of. It made more sense to call it a date than to call it anything else. While she and Hank might spend a pleasant evening discussing current affairs in Massachusetts, she didn't really see that happening. Unless *affairs* was taken to mean something a lot broader than its usual definition.

*This is headed in one obvious direction. The only real*

*question is how I feel about it.*

The truck finally moved beyond the trees, and Greta got her first view of Tompkins Lake, glimmering silver among the groves of white pine and hardwood. She could see a few picnic tables tucked in among the trees, complete with families having dinner. One or two small children waded in the shallows of the lake.

"Not exactly deserted," she murmured and then blushed. Who said Hank was looking for a deserted spot in the first place?

He grinned as he turned the truck up another short road. "It gets more deserted a little later, after all the parents leave to put their kids to bed."

She nodded absently, as if the prospect of the parents taking off was only faintly interesting. Which it was. Absolutely.

*Uh-huh. Right.*

Hank pulled the truck in next to a pine grove and turned off the engine. "This look okay?"

"Sure." Greta glanced at the aging wooden picnic table on the square of gravel and grass. The wood had weathered to silver and probably had several hundred splinters per square foot. Suddenly she really wished she'd brought a tablecloth.

"I'm not sure that table is going to work," she said slowly.

"Don't worry. I brought a blanket." He lifted a battered picnic basket from behind the seat.

"For a tablecloth?"

He shook his head. "To sit on. If that's all right with you."

"Um...sure." There was no reason not to eat on a blanket spread on the grass. None whatsoever.

Hank lifted out an even more battered cooler that he placed beside the basket. "I found the basket in the pantry. With any luck it hasn't held anything toxic."

Greta eyed the cooler dubiously. "The cooler's more suspect than the basket. It looks like it was used to transport organs."

He grinned. "The cooler's mine. No organ transport, but it's been in a few rough spots around the world. Came through fine, so far as I can tell."

"Oh." Greta swallowed. "Well, good." For some reason she seemed to be putting her foot in her mouth much more regularly now than she had been earlier. Maybe it was the weather.

He pulled a threadbare quilt from the side of the basket. "Don't know how big this is, but it should be enough for a meal." He flipped it open, spreading it across a grassy patch near the trees.

The late afternoon sunlight caught flecks of gold in his hair, turning his skin golden as well. For a moment, his muscles were outlined in shadow as he smoothed the blanket across the grass.

Greta took another in a series of deep breaths, then picked up the picnic basket and joined him.

"I hope we've got enough food. If I'd had more warning, I could probably have come up with something better than this." She set the basket on the blanket, kneeling beside it, careful not to look at Hank. "I've got sandwiches and carrot sticks. And some cherry tomatoes. There's some chips too. Would you like pickles? Because I brought some along."

*Stop talking. For the love of god, just stop.*

She licked her lips, taking a slightly shaky breath.

"Here." He handed her a beer bottle. "Have some. Relax. Whatever we've got to eat is fine."

She took a quick sip of beer, wishing it were something

stronger or possibly weaker. The last thing she needed was something that would make her babble more than she was already babbling.

"So what have we got here?" He began lifting packages out of the basket—sandwiches, chips, veggies. "Looks good." He paused, then lifted the final package out very carefully, positioning the rose geranium cake reverently at the center of the blanket. "My god, did I say good? This looks sensational."

"Thanks. It's pretty tasty. Usually. If everything worked out the way it was supposed to." *Stop talking, Greta Anne. Just stop talking.*

He arched an eyebrow. "My guess is everything worked out. And even if it didn't, I'm willing to make believe it did."

Greta grabbed a ham sandwich, pushing it in his direction. "Here you go. Dinner."

"Dinner. Right."

For the next few minutes, she managed to keep her mouth full of food, which seemed to be a good antidote to babbling.

Hank took a swallow of beer, watching her as he did. "So have you had enough time in Casa Dubrovnik to be ready to pass on a little information about yourself? Or are you still finding your footing, so to speak?"

"What do you want to know?" All of a sudden, Greta found she had no urge to babble whatsoever.

"Well, we could start with where you're from."

"Promise Harbor."

He waited for a moment, maybe to see if she'd say anything else, then shrugged. "So you live in Promise Harbor?"

She shook her head. "I'm *from* Promise Harbor. I live in Boston. Or anyway I used to." She wasn't entirely sure where she lived anymore. She'd given up her apartment in Boston at the same time she'd left for the wedding—not that it was much of a loss. "That is, I lived in Boston for a while."

"Okay." Hank narrowed his eyes. "I'm sort of confused right now. If you don't live in Promise Harbor or in Boston, where do you live?"

She ran a finger through the condensation on the side of her bottle, trying to come up with an answer that made sense. "Casa Dubrovnik?" she said with an attempt at a smile.

He frowned. "You're going to move in there permanently?"

"Probably not. I don't know. I just...it's another possibility. I'm not sure exactly where I live at the moment." Yet another decision she hadn't managed to think through before she left Boston.

Hank turned toward the lake, taking a contemplative swallow from his beer bottle. "I really thought that was one of the easy questions."

"I was sort of upset when I came here," she hedged. "I was supposed to be a bridesmaid at my brother's wedding, but then his fiancée's old boyfriend showed up at the wedding, and the two of them left together. There was a lot of chaos. My mom was having a meltdown. I decided to go for a drive until things calmed down, sort of. And then I found you in the hole and pulled you out, and it was like I saw this new direction I could take."

"Right. You already told me a little about that wedding. So did you call your mother?"

She nodded. "Twice. I haven't heard back from her, though. At least not since the last message I left."

"Okay, so we've been over the whole wedding fiasco a couple of times. How about telling me something about yourself you haven't mentioned before?"

She took a deep breath, staring down at her beer bottle. The minefield stretched before her. "I never graduated from college. I was a philosophy major at Boston University, but I started cooking for my housemates and I figured out I was happier doing that than I was doing anything else. So I switched to culinary school. My mom was furious. It took her a few months to forgive me."

"Why? Didn't she think you were a good cook?"

"She thought I rushed into it. And she was sort of right—I didn't give it a lot of thought, not like I should have."

"How long does it take to get a culinary degree?"

She shrugged. "In my case, a couple of years, plus an externship. I got my associate's degree, though. My mom had to admit I followed through on it in the end."

"So then did you get a job in a restaurant or what?"

Too late she saw the trap opening beneath her feet. *Oh well.*

"No. I've never worked as a chef. Well, not until Casa Dubrovnik anyway." She took a hurried sip of beer, wishing it were colder.

Hank rolled to his back, propping his head on his hands before he glanced over at her again. "Okay, you're dancing around something here, so before I start pressing you for details, just tell me—is it really bad?"

She blew out a breath. "Define *really bad*."

"Well..." He shrugged. "Have you been in prison? Were you on trial for murder in some Central American country? Are you actually a well-known stripper in the greater Boston area?" He grinned. "Actually, that last one might not qualify as *really bad*."

"I've never done anything like that," she said stiffly. She

took another deep breath and blew it out. "I just got married."

He froze, the beer bottle halfway to his lips. "You're married."

She shook her head sharply. "Divorced."

"Oh." He shrugged. "Why dance around it then?"

She picked up a carrot strip, nibbling at the end. "Have you ever been married?"

"Nope. Nobody ever considered me promising marriage material."

"Did you ever think about it?"

He turned his head again to look at her, green eyes suddenly dark. "Sure. I'm a functioning adult who's over thirty. If I hadn't thought about it occasionally, I'd be some kind of mutant."

"But you didn't do it."

He shook his head. "Getting tenure in archaeology isn't exactly a walk in the park. I spent a lot of years bouncing around from one archaeological site to another. I never met a woman who seemed like she'd really enjoy steaming jungles with large insects and Maoist guerillas for comic relief."

"But you're not in a steaming jungle now. You're in Massachusetts."

"Really?" He glanced around the lake. "No kidding? I thought I was in Guatemala."

Greta snorted, then rubbed her nose. "Very funny. But if you specialize in Latin America, what are you doing here?"

"Found a wall. Decided to dig it up. Got somebody to give me money. The rest is history. Or anyway, archaeology. It's all Mesoamerican anyway." He grinned again, his teeth flashing in the dimming light. "And don't think I haven't noticed the discreet way you changed the subject."

She shrugged. "Here's another new subject, then. Want some rose geranium cake?"

He rolled back to a sitting position. "I thought you'd never ask."

"Okay," she cautioned as she lifted the pieces of cake out of their container and onto paper plates. "This is a really different kind of cake. And disaster is always possible since it sort of depends on the quality of the rose geranium leaves. I figure this early in the summer they won't be quite as strong as they would be later on. But there's always the possibility that they'll be so strong they'll take the cake over the top and it'll taste like bad perfume."

He raised his eyebrows, lifting the plate from her fingers. "That's one hell of a selling job there, lady. Remind me never to have you promote anything of mine."

She shrugged. "I just want to be upfront about it so you won't have to try to save my feelings if it's a bust."

"I promise I won't try to save your feelings." He grinned, sliding his fork into the cake.

Greta took a bite. *Not too bad.* At least it didn't taste like old carrots or citronella, the way it would in a worst-case scenario. And the frosting had turned out very, very well. Everything was sort of vegetal, almost flowery. She stole a quick look at Hank.

He was chewing slowly, his expression distant. She thought about telling him he didn't have to finish it, then decided to see what would happen if she didn't.

He put his plate and fork down beside the blanket. "This is one of the most fantastic cakes I've ever tasted. You're an artist, babe. The Chagall of cake pans."

She let loose the breath that she hadn't realized she'd been holding. "Thank you. It turned out okay, didn't it?" She placed her own plate beside his.

135

He nodded, reaching toward her. She caught her breath again, this time with full knowledge.

"Frosting," he murmured. "On your nose." He touched his index finger to the tip of her nose, then her lips.

She tasted the remnants of sweetness, sucking in the tip of his finger almost before she knew she'd done it.

He caught his breath in a hiss and she pulled back, blinking. "I... Sorry," she whispered.

"Why?" He leaned closer, his eyes the color of moss in the shadows.

"I'm...not. Really."

"Good." He cupped her cheek, gently pulling her closer until his lips touched hers.

Sweetness again, frosting and cake and him. Mostly him. She opened her mouth to him, running her tongue along his, angling her head to take the kiss deeper. For just a moment, she wondered what the families at the picnic tables were thinking, and then she didn't care. A thrill of heat passed down her body, centering in her core, leaving her wet with longing.

He pulled back for a moment, running his thumbs along her cheekbones. "You taste like flowers."

She closed her eyes, trying to slow down her thundering pulse.

His hands slid along her sides, dipping beneath the edge of her T-shirt, then upward to cup her breasts.

"Just my luck," he groaned. "When did you start wearing a bra again?"

"I only have one with me," she whispered. "I wore it in your honor."

"For the future, I can think of lots of different ways to honor me." He ran his lips along her throat beneath her chin, leaving a warm line with his tongue. "Wearing a bra wouldn't be one of them."

She dipped her head, touching her own tongue to the hollow of his throat, nipping lightly at his collarbone. He groaned low in his throat.

*Parents. Kids. Picnic tables.*

She pulled back abruptly, staring back toward the beach. The suddenly empty beach. "Where did everybody go?"

"Home, I imagine. Looks like we're all alone." He slid his lips farther down her throat to her shoulder. "Does it matter?" he murmured.

She shook her head, suddenly mute.

"Good." He slipped his hands beneath her shirt again, then pulled it over her head. His thumb moved beneath her bra strap, sliding it off her shoulder. Then he pushed his hand beneath the bra to cradle her breast, freeing it from the cup. His tongue moved along the upper curve, and he took the nipple into his mouth, sucking it until the tip ached, like an arrow straight to her core.

She sank her fingers into his hair, holding his mouth tight against her until he raised his head to move to the other breast. She slid down against the blanket, her breath suddenly tight in her chest. Her body arched, rubbing her throbbing mound against his thigh.

His hand dropped to the top of her jeans, pushing the button open, then the zipper. And then his fingers slid inside her panties, stroking swollen, wet flesh.

She brought her own hands to his chest, fiddling with buttons, finally pulling the shirt loose so that she could touch him, sliding her palms over warm skin, prickling hair, the hard buds of his nipples.

He slid a finger inside her, working her clit with his thumb, and she fell back again, hooking her fingers into the waistband of his jeans. His teeth caught her nipple, pulling it taut as his thumb pushed her toward the top. Her hips arched beneath him, bringing more of her in contact with his hand as she writhed against him. Then she came undone with a moan, biting her lip to keep from crying out.

His hands eased her jeans and panties down, sliding them below her knees to free her legs. She felt cool air touching her skin, a sharp contrast against the heat burning inside.

She wished for a moment that she could see him more clearly. She wanted to know what he looked like without clothes, to see the stripes of muscle and bone moving beneath that golden skin. Her hands moved over his thighs to the button of his jeans, pulling down his zipper and reaching inside to take him in her hands.

"Easy, babe," he whispered as he dug into his pocket.

She slid her hands along his length as he groaned against her ear. And then he was tearing open the condom with his teeth and sheathing himself in what seemed to be a very fast time.

She leaned back beneath him, feeling his warm hands on her inner thighs as he spread her legs farther, the slight crinkle of fabric against her buttocks. The head of his cock pressed against her opening and then slid in slowly, thick and wide, stretching her beneath him, reminding her how long it had been since she'd done this with anyone. She sighed, then wrapped her legs around his waist, pulling him deeper.

He groaned again, louder this time, but they were all alone. Or if they weren't, it didn't matter. She refused to care. He began to move slowly, propping himself above her on his forearms. His face was almost lost in the darkness, his skin silver in the shadows. She rose to meet him, bringing him even deeper, her muscles tightening around him.

"Holy god," he muttered, his face against her hair.

She cupped his face in her hands, bringing his mouth to hers, biting his lower lip, then plunging her tongue inside.

He growled deep in his throat, his teeth grazing her lips as his hips slapped against hers. One hand moved to her breast, his fingers closing around her nipple, pulling it taut.

She sighed against his mouth, her hips jerking against him. The pressure built again in her core, the rush of blood and heat. His hand dropped down between them to touch the place where they were joined, and she flew apart.

He came with her with a strangled cry, his body thrusting into hers, their hips slamming together. For a moment all she could feel was heat and light. And then she was sliding down the other side, her arms tight around his body, her head tucked into the hollow between his chin and his shoulder.

"Greta," he murmured. "Good lord above."

She closed her eyes, trying to catch her breath. "Gosh," she whispered.

*It was never that good with Ryan, was it?*

The thought drifted through her brain, but she quickly pushed it aside. Thoughts of Ryan didn't belong here. And they sure as hell made no difference.

Hank rolled to his side, taking her with him, one hand tangled in her hair. "You can cook. You can rock a hoopskirt. And you're sexy as hell. Maybe you should tell me about your flaws now before I decide you're the ideal woman."

She sighed. "I'm not talking about flaws at the moment. Maybe later. When my bones stop feeling like elastic."

"Okay," he murmured, "later then."

*Much later.* Possibly never. But for now, she'd settle for the feel of his arms tight around her shoulders and his body pressed against hers.

# Chapter Eleven

For the first time in days, Sophie woke up without that churning combination of irritation and fear in her stomach that had haunted her ever since Greta had driven off. Late yesterday afternoon, Hayley Stone had called with the news that there was no news. No accidents had been reported with unknown female victims. No wandering amnesia sufferers had been admitted to any regional hospitals. Wherever Greta was and whatever she was doing, she appeared to be okay.

Of course, Sophie was still vaguely irritated that she'd taken off in the first place. If she'd stayed put, she could have helped out. She could have done...something, although Sophie wasn't entirely sure what that something would be. Answered the phone maybe. The phone that was still ringing with annoying frequency.

Today it was Alma Martinson from the hardware store, checking to see how Sophie was doing. *How do you think I'm doing?* Sophie wanted to ask. *How is it any of your business how I'm doing?* Instead she said she was doing just fine, thank you for asking, and hung up.

She hadn't let herself think much about Owen's suggestion for a brief escape. Greenbush Island. Spa treatments. Golf. She hadn't played golf for years, not since her husband had died.

Getting away from Promise Harbor for a week or so suddenly seemed really appealing. No Alma Martinson. No Bernice Cabot. No one calling every morning on the off chance she'd heard more devastating news and needed someone's shoulder to cry on.

She wondered if she and Owen would have adjoining rooms, then felt her cheeks flush. *Of course not! What are you thinking?*

Sophie was still blushing when she heard the doorbell. She sighed. Probably another neighbor or friend or acquaintance checking to see if she'd gone over the edge yet. At least she'd have the satisfaction of seeing their disappointment when they realized she was just fine.

Not that she really was fine, exactly. But she was...okay. Surprisingly okay.

She peeked through the front door peephole to see Ryan McBain standing on her doorstep. All dark, curly hair and broad shoulders, dressed in a light blue knit shirt and khakis, as if he'd just stepped out of a J. Crew ad.

Her heart promptly began to thump in panic. *Greta!* She threw open the door. "Ryan. What are you doing here? What have you heard?"

Ryan's forehead furrowed attractively. But then Sophie had always thought he was a handsome man. Just not a very nice one. "Heard? About Greta? Nothing. That's why I'm here. I thought maybe you'd know something more."

She took a relieved step backward, and Ryan walked into her living room, glancing toward the kitchen. "Is Josh here?"

Whatever good opinion of him she might have been considering promptly disappeared in a puff of angry steam. "No. I'm here by myself. What do you need, Ryan?"

His forehead furrowed again, as if he were considering

142

Deep Thoughts. "I'm concerned about Greta. I thought maybe Josh had had some news about her."

"Why would Josh be the one to have news?" Sophie folded her arms, knowing full well what the real answer was. *Because Josh is the responsible male in the house rather than the irresponsible female.*

Ryan shrugged. "No particular reason. So have you heard anything new?"

"The police checked for accidents. None have been reported. I'm sure Greta will let us know where she is when she's ready." She managed a thin smile.

Ryan sighed. "Well, that's good, I guess. Not as good as a message from Greta would be, but good. I'm glad to hear it."

Sophie's heart softened somewhat. At least he was concerned about her daughter. As he should be. Her good manners gave her a quick kick. "Would you like something to drink? There's fresh coffee."

"Coffee would be great, thanks. Black." He followed her into the kitchen, slumping into a chair at the table.

She poured two cups from the percolator, stirring milk into hers. At least she might be able to pump Ryan for a few more details about the divorce. "When was the last time you heard from Greta?"

Ryan frowned slightly. "A couple of weeks ago, I guess. When the final decree came down." His ears turned faintly pink. Apparently, the subject of the divorce was still sensitive.

Sophie nodded, as if she heard her daughter's final divorce decree discussed all the time. "Did you realize she was coming here for Josh's wedding?"

"No." He frowned. "Josh got married?"

"Not exactly," she said quickly. "Greta was supposed to be

the matron of honor."

"Oh." He shrugged. "I thought maybe she came back here to be with her family after...everything."

"Everything." Sophie sat down opposite, stirring her coffee, trying not to sound like a prosecuting attorney. "Just what does *everything* include?"

Ryan licked his lips. "Well, the divorce. The separation. All of that."

"So Greta was upset about all of that?" She took a sip. "I only ask because she didn't seem particularly upset when she got here, but I might not have noticed. There was a lot of confusion surrounding the wedding." And a lot more surrounding the fact that it hadn't taken place after all.

Ryan's gaze darted around the kitchen. Sophie got the distinct impression this wasn't a topic of discussion he was enjoying much. "She seemed okay the last time I spoke with her. But, as I say, that was a couple of weeks ago."

"How long were you separated before the divorce?" she asked flatly.

He licked his lips, staring down at his hands. "Around three months. It didn't take long to reach our property settlement and get the filing done."

"So you and Greta have been separated for four months now?"

"About that." He finally looked directly at her.

Sophie noted the tightness around his jaw, the slightly narrowed eyes. Something was obviously making him feel very uncomfortable indeed. She considered the possibility that it might be something Greta had done and then dismissed it. Only someone with a guilty conscience would bother to drive from Boston to Promise Harbor to find out what had happened to his ex-wife.

"Do you mind my asking what happened between you? Since Greta didn't get a chance to tell me herself before she left?" She managed to keep her voice pleasantly noncommittal, but she'd already begun considering just what choice expletives she could use on the good-looking weasel before she tossed him out. By now, she was beginning to have a very good idea what might have produced the guilty conscience that had brought him to her door.

Almost as soon as she'd had that thought, she heard the front door open. "Sophie?" Owen's voice called. "You here?"

*Oh wonderful, somebody else to put their two cents in.* "We're in here," she replied. "In the kitchen."

Owen stepped through the door, then paused, frowning slightly in Ryan's direction. "Hello."

Ryan blinked, then glanced at Sophie, clearly waiting for an introduction, which she regarded as another mark in his disfavor. How much energy did it take to say hello, for Pete's sake? Plus he should remember Owen from when he was married to Greta. "Ryan, this is Owen Ralston, a family friend. Owen, you remember Greta's ex-husband, Ryan McBain."

*Ex-husband.* Funny how much easier it had become to refer to him that way now.

Ryan nodded in Owen's direction. "Hello."

Owen nodded again, then took the chair next to Sophie. "Something up?"

"Not exactly. Ryan was just telling me about the divorce." She turned her best eagle-eyed stare in his direction.

Ryan glanced at Owen again, clearly unhappy with the idea of discussing his marriage in front of a stranger. Sophie found she really didn't care whether Ryan was happy or not. "About the divorce?"

"It was..." Ryan licked his lips. "It was sort of a misunderstanding. My fault, really. Just incompatibility. Sort of."

Sophie decided that was the lamest excuse she'd ever heard. But she also decided she really wasn't interested in hearing much more from Ryan McBain, particularly since she doubted he'd tell her the truth. "Well, I haven't heard anything more from Greta, as I said. I can have her call you when she comes back." *Assuming she does come back.* Sophie pushed that thought from her mind.

"I'm not leaving town just yet. I thought maybe I'd talk to people around Promise Harbor a little before I left. See if I could find out any more information." He was looking uncomfortable again.

"Any more information about what?" Sophie felt a slight sting of exasperation. The man made no sense at all. And she didn't much care for the thought of him stirring up more gossip in the harbor. "We've already asked the people who were at the wedding and they haven't seen her."

"Look, this is my responsibility." Ryan pulled himself up so that he was sitting very straight, the model of a responsible male. "If Greta's done anything..."

"Done anything?" Sophie stared at him. "What do you mean 'done anything'? She just drove away. She didn't knock over a liquor store."

"Suicide," Owen said flatly, staring at Ryan. "You think she's killed herself."

Ryan's face turned pink, his lips narrowing to a thin line. "I don't know what to think."

Sophie's exasperation instantly morphed into full-blown rage, with perhaps a slight tinge of fear. Had he heard about her depression after Dave had died? Was he assuming like mother, like daughter? Maybe Josh had thought she was suicidal, but he'd been wrong. She'd never come close to suicide, even when she was at her lowest. And Greta hadn't even seemed depressed. Suicide? The very idea made her want to slap him across that smug, WASPy face.

"You think my daughter would hurt herself? Over you? You conceited ass! My daughter would never kill herself over you. Or over any other man. She's got too much good sense to do something like that." She pushed herself to her feet, her hands shaking. "Get out of my house. Right now."

"Sophie..." Ryan looked scandalized.

"I'm serious, Ryan. You get out. If you think Greta would hurt herself over you, you obviously don't know her at all. Which is maybe why you're not married to her anymore." Sophie closed her hands into fists at her sides. She didn't really think she'd sock him, but she wasn't entirely sure.

Ryan rose stiffly to his feet, his expression grim. "I hope you're right, Sophie. Believe me, I'd prefer that. But I'm still going to look for her."

Owen put his hand on her arm. "Better leave now," he said to Ryan. "Sophie wants you to go."

Ryan opened his mouth again, then closed it abruptly. He started toward the front door, then turned. "Honestly, Sophie, I'd rather be wrong."

"Then you're going to get your wish," she said through gritted teeth as she watched him walk away.

Owen rubbed his hand across her shoulders after the front door had shut behind him. "Okay?"

She closed her eyes. "Yes, now that he's gone. The nerve of that man. The iron-plated nerve."

"Any news?" Owen raised an eyebrow.

"Just what Hayley said—no accidents, nobody unaccounted for at the hospitals."

"Checked your phone today?"

Sophie frowned. "She'd call on the landline, and there aren't any messages there. She knows I don't like the cell."

He shrugged. "Better check anyway."

She frowned again, but dug the cell phone out of her purse, flipping it on as she did. And saw the flashing icon.

"There's a call." Her throat felt tight all of a sudden.

"Voice mail. Click on it."

Sophie clicked, then put the phone to her ear. The voice was the one Greta used when she was trying to pretend she didn't feel guilty. Sophie recognized that voice from a long series of teenage catastrophes. "Hi, Mom. Just wanted to let you know I'm staying at a hotel up the road for a couple of days. They needed a cook. Don't worry, please. I'll be home by the end of the week."

She closed her eyes for a moment, taking a deep breath. Then she put the phone on speaker and played the message again.

Owen shrugged. "Sounds okay."

"Yes, she does." She tried to keep her voice from rising. "And when I see her again, I will tell her just what I think of her little adventure. In detail."

"So she's cooking." He shrugged again. "That makes her happy."

Sophie took a breath, ready to tell him just how angry she was. But a picture of Ryan McBain's clueless face floated through her mind. *Happy.* Had Greta been happy lately? She'd always really enjoyed cooking. Maybe she was enjoying herself now. "Yes," she murmured. "It's probably making her very happy."

"Going to tell her ex?" He raised an eyebrow.

She shook her head. "No. Let him wander around and make a fool of himself. I think that would be good for him. Or anyway, it would be good for Greta."

Owen nodded. "Sounds fair. What about Greenbush Island?"

She turned to look at him. With his blond hair and green eyes, he looked a little like Allie. But he looked more like Owen. *Dear Owen.* Such a good man.

"I think it would be a wonderful idea," she said slowly.

Greta made three dozen muffins for breakfast, leaving two dozen of them for Alice to sell in the general store. She was a little curious about how much Alice would charge today, but not curious enough to brave whatever sarcastic comments Alice might have about her activities the night before.

*Activities. Nice way to put it, Greta.*

Nadia came in while she was rolling out dough on the kitchen table.

"Pie?"

Greta nodded. "I got some blueberries at Merton."

"We have some growing in the backyard. Hyacinth could pick some—she's quite good at it."

Greta wondered briefly if Hyacinth was speaking to her again. She was betting on not. "Maybe for the next one."

"Of course."

One of Nadia's penciled brows arched as she smiled, and

Greta braced herself. Maybe she could head her off at the pass. "How was the movie?"

"Oh, all right I suppose. Some sort of cartoon. Hyacinth liked it."

"Good." Greta kept her gaze on her piecrust, willing Nadia to go away.

"And how was your evening?"

"Fine," Greta said flatly.

"Did you have your picnic?"

"Yes."

"And where did you go?"

Greta considered not answering, but she doubted that would be enough to shut Nadia off. "Tompkins Lake."

"A pleasant spot." Nadia readjusted the pink pashmina around her shoulders. "Did it work?"

Greta bit her lip. *So* not what she wanted to have a conversation about right now. "We had a good time. Thank you for suggesting it."

"You're welcome. I'm also going to suggest something else. Why don't you take Hank some lunch at his dig or his hole or whatever it is? I don't know what he eats normally, but I'm willing to bet it isn't particularly healthy." She picked up one of the leftover muffins, peeling off the paper sleeve. "I'm sure we could spare you for lunch. Also dinner, assuming you make something that can be warmed."

Greta leaned back against the sink, drying her hands. "Okay, Nadia, what exactly is going on here? Are you a total romantic or what?"

Nadia shrugged. "I'm sure Alice would say that I am, but she'd be wrong. I don't believe in pairing everybody off. Life's not like Noah's Ark, after all." She adjusted the pashmina again.

"On the other hand, when I see two people who seem compatible and who could both benefit from the relationship, what's the harm in doing a little matchmaking?"

Greta gave her a dry smile. "For the record, I sort of started this particular match myself."

"So you did. Although rescuing Hank from a hole could hardly be regarded as a strategy." Nadia's eyebrows arched again. "Unless, of course, you contrived to put him there in the first place."

"Nope." Greta picked up her dish towel again. "I'm not that forward thinking, I guess. I'm still not ready to be matched up by somebody else, though. I'd rather think it was my own idea, all in all."

"Could I ask why you're resisting? Do you object to Hank or do you object to the idea itself?"

Greta bent over the sink, washing the last of the coffee cups and very deliberately not looking at Nadia. "I just wonder..."

"Wonder?" Nadia prompted.

"If this is some kind of rebound thing," Greta finished in a rush. "I mean, I've only been completely divorced for a couple of weeks. And we were only separated for two or three months before that. It hasn't been that long since I was married."

"Do you miss your husband?"

Greta frowned, considering the possibility. "Not really. I sort of miss being married—I mean, I liked having somebody to talk to every day or so. But I could have gotten that with a roommate instead of a husband." *And the sex might have been better.* She pushed that thought to the back of her mind rather quickly.

"Companionship is an important quality," Nadia agreed.

"Still, there are more important considerations, at least in my experience."

"You were married?" Greta tried not to sound surprised.

Nadia nodded. "Twice, in fact. I outlived both of them, which wasn't entirely unexpected but still not what I'd hoped for. I came to live here with Alice after my second husband died."

"And Alice was married too, or at least I assume she was since Hyacinth is her granddaughter."

Nadia nodded. "Married for over thirty years. Divorced for a decade or so now. Her daughter Annette is Hyacinth's mother. She's currently on tour with the Boston Symphony. Plays viola."

"Oh." Greta wasn't sure what to add to that, so she settled for nothing.

"But none of this has anything to do with this rebound nonsense," Nadia continued. "If you don't miss your ex-husband for anything other than a sounding board in the evening, I'd say you're not really suffering from a broken heart."

Greta sighed. That much was definitely true. "No. My heart is bruised but intact."

"Then a nice affair with Hank should be perfectly okay with everyone, I'd say."

Greta opened her mouth to object to the "nice affair" thing but stopped. It *was* a nice affair. Very nice, in fact. And she couldn't really think of a single good reason not to go ahead with it. "Thanks, Nadia."

"Don't mention it. I like to think the two of you would have stumbled into a relationship even without my prodding. I merely speeded up the process." She smiled again. "But I'd still suggest taking him a sandwich around noon." She flipped the pashmina over her shoulder and swept out of the kitchen.

Greta stared down at the dish drainer. Surely she could make another ham sandwich or two. And surely Hank could spare her a few minutes at the dig.

# Chapter Twelve

At twelve fifteen, Greta packed up the same battered picnic basket they'd used the night before with basically the same meal—sandwiches, chips, cherry tomatoes, a couple of peaches, and two sodas. Instead of rose geranium cake (the rest of which had completely disappeared by the time they got back to Casa Dubrovnik), she included a couple of peanut butter cookies she'd baked that morning.

Alice raised an eyebrow, Nadia gave her a smile, and Hyacinth avoided her gaze just as she had ever since the Carolina incident. Greta really hoped she could get the child to talk about the whole turtle problem, but she wasn't ready to try it now. She made sure the Dubrovniks had enough soup and sandwiches for their own lunch and headed for her car.

She hadn't really spoken to Hank since they'd parted the night before. He'd asked her to come to his room for a beer, and part of her had really wanted to do just that. But the more sane part reminded her that she had to get up early to make the muffins and coffee for the general store. Plus, of course, she felt a little weird about going into his room cold-bloodedly as it were. It was one thing to be overcome with passion on the shore of a lake in the moonlight. It was quite another thing to decide to go to Hank's room because the sex had been really good and she wanted to try for a rematch.

Although, of course, that had been absolutely true.

Now she drove carefully down the bumpy gravel road to the field where Hank's truck was parked under a maple. There was another car there too for once, an ancient Toyota with a rusted fender and bald tires. Greta wondered if it had actually been parked there deliberately or if the driver had simply abandoned it where it had finally reached the end of its lifetime.

She hoisted the picnic basket out of the backseat and headed up the path with the *Danger* signs. At least now she knew they didn't apply to her.

She stepped into the clearing and stopped abruptly. A strange man was climbing up the ladder out of the excavation, carrying a sack of rocks over his shoulder.

For one insane moment, she thought he might be some kind of criminal. A serial killer. A rock thief. A tomb robber, although that made no sense at all since Hank's hole wasn't a tomb, or at least she didn't think it was.

He looked to be about medium height, although it was hard to tell since he was still partly in the hole. He wore a tank top and jeans, with a blue bandanna wrapped around his head. After a moment he turned and saw her, his forehead furrowing. "Hello?"

"Where's Professor Mitchell?" she blurted.

The man stepped out of the hole and lowered the rocks to the ground. Once she got a good look at him, she revised her estimate downward—more like a boy than a man. Long, stringy blond hair hung below the edge of the bandanna, and he had a sprinkling of acne across the bridge of his nose. "Dr. Mitchell?" he called. "Somebody here to see you."

Hank's head popped up at the end of the excavation. Fortunately for her ego, he broke into a grin as soon as he saw her. "Hey, Greta. What's up?"

"I brought you some lunch." She lifted the picnic basket.

"Great. Hang on a minute." He disappeared into the excavation again, then climbed up the ladder much more quickly than the boy had. But then he didn't have a sack of rocks on his shoulder.

The boy stared longingly at the basket. "Lunch break?"

Hank glanced at him. "Give it another twenty minutes."

"Oh." The boy's expression turned tragic.

Hank rolled his eyes. "Meet my missing intern, Marty Petersen. Marty, this is Greta Brewster. And no, the lunch she has in that basket isn't for you."

Marty looked even more tragic. "Figures."

"Marty here apparently landed in the college infirmary without bothering to tell anyone. He just got out yesterday, right, Marty?"

The boy nodded morosely. "Flu. Flat on my back for a week. Still don't have all my strength back." He cast another longing look toward the picnic basket.

"You'll have to remember to bring your lunch with you tomorrow, then," Hank said crisply. "Bring up the rest of those rocks and then you can take a break."

Marty headed back down the ladder with considerably more energy.

"You're mean," Greta murmured, hiding her grin.

Hank made a sound that was remarkably close to a growl. "He deserves it. Little jerk didn't tell his adviser where he was and he didn't even try to send me a message. Says he was too sick. I'm thinking he was enjoying being waited on hand and foot by the infirmary staff. He's got a lot of digging to do to make up for it."

He headed toward the battered table at the end of the

clearing, pushing aside enough rocks to make room for the picnic basket. "What have we got here?"

"Pretty much the same thing we had last night, unfortunately."

"What we had last night was great." He glanced her way, smiling, and she suddenly had a quick vision of just what last night had been like. Her cheeks promptly heated to something that was probably close to brick red.

"Sit down." He waved toward the camp chairs at the side. "Let me clean up a little bit, and then we can eat." He poured water from the cooler on his hands, rubbing them on a bar of soap and scrubbing with a rag from the table.

"When did you find out you still had an intern?"

"When he showed up this morning." He opened the basket, handing her a sandwich, then grabbing one for himself before he sat down on a camp chair. "If I didn't need him so badly, I'd tell him to forget it. But I need somebody for scut work if I'm going to get anything done by the end of the summer."

He smiled up at her again, the sunlight through the leaves still catching glints of gold in his hair, his teeth white against his tanned skin. "How are you? I missed seeing you this morning."

She felt suddenly shy, staring down at her sandwich. "You were gone before I got up, and I got up really early."

He shrugged. "Should have joined me for a nightcap. I might have stayed in bed all morning." His teeth flashed again.

She could feel her cheeks flaming. "At least I didn't keep you from meeting Marty."

His smile turned wry. "Yeah. That would have been a tragedy. What are you doing tonight?"

"Tonight?" She frowned. "Cooking dinner. I haven't thought

much beyond that."

"Have dinner with me."

"You mean tonight?" Which was an incredibly dumb thing to say, of course. When else could he be thinking of?

Apparently, he thought so too. The grin was back. "Yes, tonight."

"Like I said, I have to cook dinner."

"So? Make dinner for the Dubrovniks and then let's go out."

She did a quick mental review of what she'd planned— Asian shrimp salad with spring rolls. All of which could be made in advance and left in the refrigerator, along with the gratin from last night if they wanted something hot. "Okay. Where shall we go?"

He rubbed the back of his neck. "There's an inn in Promise Harbor."

"No," she blurted, then shrugged when he narrowed his eyes in surprise. "The food's not very good." Plus the last time she'd been there she'd been wearing a hoopskirt and carrying a bridal bouquet. Not exactly a moment to revisit.

"Okay, well, there's a place on the edge of town. Seafood, I guess. Would that be all right?"

"Barney's Chowder House?" She shrugged again. "Yeah, sure. They've got good diner food."

"Okay then." He took another bite of his sandwich. "I'll see if I can get Marty moving enough to finish up around five or so."

Greta glanced down at her T-shirt and shorts. There might be time to go into Merton and buy something more suitable. Somehow she didn't think the braless look would go over big at Barney's. Although now that she thought about it, Hank probably wouldn't mind.

He finished the last bite of his sandwich and smiled again,

licking mustard from his fingers. "Very nice. Delicious, in fact. Thank you. I guess I'll give my peanut butter and jelly to Marty, assuming I don't want to starve him."

"Dr. Mitchell?" Marty called from the hole. "I think you need to see this."

Hank rolled his eyes again. "He's been doing that all morning. So far, he hasn't shown me a damn thing I haven't seen twenty times already."

"Maybe I'll get going," Greta said quickly. "I've got a few things to take care of before we go out. Do you want me to leave the basket?"

"What's in it?"

"Chips, soda, cherry tomatoes, and cookies."

"Cookies?" His eyes grew wide. "Homemade? What kind?"

"Of course homemade. Peanut butter."

He gave her a slow grin. "Leave the basket, sweetheart. I can always use a cookie to bribe Marty into getting something done. Assuming there's enough for me too."

"There's enough. I packed extra. I thought you might like an afternoon snack."

Hank's eyes took on a faint gleam. "Woman, you are worth your weight in whatever cooks regard as most valuable— saffron? Anyway, whatever it is, you deserve it." He leaned over quickly and brushed his lips across hers. "Thanks."

Her heart rate kicked up a notch. "You're welcome. Now I've got to go. Give Marty a cookie for me."

"Right," he muttered. "Only if he doesn't piss me off too much. Of course, I've always got tonight to improve my mood." He gave her a last grin before he headed back toward the excavation.

She took a quick breath. "I'll look forward to it."

*Oh yes, definitely time to go to Merton for some new clothes.*

Normally, the drawbacks of the showers at Casa Dubrovik didn't bother Hank too much. All he really asked was that the water be clean enough to rinse off dirt and sweat, of which he usually had quite a bit. Now he found himself simmering with exasperation at the low flow trickling from the showerhead and the distinct lack of heat. He had a feeling his hair was going to be standing on end, particularly since he had no way to dry it except with one of Alice's limp towels.

But, of course, those towels had never bothered him before. Greta Brewster was having one hell of an effect on his routine and his general satisfaction with life. Not that he minded all that much.

He checked his closet, settling on a clean pair of jeans and one of the Hawaiian shirts he wore when he wanted something besides a T-shirt. This one had some kind of vaguely tropical white flowers against a turquoise background. Spiffy.

It was a little weird going out with somebody who lived in a room across the hall. He wasn't sure whether he should knock on her door or wait for her at the foot of the stairs. He'd peeked across the hall once before he'd changed his clothes, but it looked like she wasn't there. Well, that eliminated option one anyway. He headed downstairs.

Alice stood waiting for him at the bottom of the stairs with her perpetual sardonic smile. "Going out?"

He nodded. "Taking Greta to Promise Harbor."

"Don't bring her back too late. She's got muffins to bake for the store tomorrow."

*Yes, Mom.* "She'll know when she needs to be back so that

she can get up in time."

"Maybe." Alice shrugged. "You know this is all Nadia's idea, right?"

Hank gritted his teeth. "Believe it or not, Alice, Nadia's plans have very little effect on my social life."

"You just keep telling yourself that." She gave him another grim smile.

The door to the kitchen swished open behind them, and Hank turned to see Greta wiping her hands on a towel as she turned toward Alice. "Your dinner's in the refrigerator—it's salad and spring rolls. No heating required. But there's a potato gratin in there too if you want something hot. In that case, put it in the oven at three seventy-five for forty-five minutes or so. Then just set the table and serve." She paused when Alice narrowed her eyes. "Or have Nadia put it in the oven while Hyacinth sets the table. What I'm trying to say is you're all ready to go here."

Hank worked on controlling his slightly elevated pulse rate. Greta was wearing a short-sleeved, emerald-green sweater along with slacks in a lighter shade. The color somehow made her brownish hair glow red, while the slacks hugged her hips and thighs in a way that gave him a very vivid flashback to the blanket they'd shared under the full moon. He wasn't sure about the bra situation yet, but right now it looked like she'd gone without again.

He wondered if it was too late to suggest another picnic.

Greta flashed him a quick smile, turning to toss the towel on the desk. "Ready?"

*Oh my god, yes!* "Sure." He reached for her hand, ignoring the annoying way Alice's lips had quirked up. On closer inspection, Greta was wearing a bra, but at least it looked easier to dispose of than the one she'd had on last night.

The drive to Promise Harbor was surprisingly quiet. He had the feeling Greta was thinking about something else. "You're from Promise Harbor, right?"

She gave him a quick smile. "Right."

"Does your family still live here?"

She nodded. "My mom and brother do." She paused for a moment, seeming to consider something. "Want to see the house where I grew up?"

"Sure."

She directed him through a series of neighborhoods—nice midsized houses, lots of elm trees. "There it is," she said, leaning forward quickly.

The white clapboard house sat on a large lot with its own set of spreading maples. "Nice. Your mother still lives there?"

She nodded, squinting. "I don't see her car. Looks like nobody's home."

He gave her level look. "Would you have gone inside if she had been here?"

Greta shrugged. "Yeah. Maybe. I'm not sure."

"You're not ready to talk yet?"

"My week's not over yet," she said flatly.

He nodded slowly. "So what happens when it is over? You come back here to Promise Harbor?"

"I haven't thought that far ahead." She shrugged again. "I'm not making any decisions at the moment. I'll figure it out when the time comes. Meanwhile, why don't we head over to Barney's for some chowder?"

"Sounds good to me."

Ten minutes later, he pulled in to the parking lot next to what looked like a classic silver-sided diner with a red brick addition at the far end. Judging from the number of cars in the lot, the addition was justified. "Popular place."

"Yeah. There's not a whole lot going on in the harbor in terms of entertainment. Barney's sort of fills the gap." She gave him a quick smile. "Ready?"

"Sure."

He took her hand, leading her toward the building. "Do you know people who work here?"

"Maybe." She sighed. "I'm not exactly looking for old acquaintances right now. I'll probably keep my head down."

He paused, glancing at her tight smile. "We don't have to do this, you know. We could go back on the highway and see if we can find an Applebee's or something."

She shook her head. "No. It's a good place to eat. And I'm a big girl."

His lips spread in an involuntary grin. "Yeah. Thank the good lord." He drew her to the door while she was still laughing.

Inside, the place was packed. The harried hostess grabbed a couple of menus and led them down a narrow aisle to a booth tucked beside one of the windows. "This okay?"

"Great." He slid in one side, watching Greta slide in opposite him. Given his choice he'd have preferred to have her sit alongside him, but he'd take what he could get.

"What's good here?" He picked up the vinyl-covered menu.

She shrugged. "Clam chowder and fried clams are the two big things. The lobster roll's respectable. My brother likes the hickory burger."

"Are we likely to run into him?" Hank worked on keeping his voice neutral. In reality, he was beginning to be very curious about her family. The family she was apparently trying to avoid at the moment.

She shrugged again. "Not likely. He took off after the wedding that didn't happen. I'm not sure where he is right now."

He nodded. "Because your phone is dying and you're keeping it turned off."

"That's right." She narrowed her eyes.

"You know, I've got a universal charger. I'd be glad to lend it to you."

She rolled her eyes. "Thanks a bunch. That would really simplify my life."

A waitress stepped to the their table. For a moment she frowned at Greta, as if she were trying to remember her. Then she seemed to shrug it off. "What'll you folks have tonight?"

"Fried clams," Hank said. "And the largest, coldest beer you've got."

Greta gave him a tight smile. "That sounds great to me."

He deliberately moved away from the topic of Greta and her hometown during dinner. He wanted her real smile back, if only until he finished his order of fried clams.

"Good," he muttered through a mouthful. "Tasty."

She frowned, moving a fried clam with her index finger. "Not bad. A little greasy. Either the oil needs to be hotter or the clams need to be warmer when they cook. My guess is they dump them in straight from the freezer. Which, of course, is the way most people cook them. I mean, it's not like Barney's is doing anything wrong. And when I was a teenager I ate a ton of these with no complaints at all."

"Right." He took a swallow of beer. Very good, very cold. There was even frost on the glass. "Can you enjoy eating in a restaurant anymore, or do you always find yourself doing a critique?"

She gave him a rueful smile. "Sorry. Occupational hazard. Yeah, I can turn this kind of thing off sometimes. And for the record, I really do like Barney's clams. It's just that they're better in my memory than they are on the plate."

"That's the way with a lot of food, I guess. Hot dogs were a hell of a lot better when I was a kid."

"And we liked it that way," she said in a little old man voice. "Where are you from, Doc?"

"Omaha. Haven't been back in a while, though. My folks moved to Texas when the winters started getting to them."

"How did you end up here?"

"I got a job. In archaeology, you don't worry much about where the job is. You know you won't spend much time there, unless it's in someplace like New Mexico."

"But now you're digging here in New England."

"I lucked out. Most of the big digs in the area are in historic sites, and the guys who have the grants aren't interested in sharing." He gave her a slightly sour grin, shoveling in a few more clams.

"Well..." she began.

"Greta?"

The voice came from a few feet away. Hank turned to see a rather plump blonde working her way down the narrow aisle toward their table.

Greta sighed. "Oh, swell."

"Greta. It *is* you." The blonde gave her a triumphant smile, as if she'd just proved her case.

Greta's smile was more like a twitch of the lips. "Hi, Bernice. How are you?"

"Oh, I'm just fine." The blonde turned her gaze on Hank, skewering him with a suspiciously bright-eyed glance. "Who's this?"

Greta looked like she was gritting her teeth. "This is my friend Hank Mitchell. Hank, this is Bernice Cabot." He noticed she didn't describe Bernice as her friend, but maybe that wasn't significant.

Hank nodded in Bernice's direction. "Pleased to meet you."

"Likewise." Her greenish-hazel eyes looked both avid and slightly suspicious, like she wanted to see his ID. If so, she was destined for disappointment. "Are you from Boston?"

Hank shook his head. "Nope."

She waited for him to elaborate. He didn't.

Bernice turned back to Greta. "Where did you go after the wedding? Your mother was looking for you. Have you heard anything from Josh? Did he go after Allie? What about Gavin?"

"I haven't heard anything from Josh or Allie," Greta said quietly. "I don't know what they're doing. I took off for a few days."

If she was hoping that statement would bring the conversation to a close, she'd underestimated Bernice's persistence. "So are you home now?"

Greta's smile looked transparently annoyed. "I'm around."

"Well good, because once Josh and Allie come back, there's going to be fireworks. Your mom's going to need your help. Unless you need to get back to your husband in Boston?" That bright-eyed look was back again.

"Mom can handle stuff like this better than I can." Greta shrugged, her smile sliding into something that looked more like a grimace.

Bernice's own smile suddenly seemed annoyingly self-righteous. "Even so, you should be there to help. It's your responsibility, Greta."

Greta gave her a steely-eyed look but said nothing.

Bernice's ample bulk had effectively blocked the passage, making it almost impossible for the waitresses to get by. "Bernice," one of them snapped. "Move. You're in the way."

Bernice snugged herself more tightly against the table, which only moved her rear end into a more prominent position. "You can scrunch by."

The waitress narrowed her eyes, giving Bernice a death-ray stare. "Only if I lose fifty pounds. I'm serious, Bernice. You have to move."

"Well, there goes her tip," Bernice muttered. But she turned back toward the front of the restaurant. "I guess I'll see you later. Call me."

"Sure." Greta gave her another tight smile. "In about a hundred years," she murmured as Bernice moved away.

"Friend?" Hank asked.

"Acquaintance."

"Want to get out of here before you meet anybody else?"

Greta gave him a thin smile. "I thought you'd never ask."

He followed her toward the cash register at the end of the counter. She seemed to be keeping her gaze fixed on the door deliberately, as if she really didn't want to see anybody else she knew. Fortunately, no one else seemed interested in them. He paused at the cashier to pay the check, making one last survey of the restaurant. Bernice was tucked back in her table at the side, casting furtive glances in his and Greta's direction while she muttered to her dinner companions. He glanced back toward Greta.

Only to have his gaze caught by a guy sitting by himself at the far end of the counter. Dark hair. Medium height. Clothes that looked expensive, although Hank had no way of knowing, really. He bought his own stuff off the rack with as little thought as he could manage. Judging by his expression, the guy had developed an instant hatred for him, although Hank wasn't sure why. Maybe he objected to Hank's choice of shirt.

*Oh well.* He pushed his money toward the cashier, turning to follow Greta out the door. But he felt as if someone's gaze was burning into the middle of his back until they climbed into the truck.

# Chapter Thirteen

The ride back to Tompkins Corners was even more silent than the drive over had been. Greta stared out the window at the darkening trees alongside the road, wishing she could have the last couple of hours back to start over again. She should have known going to Barney's for dinner was a bad idea. She was just lucky she hadn't run into anyone besides Bernice, although actually running into somebody other than Bernice would probably have been an improvement.

She'd deliberately avoided looking around Barney's so that she wouldn't lock eyes with anybody who knew her. She'd reckoned without Bernice's ability to find her prey, however. Bernie could smell gossip a couple of miles away. And there Greta was with somebody other than her husband. Granted, Ryan wasn't her husband anymore, but Bernice didn't know that. Thus all those pointed references to Boston.

She only hoped Bernie wouldn't tell her mom she'd been at Barney's. She was pretty sure Mom's feelings would be hurt even though she had tried to stop by. And that might be the least of it.

"So." Hank's voice sounded blessedly normal in the gathering twilight. "I guess Promise Harbor, in spite of it being your hometown, is not one of your favorite spots."

She sighed. Given the way she'd acted with Bernice, that

was probably a fair assumption. "I like the town. I'm not crazy about some of the people who live there, but it's home."

"What's the problem with the people who live there?"

"They still think of me as a high school screwup." Also college. Also culinary school, although in reality she'd done pretty well there.

"Dare I ask what that involved?" He turned off the highway on the road toward Casa Dubrovnik.

"Oh, the usual. I borrowed my parents' car without asking and ended up in a snowdrift. I dyed my hair purple and had to let it grow out instead of washing it out because it turned out to be permanent dye. I painted my room black without checking with my parents first. My prom dress had a wardrobe malfunction."

His eyebrows raised. "An interesting wardrobe malfunction?"

She shook her head. "Not so much. My date caught my skirt in the car door and it ripped up the back. I had to go home and change into one of my mom's party dresses. So I ended up looking like I was channeling Joan Collins." She sighed. "It wasn't one of my best nights."

"But your brother's the one who's in the spotlight after this wedding, right?"

"At the moment."

He pulled to a stop in the carport, shutting off the headlights, then turned toward her. "So what's really going on here, Greta? I mean, I'm guessing it was more than just your friend Bernice, although god knows she strikes me as someone who'd depress the hell out of anybody."

"Yeah, well, she's not exactly my friend. More like an acquaintance." She sighed. "I'm sorry about this. I should probably have steered you away from Barney's. But I didn't know being there was going to be such a downer. Actually, it wasn't much of a downer until Bernice reminded me why I took off after the wedding." The whole decision-free zone thing was looking like another disaster.

"Come on." He opened his door. "The moon's still up. Let's walk around Nadia's garden."

The faint smell of lavender still perfumed the night air, slightly humid against her cheek. Hank interlaced his fingers with hers. "Nice night. Nadia's plants always smell great."

The lavender scent was replaced with mint. Greta closed her eyes, letting the aromas and the feel of the night air drift over her.

"So I'm guessing a lot of what you're not telling me has to do with your divorce. And the fact that the people back home apparently don't know about it." His voice was soft. "Would I be right about that?"

Her eyes popped open again. "Well, crap."

"Sorry." He gave her a rueful smile. "Didn't mean to exactly drop it in your lap like that. Am I right?"

She sighed. "Yeah. For what it's worth."

"So having wandered into this minefield, I guess I'll just keep going." He guided her to a bench, half hidden beneath a maple at the side of the garden, pulling her down beside him. "Tell me about it."

She stared off into the darkness toward the garden shed. Just her luck to have what should have been a great date turn into a confessional. "My divorce was final about two weeks ago. We were separated for two or three months before that. He cheated on me. I threw him out. That about sums it up." She glanced back at him, trying to see his face in the gathering darkness.

His hand moved across her back, rubbing gently. "Okay. Sounds messy, but not all that unusual, unfortunately. Did you love him?"

She blew out a long breath, thinking. Did she love him? Had she ever? "No," she said slowly. "I didn't at the end. I might have loved him, or sort of loved him, when we first got married. I'm not sure I remember."

"How long were you married?"

"Around two years." She leaned back against the bench, letting her head rest against his shoulder. "No big love story. Just...sort of typical, I guess."

"Okay." He rested his hand on her arm, holding her against him. "So why is this something you don't want to tell your mother? Did she really like this guy?"

She shook her head. "Not especially. And she's already found out about it, by the way—she left me a message on my voice mail. She always said he was really good looking, but that was about as far as she went in terms of compliments. He's from this sort of wealthy family, and I think Mom thought he was a snot."

"Was he?"

She turned to look up at him, smiling faintly. "Yeah. Now that I think back on it. He really was a snot."

"So your mother might not be all that upset that he's no longer related to her."

Greta shook her head again. "No. But that's not the problem. It's the whole screwup thing. It's something else I rushed into against everybody's advice, including hers. When I talk to her about it, Mom's going to sigh. When I told her I was dropping out of college to go to culinary school, she sighed. When I told her the purple dye wouldn't come out of my hair, she sighed. She always sighs. It's like she's saying 'You've done
172

it again, haven't you?' And she's right, of course, which is what makes it worse. I just...I wish I wasn't the one who always made her sigh."

They sat for a few moments, listening to the rusty sound of the crickets in the grass. "I don't exactly have a solution for you," he said finally. "But it doesn't sound like this was totally your screwup. My guess is your mom will be okay with it. Hell, knowing mothers, she'll probably be ready to cut the guy's nuts off."

"There's a thought." She fought back a grin. *Totally inappropriate.*

His hand cupped her shoulder again, gently pulling her closer. "If I kiss you now, you're not going to think it's some kind of half-assed pity thing, are you?"

She frowned. "It isn't, is it?"

"Nope. Definitely, nope." His lips touched hers lightly, almost a brush and then something more.

She opened her lips to him, letting her tongue slide along his for a moment. Then his lips pressed more firmly. She felt the edge of his teeth as he angled his mouth, one hand moving to the back of her head, holding her in place as his tongue plunged deeper.

She could barely see him in the darkened garden—just the dim shape of his body. It was almost like making love to a ghost. She moved her hands across his chest, feeling the smooth weave of his Hawaiian shirt, her fingers fumbling with the buttons.

He pulled back, resting his forehead against hers, his chuckle more like a groan. "Should have known better than to wear a shirt that buttoned."

"I like it," she whispered. "I'll like it even better when it's off."

He pushed her fingers away, undoing the buttons quickly. She smoothed her hands across the warm skin of his chest underneath, feeling the slight tickle of hair against her palms and then the hard points of his nipples. She ducked her head, running her tongue across one while she rubbed the other with her thumb.

His breath came out in a whoosh, and he grasped the bottom edge of her sweater. "The sweater goes." He pulled it up and off in a single jerk, dropping it on the bench, then squirming out of his own shirt so that he could lean against her.

The feeling of skin against skin almost sent her into instant orgasm. She caught her breath in a gasp, clasping her hands around his neck and bringing her mouth to his again. She nibbled on his lower lip as his tongue slid into her mouth again. And then she was sucking hard, drawing him deeper, groaning against his mouth.

She felt cool air against her back and realized that at some point he'd unfastened her bra. His fingers moved along her upper arms, sliding the bra straps down until it dropped in her lap.

"Is anybody likely to come out here?" she murmured. It was, of course, sort of late to be asking that question. *Oh well.*

"I doubt it. We're the only guests, after all. And all three of the Dubrovniks should have gone to bed by now."

He dipped his head and she felt warm breath on her nipple, then the rasp of his tongue. Her whole body seemed drawn to a single point, a shaft of desire flying straight to her core. He sucked hard, drawing her nipple taut between tongue and teeth.

Her body shifted restlessly. Somehow she had to get out of her capri pants. And she had to do it very, very soon. She started to unbutton the waistband.

Again, he pushed her hands aside, unbuttoning, then pulling the zipper down and lifting her into his lap as he tossed the capris on the rapidly growing pile of clothing on the bench beside them.

She turned to face him, spreading her legs with her knees pressed against his sides. Her hands were braced on his shoulders so that she could look at his face, or as much of his face as she could see in the darkness. The dim light made everything surreal, as if what she was feeling was somehow disconnected from her body.

Then he rubbed his thumb against her, back and forth, slowly, until the wisp of fabric between her legs was damp and she was panting as hard as if she'd just run a fifty-yard dash. Suddenly, she didn't feel disconnected at all.

He pushed her panties aside, his fingers suddenly delving into moist, warm flesh, and she managed to strangle the cry by sheer will. One finger slid deep inside her and began to move slowly in and out. She bit her lip to keep from groaning, moving her hips along with his hand. Another finger joined the first. He rubbed his thumb across her clit and the heat rose to a starburst. She came undone, her hips jerking against him as she whimpered.

"Ssh," he whispered, "it's okay." His lips brushed hers again as he took his hand away, leaving her aching and empty.

He dropped his hand to his pocket, but she touched his arm, shaking her head. "You don't need it. It's okay."

"You're on the pill?"

She nodded. "I should have told you last night."

"Doesn't matter. Just a nice bonus." He leaned forward, taking her nipple into his mouth and sucking again. He pinched the other nipple between thumb and forefinger, pulling until it was diamond hard.

She reached for his belt, pushing the buckle open, pulling down his zipper at the same time she felt him tug at her panties. The material at the crotch gave way with a snap.

*Crap.* She had another pair from the package she'd gotten from the general store, but that was it.

"Sorry," he murmured.

"I'm not." *Not exactly, anyway.* She pushed his pants and shorts down, letting his cock spring free. She moved her hand up and down his length, enjoying the feel of him, softness on granite, until he brought his thumb against her again, brushing back and forth across her clit until she gasped. Her inner muscles clenched tight.

"Wrap your legs around me." His voice sounded gritty, as if the words were being ground out.

Her legs locked around his waist, bringing her hips close so that she could feel the head of his cock grazing her opening. And then he was moving inside her slowly, letting her inner muscles adjust to his size. She kept her hands braced on his shoulders, her gaze fastened on his, moving her hips up and down to meet him.

She could feel the heat rising again, the aching need in her core. But this time she was going to wait, to make him come with her. Feel with her. His face was lost in darkness, then caught in moonlight as he moved, the skin slicked with sweat, his jaw tense. He leaned forward again, catching her nipple between his teeth, and she groaned.

The feeling blossomed like a hot rose, pushing her further toward the edge, almost beyond what she could hold back as he plunged deep again and again.

His forehead dropped to her shoulder, the harsh sound of his breathing echoing in her ear. And then he was jerking against her, hard, his fingers digging into her buttocks as he thrust deep.

She gave way then, pressing her heels against him as she came in a blaze, heat and light that seemed to go on for a long time. If they hadn't been in a darkened garden behind a house with three sleeping people, she would have given a war whoop.

Two years of marriage, and a lot of years of dating before that, and she'd never felt anything remotely like this. She really wanted to yell. She settled for nibbling his earlobe instead.

Hank leaned back so that he could look up at her. "Wow."

She nodded. "Wow."

"I don't know what it is about the combination of you and the moonlight, but it seems to send me into some kind of hyperspace." His lips turned up in a faint grin. "Not that I'm complaining, you understand."

"Good." She leaned forward, nestling against him as he moved his arm around her waist. They were still connected, and the connection made her glow. She wasn't quite ready to lose him yet.

He nuzzled her ear, biting the lobe gently. "You need to come to my room. Doing this in the moonlight is fine, more than fine in fact. But doing it in a bed has a whole range of other possibilities."

She blew out a breath. "I'd like to. But I'm a little worried about what the Dubrovniks might think."

He tilted his head so that he could grin up at her. "You're kidding. You really think Alice or Nadia gives a rat's ass?"

"Well, there's Hyacinth."

"True. But I have no intention of doing anything in front of her. Actually I have no intention of doing anything in front of Alice or Nadia either. I'll lock the door. Hell, I'll even put a chair under the doorknob if you'd prefer." He stroked his hand along her side, letting his thumb graze her nipple.

She snickered. "I just had an image of Alice enforcing bed check. Sort of like a dorm mother. I don't think I've ever seen her up in the hotel part. Does anyone even clean the room?"

"Alice does. Once a week." He paused for a moment. "You might not be here to see her do yours."

She felt a quick pang that she ruthlessly suppressed. "Probably not."

He was silent for a moment, gently running a hand over her hair. "I assume this would not be a great time to discuss what you're going to do when you leave here."

Her chest tightened. "You assume correctly." *No decisions tonight, Doc. Absolutely none.*

They sat in silence, listening to the crickets creak around them. She could feel the steady beat of his pulse where she rested her cheek against his shoulder. The warmth of his skin. The smell of Nadia's herbs. Her eyelids began to drift down.

"Okay," he said slowly, his voice rumbling in his chest. "I won't ask. I'll wait until the end of your week. But I'm still going to wonder about it, Greta. I might even worry."

She sighed. "I'm really tired of people worrying about me. There's nothing to worry about. I'll probably go back to my mom's house for a while until I get my bearings." Which would be loads of fun since every other citizen of the harbor would be watching to see how she screwed up next. "I've got a part-time job at a bakery in Boston that I could go back to. Or I could look for a job around the harbor. I mean, I've now got experience as the head chef of the Tompkins Corners Hotel Grand. That ought to count for something." She flexed her suddenly tense shoulders. Another decision she'd need to make. And soon too.

He tightened his arm around her shoulder, pulling her closer. "You could always stay here for a while longer."

She closed her eyes, ignoring the sudden surge of longing. "No, I couldn't. This is a fantastic escape. But that's all it is. It's not like it could ever be permanent."

He shrugged. "I don't think anybody said anything about permanent. But it's great for now. And who knows, you might find something else if you looked around."

A sudden breeze made the leaves rattle above them. She sighed. "We'd better go in. If nothing else, I'd better put my clothes back on. You never know when Hyacinth might decide to look at the moon."

He caught her face in his hands, his mouth covering hers, and she looped her hands around his neck, pressing herself close to him.

After a moment, he lifted his mouth again. "You are coming to my room now. No discussion. The mattress isn't the greatest, but it's soft. And I can promise you a beer."

"Beer and a mattress. How can I resist?" She smiled up at him as she reached for her sweater, her heart speeding up slightly at the sight of him in the moonlight, shadows outlining the slabs of muscle across his chest.

"I was hoping you wouldn't try." She saw the flash of his smile. Then he reached toward her, pulling her to her feet.

She tugged on her clothes, then followed him toward the back door, feeling the cool of the grass against her bare feet. He turned when they reached the back steps, scooping her up in his arms.

She wound her arms around his neck. "What are you doing?"

"You came here looking like Scarlett O'Hara. I thought I'd

just carry the theme along a little."

She was still laughing as he carried her inside, but a voice at the back of her mind whispered *decision-free zone* over and over.

# Chapter Fourteen

Greta woke in Hank's bed, which was neat but couldn't last, given that both of them had work to do. She sat up, pushing her hair out of her eyes, and tried to figure out how to get to her room without waking him.

"What's up?" he mumbled.

"Me. I've got breakfast to fix." She slipped out of bed, searching for her bra in the pile of clothes on the floor.

He reached for her, running one hand up and down her hip. "Ten minutes."

She raised an eyebrow. "Really?"

He nodded, his lips moving into a lazy grin. "If we both concentrate."

"You're on." She dropped her clothes and slipped back between the sheets.

In reality, when they finally got out of bed, Hank had to hurry as much as she did. At least he had enough time for sour cream pancakes with strawberries. "Got to get there before Marty does. God only knows what he might do on his own. See you tonight." He grinned. "Unless you want to do lunch."

"I'll think about it."

She was still humming "I'll Be Your Baby Tonight" when Alice came in. Alice cocked an eyebrow in Greta's direction.

"Having a good morning?"

"So far." Greta turned back to the stove. "Pancakes?"

"Sure. I'm always glad to take advantage of somebody else's good luck." Alice took a seat at the table. "What do you have to sell in the store? I'm assuming pancakes won't move all that well."

Greta shrugged. "They might, but no, there are cookies from yesterday, and I'll make muffins once everybody's had breakfast."

Alice nodded slowly. "Should work. It's all selling well, you know. We could probably double the number of muffins and still move them all. Hell, we've got people coming in from two towns over."

"Do you actually want me to double the number?"

"Sure. Why not take advantage while we can?" She narrowed her eyes. "Of course, doing this probably violates every board of health regulation on the books."

"Probably." Greta shrugged. "If you wanted to go on doing this with somebody else, you'd need to get the county to inspect the kitchen and make sure it's up to standard. But just on a guess, I'd say you could get a license without too much trouble. This kitchen looks like it used to be set up for commercial work."

"What about serving meals?"

Greta turned, flipping a stack of pancakes onto a plate. "Serving meals is trickier. You'd need a restaurant license and the rules are a lot more stringent. Still, as I say, it looks like this was once a professional kitchen or close to it. You've got the restaurant stove and the walk-in pantry and the prep sink. And the dining room looks like it was once the hotel dining room. You'd need a better refrigerator and a dishwasher and probably some renovation to what you've got here."

Alice gave her a sour smile. "Putting out money to make money. Always a risky proposition."

Greta shrugged. "You could talk to a restaurant consultant. They could at least tell you whether you stood to make any money selling meals or not."

Alice sawed off another bite of pancake. "Maybe we could do meals for the guests and anybody in the neighborhood who might happen to just drop in, accidentally so to speak."

Greta considered pointing out that Alice currently had only two guests, one of whom was her cook. But she decided to let it go. She had a feeling the conversation might veer into one of those "what are you going to do after this week" discussions that she was so determined not to have just yet.

Hyacinth walked in, rubbing sleep from her eyes just as Alice was finishing. "Good morning."

Greta smiled in her direction, hoping she could get the child to be friendly again. "Good morning, Hyacinth. How are you today?"

Hyacinth glanced up, blinking. "I'm all right," she mumbled.

"We have sour cream pancakes and strawberries. How many would you like?" Greta kept her smile in place, willing Hyacinth not to look away.

She shrugged. "Two, I guess. How big are they?"

"I can make them as big as you want," Greta grabbed her ladle. "Come and tell me what you'd like."

Hyacinth hesitated for a moment, regarding her suspiciously. Then she stepped up next to her at the stove.

Greta dipped the ladle in the batter, then dropped a small amount onto the griddle. "Bigger?"

Hyacinth nodded.

Meg Benjamin

Greta added a bit more. "Now?"

Hyacinth's brow furrowed as she studied the pancake. "A little more."

"Right." Greta poured the rest of the ladle onto the griddle, smoothing the pancake with the ladle's back. "Okay?"

"Yes, ma'am." Hyacinth smiled up at her.

Amazingly enough, Greta's heart seemed to do a little flip. She began humming again.

"Good morning," Nadia trilled, gliding into the room as she adjusted a turquoise pashmina around her shoulders. The woman must have bought out the entire stock at some random pashmina place.

"Time for work," Alice said flatly, pushing herself to her feet. "Cookies ready to go?"

"In the pantry on a sheet pan. All wrapped and ready." Greta added more batter to the skillet for Hyacinth's second pancake.

Hyacinth took her seat at the table as Nadia poured a cup of coffee. "Aunt Nadia, did you hear the owls in the garden last night?"

Nadia shook her head absent-mindedly. "I was probably asleep, dear. What did they sound like?"

"Sort of like somebody groaning," Hyacinth explained helpfully.

Greta gritted her teeth, flipping the pancakes. There could have been owls out there last night. It was always possible.

"Do tell." Nadia was smiling in her direction.

Greta spooned a good-size helping of strawberries onto Hyacinth's pancakes, then turned toward Nadia, her expression deliberately bland. "Pancakes?"

"Yes, please. Two. Tell me more about the owls, Hyacinth."

"There must have been more than one because one sounded high and the other sounded low. Unless one owl could be both high and low, I guess." She shoveled a bite of pancake into her mouth.

Greta's ears felt as if they were flaming. She poured out two more pancakes for Nadia.

"Did you get a look at them?" Nadia hid her smile behind her coffee cup.

Hyacinth shook her head. "It was too dark. I'll watch for them tonight."

"Do that." Nadia smiled again, taking the plate of pancakes from Greta.

Greta devoted herself to mixing up the muffins once Nadia and Hyacinth were seated with their pancakes. She figured she could avoid looking at Nadia if she concentrated on getting the proportions of wet and dry ingredients perfectly aligned.

Hyacinth finished eating and put her plate in the sink. "Thank you for the pancakes." She gave Greta a polite smile. "They were delicious."

"You're more than welcome. Come back later and I'll have muffins."

"Okay." She smiled again, heading for the back door, and Greta felt her shoulders relax. At least Hyacinth seemed to have forgiven her for wanting to free Carolina.

Nadia leaned back in her chair, sipping her coffee. "I do hope Hyacinth doesn't see the owls tonight," she said finally. "Or whatever they were."

"I can pretty much guarantee she won't." Greta sighed.

"Good. Did you have a nice dinner last night?"

"Sure." She gave the muffin batter a quick stir. "Good food, anyway."

"Surely the company was pleasant, too."

Greta turned to face her, leaving the batter on the counter. "Hank is great. Between him and this place, I've had a really wonderful week. But the thing is, I have to go home and face the music."

Nadia shrugged. "Of course you do. That was never in doubt, at least so far as I was concerned."

"And then I have to figure out what comes next. Without having you or Hank or Hyacinth to hide behind." *Decision-free zone. Yeah, right.*

"Well, I wouldn't call what you've been doing here hiding exactly. And you can always come back here if you want to. It's not like Promise Harbor exists in another dimension." Nadia took a last bite of pancakes. "These are superb, by the way. Whatever you do next, it should certainly involve preparing food."

"I'm sure it will. I don't want to do anything else." She sighed, pouring the last of the batter into her muffin cups. "Now all I have to do is find somebody who wants a cook."

"Well, we do, of course. But I imagine you're looking for something a little more challenging. Or something that at least pays real money. And what kind of muffins are you fixing today? Blueberry?" She raised a hopeful eyebrow, watching Greta slide the muffin tins into the oven.

Greta shook her head. "I'm trying peach. They're too wet sometimes, but I think I found a way to make them work."

"My dear, even if they're sopping they'll be consumed with gusto. The demand for fresh baked goods in Tompkins Corners has skyrocketed." Nadia frowned. "I don't know what we'll do when we can't supply them anymore, since there's no way in heaven or hell that either Alice or I could bake anything like this."

Greta leaned back against the counter again, narrowing her eyes. "I wonder how many other little towns around here have stores that might be interested in selling fresh muffins and cookies, with maybe the occasional cupcake thrown in?"

Nadia put down the fork she'd been using to scrape the last of the strawberries off her plate, blinking up at Greta. "That's a very interesting question. I'm sure the answer would be even more interesting."

"Of course, you'd have to have a kitchen that could be okayed by the county board of health. And it would have to have enough capacity to produce several dozen baked goods every day."

"Rather like this one, I suppose." Nadia glanced around the kitchen, smiling. "This used to be a real hotel, you know. With a kitchen that produced meals. It was almost derelict when Alice found it. She's done a great deal of work herself. I'm sure she'd be interested in doing more, given the right incentive." Nadia's smile turned dry. "In this case, of course, the right incentive would be money."

"It's...a thought." Greta paused. She closed her eyes for a moment, trying to fight down the rush of excitement. *Don't get ahead of yourself. Don't rush into anything. Stop and think for once.*

She might be able to find a job around the harbor somewhere. Frying clams at Barney's, for example. Or she could stay in Boston and go on working at the bakery. Of course, most of the people she knew in the city were either Ryan's friends or Ryan's business contacts, so her social life might be nonexistent.

Or she could open a contract bakery business in the kitchen of the Hotel Grand in Tompkins Corners. Working with people she'd known for less than a week. In a town she hadn't even realized existed before. *Another leap, Greta.* Her chest contracted almost painfully.

"Take some time," Nadia said quietly. "Think about it. But I'd say the possibilities are there."

"Possibly." She turned back toward the stove again, setting the timer. "Quite possibly."

Thirty minutes later, she was still thinking about the possibilities—and trying to fight off her rising panic—when she carried the first tray of muffins into the general store. The usual crowd of coffee drinkers was gathered around the front counter, although she noted that Alice or someone else had set up a makeshift café area at the side with some rickety tables and chairs. The crowd surged forward when she appeared, earning pointed comments from Alice about their parentage and their general lack of good sense. Greta spent a frenzied ten minutes or so passing out muffins while Alice collected money.

After they'd sold most of the tray to the first wave, Alice turned toward her. "Somebody was asking for you. Or anyway, I guess it was you. Somebody asking for Greta, anyway."

Greta's heart fell. Oh well, it was probably inevitable that somebody from the harbor would find her eventually. And at this point, it really didn't matter. She'd be going back there in a couple of days. Of course she would. "Man or woman?"

"Man. He's around here somewhere." Alice peered through the throng of people drinking coffee and eating muffins at the front of the store. "Move it, Hiram, I can't see to the back of the store with you there."

Hiram moved to the side, grumbling about the shortage of seating, and Alice peered toward the end of the room. "There," she said. "Over by the motor oil."

She pointed toward a dark-haired man standing next to the auto supplies rack. In the dim light of the store, he looked vaguely familiar. A sliver of ice slid down Greta's spine. More than vaguely familiar. Much more.

"Ryan," she whispered.

His head rose suddenly, almost as if he'd heard her. Their gazes locked as he moved toward the counter.

Alice glanced at her as Ryan walked in their direction. "Do I need my baseball bat?"

"Only if you want to hit a few pop flies," Greta muttered.

Ryan stopped in front of the counter, staring down at her, his smooth forehead slightly crinkled in concern. "Greta?"

He really was a very handsome man, with those cobalt eyes and that dark, curly hair. He'd managed to stay fit too, even though he'd spent most of his time at a desk in his father's firm. Quite a catch. No wonder she'd fallen for him. Of course, right now he didn't even raise a slight spray of gooseflesh.

She rested her hands on her hips. "What are you doing here, Ryan?"

He blinked. At least she'd managed to surprise him. "I've been looking for you. Your mother was worried."

"I left her a couple of messages. I don't think she's particularly worried anymore." She folded her arms across her chest. *Defensive move, Greta.* "Was that all you needed to know?" She managed to keep her voice neutral. With any luck she sounded polite and perhaps slightly bored.

His forehead creased a bit more. "Well, I just wanted to know that you were all right. I mean, you sort of disappeared."

"I'm all right. I just needed some time off." She could sense Alice leaning forward beside her. Maybe she was reaching for the baseball bat. Maybe Greta would help her if she found it. "How did you find me anyway?"

He looked slightly uncomfortable all of a sudden. "I saw you last night," he began.

Greta's jaw clenched. When exactly had he seen her? And what had she been doing at the time?

"That is, I think I saw you," he went on. "At that place in Promise Harbor, the restaurant."

"Barney's Chowder House?" The tension in her shoulders eased, but now her curiosity took hold. "What were you doing there?"

"Having dinner. And then I saw you. With...who was that?" He narrowed his eyes slightly.

Curiosity was promptly replaced by irritation. "That was a friend."

"Oh." He paused, waiting for her to go on.

She let him wait.

After a moment, he blew out a breath. "I asked around at the diner and one of the guys at the counter said this place had a new cook. I figured it was worth a look."

"Right. Well, as you can see, I'm perfectly fine. And cooking. You can go back to Boston now."

He drove his fingers through his hair, leaving the curls tangled across his forehead. Greta narrowed her eyes. She wasn't sure she'd ever seen Ryan with messy hair in public before.

"Look," he said, "we need to talk. We should have talked before this, but, well, things sort of got in the way. So could we talk now?"

"I don't—" she began.

"Use the lobby," Alice cut in. "Nobody's around. Except maybe Nadia. And you can ignore her." She gave Greta a quick grin.

"Thanks." Greta managed not to snarl.

"Get it over with," she said softly. "Then you can do whatever you need to do."

Greta sighed. Things were at a pretty pass when Alice was providing Significant Life Lessons.

She led the way back into the lobby, trying not to grind her teeth. This was so not a conversation she needed or wanted to have. Once they reached the leather couch and chair in front of the window, Ryan sank onto the couch, his lips twisting slightly in distaste at the small puff of dust that went up from the seat cushion.

Greta restrained herself from hoping he got dust stains on his khakis. The thought was unworthy of her.

She took the chair opposite him. "Okay, we're here. What exactly do you want to say?"

He stared down at his hands for a moment, then shrugged. "I never really had a chance to tell you how sorry I am. About how all that turned out."

She gritted her teeth. "By *all that* I assume you're referring to our marriage."

He nodded. "What I did... It was... Crap, Greta." He ran his fingers through his hair again. "I screwed up, okay? And I'm sorry. That thing with Dorothy and the restaurant? I didn't know anything about that. I wouldn't have let her do it if I had."

"Yeah, I sort of figured as much." She shrugged. "It's over now. It hurt, but it's over. I don't hold a grudge." Not much, anyway.

"Well, that's good." He sighed, going for the hair again. At this rate he'd look like a punk rocker in another five minutes.

Greta managed to give him a tight smile. "So, as I said, you can go back to Boston now."

He gazed at her, forehead furrowing again. "I'm not so sure

about that."

"What do you mean?" Her hands automatically contracted into fists, her nails digging into her palms.

"I mean, I'm not sure you're as okay as you say you are. I'm worried about you, Greta." He gave her one of those soulful looks she'd thought were so appealing when they'd first met. Now she found it vaguely annoying. All big blue eyes and pouting lips. *Grow up, bond trader boy.*

She leaned back in her chair. "Why would you worry about me? It's not like I'm your responsibility."

He looked down at his hands. "You moved out of your apartment."

She shrugged. "So? I didn't have any particular ties to Boston once the divorce was final. I came back to Promise Harbor for the wedding."

"Your landlady didn't know where you'd gone." He gave her a long look. "She said you put your things in storage."

"You talked to Mrs. Falconetti?" Greta managed not to snarl. "Look, Ryan, I don't appreciate you checking up on me."

He gave her a long look. "You left Boston. You ran away from Promise Harbor. You packed up everything you owned and put it in a storage locker. What was I supposed to think?"

Her jaw firmed. *I will not snarl. I will not point out who cheated on whom.* "My life really isn't any of your business, Ryan. We're divorced. That means the whole thing about keeping track of each other till death do us part is no longer in force." Not, of course, that he'd paid much attention to it when it had been.

He grimaced. "I deserve that, I guess. I screwed up. All I'm asking for here is a chance to make it right. And to know that you're really okay."

She closed her eyes and counted to ten silently. "Ryan, look, there is no 'making it right' here. It's over between us. We're divorced. I'm not coming back to Boston. I'm going to go off and be a cook somewhere. It's what I want to do." Greta frowned. When had she decided all of that? Apparently, within the last three minutes. Which didn't make it any less accurate. "And I just told you I'm okay. Really, really okay."

"Well, that's good." He frowned slightly. "I'm glad you've made some decisions about your life. Although you realize you could find a lot more opportunities in Boston if you really want to do this cooking thing."

*This cooking thing.* Greta's jaw hardened. "Why should it matter to you whether I've made decisions about my life or not?" She folded her arms across her chest. "Go home. I can't make it any clearer than that."

They stared at each other for a moment. Then he shook his head. "No. I can't do that yet."

"What?" She blew out a breath, holding on to her patience with her fingernails. "Why?"

"Because I'm still worried about you."

She closed her eyes again. "Ryan, what do you need exactly? A letter from a shrink saying I'm not certifiable?"

The door to the general store swished open and Alice leaned into the room. "Everybody still alive? Just checking."

Ryan pushed himself to his feet. "Do you own this place?"

Alice raised an eyebrow. "I do. Any problem with that?"

He shook his head. "No. I want a room for the night. Is anything available?"

"A room?" She glanced at Greta, who was now also shaking her head vigorously. "Possibly. Let me check the register."

Ryan followed her across the room to the check-in desk.

193

Greta got up, folding her arms across her chest again. "Alice..." she began, trying to make her voice sound ominous.

"Ah." Alice smiled up at him. "We have a vacancy. Hundred dollars a night. In advance."

To his credit, Ryan managed not to choke. Nor did he take a second look around the Hotel Grand lobby. He pulled out his wallet, plunking his gold card on the desk.

Alice shook her head. "Cash only."

This time he did narrow his eyes, but after a moment, he pulled a bill out of his wallet. "Here. One night."

"Right. Sign the register, and I'll give you the key." She pulled open the desk drawer, rummaging through until she found a key she plopped onto the desk blotter while he signed.

Ryan picked up the key. "Where's the room?"

"Up the stairs, end of the hall."

He turned toward Greta, his chin raising to a heroic angle. "Give me some time," he said. "Give me a chance."

She watched him climb the stairs out of sight, her jaw tensing. *A chance for what exactly?* "Thanks so much, Alice."

Alice shrugged. "Couldn't turn him away, could I? Not when he's willing to pay four times as much as Hank. Was he always that much of an asshole?" She raised one gray eyebrow.

Greta sighed, rubbing her eyes. "Actually, yeah. I very much fear that he was."

# Chapter Fifteen

Hank managed to get Marty moving productively after enduring forty-five minutes of whining and dragging feet. At least he'd gotten there early. He wasn't the worst intern Hank had ever dealt with, but he was definitely in the running. Apparently, the deep and abiding enthusiasm he'd expressed for archaeology in his internship application hadn't extended to the actual digging. Or carrying rocks. Or sifting soil. All of which were the duties that Hank had hoped to drop onto his ever more unwilling shoulders.

"I'm still weak from the flu, you know," Marty whined after an hour.

"Well then, it's a good thing sifting doesn't take much muscle power." Hank gave him a dark look and Marty returned to his sifter, muttering something about incipient asthma.

By eleven, Hank had begun to think about lunch. He'd been working more or less nonstop since a little before seven, and his stomach was rumbling regularly. He wished he'd made firmer plans with Greta. As it was, he had his usual peanut butter and jelly ready, but he'd be much happier with some female company.

As if she'd been summoned, Greta walked into the clearing just when he'd begun to think he might need to give in and eat his own cooking. "Hey," he called. "Just who I was hoping to see."

She turned toward him, her expression thunderous.

"I mean," he stammered, "I thought maybe you might... Is anything wrong?"

He heard a step behind him, and Marty's nose appeared above the edge of the excavation, looking a little like a hungry basset hound. "Hi, Ms. Brewster. Did you maybe bring any more of those cookies?"

Hank felt a little like kicking him. In her current mood, he figured Greta might stomp off and leave them both hungry.

She gave them another scowl. Then her expression softened. "Sure, Marty. I brought you a cookie. They're a little stale by now, though." She reached into her picnic basket and pulled out a plastic-wrapped cookie.

"Doesn't matter," Marty said loyally. "They'll still be delicious." He heaved himself up the ladder with more energy than he'd shown all morning.

"Okay, Marty, lunch break." Hank sighed. "Be back in thirty minutes."

Marty gave him a mournful look, then headed for the parking lot, already unwrapping Greta's cookie.

Hank climbed the ladder more carefully. If Greta was mad at him for some reason, he needed to do a quick reconnaissance mission to find out why before he stepped even further into this particular briar patch. "Thanks for bringing lunch." Surely that wasn't anything that would get him into trouble.

"No problem." She sighed, sinking onto one of the camp chairs. "I need to talk to you."

Oh lordy, words that no man ever wanted to hear. Hank's internal alarm system immediately swung into full alert mode. "Oh? Problems?"

"You might say that." She grimaced. "My ex-husband showed up at Casa Dubrovnik this morning."

Hank flopped into a camp chair of his own. Whatever he'd expected her to say, that wasn't it. "Why?"

"Well, that's the fifty-thousand-dollar question, isn't it?" She gave him a sour look, then shrugged. "Don't mind me. I'm still pissed and I can't take it out on Ryan at the moment."

"Ryan being the ex?"

She nodded. "He showed up in the general store when I was selling muffins."

"And said what?"

"And said he was worried about me and wanted to make sure I was all right." She rubbed a hand across the back of her neck. "I told him I was fine and to go back to Boston, but apparently he doesn't believe me."

"Meaning?"

She sighed again. "Meaning he rented a room at the hotel. From Alice."

"A room? On our floor?" In the month he'd been in residence at Casa Dubrovnik, Greta was the only other tenant he'd ever seen. He didn't think Alice even tried to attract renters.

"On our floor. Which figures, since it's the only floor with rooms at the hotel." Apparently this was her day for sighing. "I can't really blame Alice. She's charging him a hundred dollars a night, cash."

Hank whistled softly. "Not bad. Major profit there. Alice must have scented a sucker."

"Whatever she scented, she's now got Ryan. And me. And you." Greta closed her eyes, sliding down to lean her head back. "To tell you the truth, part of the reason I brought you lunch was just to get out of there."

He shrugged. "Doesn't matter. Food's food. Although yours is way above the average. And I was getting hungry." He lifted the picnic basket up on the table. "What have we got today?"

"Leftover shrimp salad plus some spring rolls. Hope you like Asian."

"At this point, I'd eat anything you brought. Although I'm sure this is terrific and Asian food is great," he added hastily.

"Nice save." She gave him a dry smile, pushing herself to her feet. "Wash your hands. I'll serve you up a plate."

They ate in silence for a few minutes. Fortunately, the shrimp salad was indeed great. Even the spring rolls were good, and normally he wasn't a big fan of rice paper. After he'd managed to calm his inner ravaging beast, Hank leaned back in his chair again. "So why do you think he's really here?"

She shook her head. "I've got no idea. He keeps talking about how concerned he is about me, but hey, if he was that concerned he wouldn't have slept with his secretary. Or anyway, that's my point of view."

"Did he come to your brother's wedding?"

She shook her head. "He was invited because I didn't have the *cojones* to tell my mom we were divorced, but I managed not to tell him about the invitation."

"So how did he know you were here?"

"Oh yeah, I forgot that part." She grimaced again. "Apparently, he saw us in Barney's last night. And somebody told him Alice had a new cook. So he put one and one together and got me."

Hank rubbed a hand across his jaw, trying to kick back the uneasy feeling in his gut. "Okay, this still doesn't make sense. He didn't go to the wedding, but he was in Promise Harbor. You haven't had any communication lately, but he tracks you down. Why?"

She shrugged. "Got me. He even went to the place I used to live in Boston and talked to my landlady. Which is really annoying since she wouldn't give me back my damage deposit and I'm pissed at her."

He took a few more bites of shrimp salad, trying to figure out how to frame his question. But sometimes it was best to just put it out there. "Does he want you back?"

"Back?" Her eyes widened. "You mean as in get back together again?"

He nodded. "I mean, it sounds a little like he's following you around."

She shook her head vigorously. "No way. He had lots of time to talk to me back in Boston and he didn't. He didn't even ask for mediation before the divorce was final. He doesn't want me back. Definitely not."

"Maybe he changed his mind," Hank said slowly. "Maybe he didn't realize how much he wanted to be with you until he wasn't."

"No." She shook her head again. "And even if that were true, it wouldn't matter because I don't want to get back together with him. Ever."

Hank stared down at a spring roll he suddenly had little interest in eating. "Are you sure about that?"

She frowned, chewing on her lower lip in a way that made his groin ache. "Yes, I'm sure about that. Absolutely. Breaking up with him was painful, but not nearly as painful as it should have been. I realized then that I really didn't want or need to be with him. Read my lips. I do not want to be back with Ryan. Ever."

"I can think of things I'd rather do with your lips." The groin ache was definitely distracting. "Is this going to put a crimp in our evening?"

"You mean having Ryan down the hall?"

Hank nodded. "Will you feel weird?"

"Maybe." She shrugged. "It *is* weird, no matter how you think about it."

"Right." He blew out a breath. "We could go to a motel."

She frowned. "A motel? When you're already paying for a room at Casa Dubrovnik?"

"If necessary." He leaned forward, catching her hand in his. "The thing is, we've only got two more nights before you head back to the harbor, or wherever you've decided to go. I'm not willing to let your ex-husband screw that up."

"I like your room," she said slowly, her fingers brushing his palm. "I don't want to go to a motel. I want to do what we did last night. If Ryan doesn't like it, he can always complain to the management."

Hank's lips spread upward in a grin. "Actually, I'd like to see that. Alice's reaction would probably be classic."

"I want to make love with you," Greta said softly. "These last two nights should be our time. Let's pretend Ryan isn't there."

"Okay by me." He managed to keep his grin in place, but he was pretty sure wishing Ryan away would be a lot easier said than done.

Greta kept Ryan out of the kitchen by the simple expedient of snarling at him whenever he tried to come in. She was fixing a strawberry bombe since it would take most of the afternoon to assemble, thus making it impossible for them to have another of those conversations she was coming to dread.

*Does he want you back?* She was pretty certain he didn't, and even more certain that she herself didn't want to go back to him. But the question made her feel uncomfortable, as if she had another unpleasant conversation looming in the future.

Why couldn't he just have stayed in Boston? Why had he come to Tompkins Corners, just when things might be getting better for her? Or beginning to, anyway.

Nadia breezed in while Greta was waiting for the gelatin mixture to cool for the mousse. "Well, this is an interesting development. I assume you had no idea your ex-husband was coming here."

"None at all." Greta began whipping cream with a whisk. There was actually an electric mixer in one of the drawers, but right now she really needed to beat something.

"Do you have any idea why he chose to find you?"

She shook her head.

"Would you like me to have Hyacinth put frogs in his bed?" Greta did a double take. Nadia smiled. "Just checking. That probably wouldn't be as effective as some other possibilities."

Greta put the bowl down, sighing. "Let's just have dinner. Maybe he'll explain himself then. Or not. I really don't care, to tell the truth, as long as he goes away as soon as possible."

At five, Hank stuck his head in the kitchen door. "Do I need to wear protective gear for dinner?"

She shook her head, chopping mushrooms at Jacques Pepin speed. "Not as far as I'm concerned. And if Ryan tries anything, there's always Alice's baseball bat."

He stepped inside the room, leaning back against the counter, his arms folded across his chest. "How are you holding up?"

"I'm fine. I made him stay outside all afternoon. Maybe he left. I don't know."

Hank glanced back at the garden window. "If he's a medium-sized guy with black hair, he's still here. Of course, right now he's in danger of stepping on Nadia's lemon verbena, so he may not be long for this world."

Greta rested her knife on the cutting board, peering out the window. Ryan was wandering along the edge of the garden, looking bored. After a few moments, Hyacinth appeared, watching him dubiously. She said something to him, probably pointing out the lemon verbena. Ryan stepped back. Now he looked annoyed.

"Hell," Greta muttered, "I probably should let him in here so he doesn't create problems elsewhere."

Hank shrugged. "We could always ask Nadia to make dinner. That would probably send him screaming into the night."

"Nope. As long as I'm here, nobody cooks but me."

"How about I hold him down and you force-feed him brussels sprouts?"

"Roasted brussels sprouts are actually very good. But they're out of season right now."

"Alice rented him a room. Let Alice suffer."

"Works for me." She sighed again. She'd spent the day sighing, and she had a feeling this would be an evening of more sighs. And they'd be the result of exasperation rather than passion. "Look, whatever happens tonight, I'm sorry. I really didn't plan on this."

"Do you usually apologize for random events?" He shrugged. "If you didn't plan it, it's not your problem, sweetheart."

She looked at him, her shoulders unclenching slightly for the first time since she'd come back from lunch. "You're a very nice man. Have I mentioned that?"

"Thanks." His eyes widened slightly, either in surprise or alarm, she wasn't sure which.

*Whoa. Too much. Over the top.*

"Now you need to get out of here so that I can finish dinner." And so that she could regroup.

He pushed himself up. "Okay. I guess a shower is in order anyway. Nadia would give me the evil eye if I showed up at the dinner table like this."

"Good point." She dumped the mushrooms into a bowl. "Dinner's in thirty minutes. Drama is pretty much guaranteed. Don't be late."

"Wouldn't think of it." He headed across the kitchen toward the lobby door.

Thirty minutes later, Greta carried the last platter of food to the sideboard in the dining room. Nadia apparently had dressed for dinner. She wore a full-length black skirt of some shiny fabric, along with an embroidered peasant blouse and a paisley pashmina. She'd even put on gold hoop earrings. Apparently Ryan warranted the complete package.

He stood at the side of the room sipping something out of a small glass. Whatever it was must not have measured up to his standards, judging by his expression.

"Aperitif, dear?" Nadia handed her a small glass identical to his.

Greta glanced down at the clear liquid. It smelled a little like cough syrup. "Thanks. I'd better stay in the kitchen to make sure everything gets on the table at the proper temperature." Even she recognized that as a lame excuse.

Nadia gave her a glittering smile. "Nonsense. These plates look scrumptious. We'll take our seats as soon as everyone else is here. Drink up."

Greta took a very small sip. Not only did it taste like cough syrup, she had a feeling the alcohol content in the glass was probably close to lethal. She managed not to gag.

The kitchen door swished open behind them, and Hyacinth entered, pushing her glasses up her nose. "Why are we eating in here? I like it when we eat in the kitchen."

"We have too many people for the kitchen table tonight," Nadia explained. "We have another guest."

Hyacinth narrowed her eyes at Ryan. Clearly, along with the lemon verbena incident, he'd just gotten another black mark in her book.

Alice followed her through the kitchen door. If Nadia had dressed for dinner, Alice had gone in the opposite direction. She wore the same pair of jeans she'd worn all week, judging by the smudges near the knees. Her green plaid flannel was tucked in at the waist, showing off her battered leather belt. At least she had on tennis shoes rather than flip-flops.

She gave Ryan a faintly derisive smile. "Enjoying the home brew? My sister whips it up in the basement."

Nadia arched a single eyebrow. "My sister considers herself a comedian. Would you care for some more, Mr. McBain?"

Ryan shook his head quickly. "No, no. That's fine. I'm good."

Hank stepped in through the lobby door, glancing quickly around the room. "Sorry I'm late."

"Not at all." Nadia gave him one of her glittering smiles. "Let me pour you an aperitif."

Greta thought about warning him, but he was a big boy. Besides, he'd been in all those jungles digging out ruins. He'd probably tasted worse.

Or not. Hank's expression after the first sip reminded her of one of the instructors at culinary school who'd accidentally sampled overfermented kimchi.

"Don't let me hold up dinner," he said in a strangled voice.

"Not at all. Have you met our new guest, Mr. McBain?" She turned toward Ryan, smiling politely. "Mr. McBain was married to Greta at one time, or so I understand."

Hank took another swallow of Nadia's elixir. "Hi," he gasped.

Nadia turned toward Ryan. "Professor Mitchell is an archaeologist. He's excavating one of our local sites."

Ryan narrowed his eyes, then stuck out a stiff hand. "Pleased to meet you."

"Yeah, me too." Hank shook his hand limply.

"Let's sit down, everyone." Nadia took her seat at one end of the table while Alice moved to the other. "Sit here by me, Mr. McBain." She gestured toward the chair beside her while Hyacinth dropped into the chair next to Alice, leaving the far side of the table to Greta and Hank.

Greta managed not to grin. She passed the first platter to Alice. "Chicken cutlets with sherry mushroom sauce."

Alice plopped a piece of chicken on her plate, passing the platter to Hyacinth. Greta supplied the remaining bowls of green beans and fingerling potatoes, along with a plate of crudités, then slid into her chair next to Hank in time to help herself to chicken.

"It looks sublime, dear," Nadia purred. She turned to Ryan. "How lucky you must have felt to have someone preparing such wonderful food for you every evening."

Ryan's face turned slightly pink. "We...ate out a great deal. Boston has some wonderful restaurants."

"Indeed?" Nadia's eyebrows elevated again. "And yet I'd wager Greta is the equal of many Boston chefs."

Ryan glanced up at her and then down at his plate again as he took another bite of chicken. "This is very good." He sounded slightly surprised.

Alice narrowed her eyes. "Haven't you tasted her food before?"

All eyes were suddenly on Ryan, who swallowed hard. "Of course. I...must have."

Greta considered rescuing him and then decided not to. He'd gotten himself into this. He could jolly well dig himself out.

He took another hurried bite. "Delicious," he mumbled.

Greta started to reply, then pulled up short. "Oh gosh, Hyacinth, I forgot your sauce. I'm sorry. Be right back."

She sprinted into the kitchen, then returned with another bowl of sherry mushroom sauce.

Hyacinth gave her a radiant smile. "Thank you."

Ryan glanced at the sauce somewhat suspiciously.

"Hyacinth is a vegetarian," Greta explained. "That's her version of the sauce. It hasn't touched the chicken."

Alice gave her granddaughter a dry smile. "You'll let me know when this phase ends, won't you?"

Hyacinth ignored her, pouring a small puddle of sauce in the middle of her plate.

"Well, I think it's admirable." Nadia waved her fork rather like a conductor's baton. "Hyacinth is a budding naturalist. She spends a great deal of her time looking after the local fauna.

She's rescued several birds and small rodents."

Hyacinth's eyes grew suddenly wide. She stared down at the puddle of sauce, her fork poised over a fingerling potato.

"Do you still have the turtle, Hyacinth?" Hank asked quietly.

After a moment, Hyacinth nodded without raising her eyes.

"Could I see it?"

Hyacinth stayed still for so long that Greta wondered if she'd answer at all. The she nodded again, very slowly this time.

"Thank you. Maybe we could go look after dinner."

"Maybe," Hyacinth mumbled.

Alice watched them, frowning. "What turtle is this?"

"Just a box turtle," Hyacinth said quickly. "One I found in the woods."

"Oh." Alice didn't look convinced. "You're not keeping it, are you?"

"Would anyone like more vegetables?" Greta asked a little desperately.

Alice spooned a few more green beans onto her plate, then passed the platter to Hyacinth. "Here. Knock yourself out."

"Thank you." Hyacinth emptied the platter onto her plate. She still hadn't looked at either Hank or Greta.

Greta felt like sighing for an entirely different reason as she watched the adults finish their chicken. Looked like she was back to ground zero with Hyacinth.

Nadia scooped up her final green bean, then turned in her direction. "Wonderful, my dear. Absolutely superb."

Ryan glanced up a little guiltily. "It was...good. Really good. Tasty."

She wondered if she'd ever heard him use the word *tasty*

before. She was pretty sure she hadn't. "Dessert anyone?"

Hank glanced up at her, his lips spreading in a lazy grin. "Sure. Anytime."

Across the table, she heard Ryan's faint huff of disapproval, but she decided she didn't care. She only had two more nights. And she wasn't going to waste either of them on him.

# Chapter Sixteen

Ryan followed her into the kitchen after most of the bombe had been enthusiastically consumed. "That was really good."

"Thanks," she muttered between her teeth.

"I guess I never realized you could do that."

She wheeled around to stare at him. "I'm a culinary school grad, Ryan. Being able to cook a meal like that is pretty much a given. Let's be frank—you never wanted to know if I could do that. You didn't want me to cook for you at all."

"Well, maybe that's true. I guess I just didn't think of it." He rubbed a hand across the back of his neck. "Look, could we go somewhere and talk?"

She folded her arms across her chest. She seemed to do that a lot when he was around. "Talk about what?"

He grimaced. "About, you know, us. Our situation."

"We've already talked. We don't have a situation, Ryan." She sighed. Something else she seemed to do a lot when he was around. "We're divorced, as I keep pointing out. I don't see that there's much left to talk about. And I really, really wish you'd go home."

"Are you happy?" he blurted.

Greta sighed again. "I'm as happy as I know how to be at the moment. And I'm learning to be happier than that. So yeah, short answer? I'm happy."

"Well." He rubbed the back of his neck again. "That's good, I guess."

"You guess?" She narrowed her eyes.

"No, I mean, that's great. See, I was worried about you. Your mom called and said you were gone, and I thought..."

The kitchen door swished open behind them. "Want to see Carolina?" Hank leaned into the room. "Hyacinth's going to take me to visit her."

Greta turned. "Sure." Seeing a turtle seemed like a much better use of her time than any further dead-end dialogue with Ryan.

She followed Hank out the door, then glanced back over her shoulder to see Ryan walking along behind them. *Well, crap.* She really hoped he didn't plan on following her around all night. There were definitely places where his presence wasn't desirable.

The crickets were back, augmented now by some frogs down near the creek. Hyacinth's back looked very straight as she tramped toward the shed. Something about her posture made Greta think of Joan of Arc marching to the stake.

"Nice night." Hank grinned at her, reaching for her hand.

*Oh yeah.* She slipped her hand into his, ignoring the grumbling presence clumping along behind her.

Hyacinth propped the door open in front of them, moving purposefully forward. Hank paused, fumbling for the light switch at the side, but she turned, shaking her head. "Leave the light off. It upsets Carolina."

Hank shrugged, moving closer.

Carolina's shell still sat in the middle of the aquarium, presumably containing Carolina herself. Hank bent down for a better look. "Box turtle."

"Eastern box turtle. *Terrepene carolina*," Hyacinth corrected.

Hank studied the turtle for a moment longer, for what purpose Greta wasn't sure. Then he shrugged. "It's a nice turtle, but you probably need to let it go now. They don't do well in captivity. It's not happy, and it could get sick and die."

Hyacinth's chin went up. For a moment, she looked remarkably like her grandmother. "It's endangered. I'm keeping it safe. And it's not a captive, it's a guest."

Hank shook his head. "That's not the way a turtle would see it. Plus I really doubt it's endangered, Hyacinth. Box turtles are plentiful. There's one type or another in every state in the country."

Hyacinth's lower lip began to tremble. *Uh-oh.* "It *is* endangered. It's on the list from the Massachusetts Division of Wildlife. I looked it up on Grandma's computer."

"Let's check again." Hank pulled out his phone, clicking away on the Web browser, narrowing his eyes in the dim light. After a few moments, he smiled. "Oh, okay, I see what's going on. It's not endangered."

Hyacinth glowered. "It's threatened then."

Hank shook his head. "Not that either. It's what they call a 'species of special concern'. They want people to look out for them, but they're not in danger of going extinct."

Hyacinth didn't smile. "So I'm looking out for Carolina. I'm keeping her safe. If I let her go, somebody could run her over. Or an animal could eat her. A bear or something."

Hank shook his head again. "I don't think bears are interested in turtles. It would take too much work to get them out of their shells."

"Alligators." Ryan's voice sounded from the other side of the shed. "They eat turtles."

Hyacinth's eyes widened again.

"There are no alligators in Massachusetts," Greta said quickly. "Except in zoos. They're tropical. It's too cold for them up here."

"Coyotes maybe," Ryan mused. "They eat lots of things."

Greta turned, giving him the kind of look she hoped would turn his blood to ice, but he wasn't watching her.

He stared off into space. "And people do too, of course."

"People?" Hyacinth stared at him in horror. "No! They couldn't."

Hank narrowed his eyes at Ryan. "Nobody here is going to eat your turtle, Hyacinth."

"People don't eat box turtles anyway," Greta said firmly. "I'm a cook, and I know. Nobody is going to eat Carolina. Don't worry, Hyacinth."

"And the thing is, turtles are really well protected." Hank stood up again, tucking his phone back in his pocket. "They've got their own armor, which is perfectly designed to keep predators from eating them. Carolina can take care of herself in the wild, honest."

"She could still be run over." Hyacinth stared down at the turtle, her lower lip jutting out.

"She could." Hank nodded. "You'll have to trust that she won't be. You can't keep her safe from everything, and she'd be a lot happier back in the wild with other turtles. The aquarium just isn't her environment. It's not healthy for her."

"I don't want to let her go," Hyacinth whispered. "She's my friend."

"I know," Hank said softly, nodding again. "But sometimes

you have to think about what's best for the animal, not what's best for us."

"Would you like us to help you?" Greta knelt down beside her.

Hyacinth shook her head quickly. "No. I don't want anybody around when I let her go."

Greta blew out a breath, then stood up again. "Okay, then. We'll leave you." She turned back toward the door.

"People do too eat turtles." Ryan sounded triumphant. "Turtle soup. They eat turtle soup."

"Oh for Christ's sake, Ryan," Greta exploded. "Not now. You can correct me later. For now, zip it!"

"No," Hyacinth wailed. "No, no, no! You can't eat Carolina."

Hank took hold of Ryan's elbow, propelling him speedily toward the door. "Who are you, Anthony Bourdain? Let's go for a walk."

Greta turned back quickly toward Hyacinth. "Nobody will want to eat Carolina. She's not the kind of turtle people eat. Besides, turtle soup isn't something people like to eat much anymore. That was a long time ago. Don't worry, Hyacinth. Nobody will use Carolina for dinner." She hurried outside after Ryan and Hank.

They stood on the path outside, their shadows caught by the lights from the hotel. Hank had Ryan's collar bunched in his fist, yanking him up so that he was resting on his toes. "What the hell is it about you and eating turtles? Hasn't anybody ever taught you how to keep your friggin' mouth shut? When the lady says zip it, she means zip it!"

"We ate snapper soup, Greta and me," Ryan retorted, squirming against Hank's grip. "In Philadelphia."

"You heard the man," Greta said through clenched teeth.

"Zip it! I do not care what we ate anymore. Besides, those were snapping turtles and we're a long way from Philadelphia. And people don't really eat it much anymore even there."

"But—"

Greta balled her hands into fists. "Ryan, for the love of heaven, stop trying to get the last word. If you say anything more on this topic, either Hank or I will bash you. Possibly both of us. And we will enjoy doing it. Do I make myself clear?"

He narrowed his eyes, his chin squaring mutinously, but then he nodded.

Greta stepped back inside the shed door. "We'll leave now, Hyacinth. I know you'll do the right thing. If you love Carolina, you'll want what's best for her."

She turned without looking at Ryan. He wouldn't have any reason to stay outside the shed to wait for Hyacinth and Carolina once she and Hank had left. Unless he just wanted to cause trouble, in which case she really would bash him.

Hank stepped beside her, taking her hand again as they walked. "Snapper soup?"

She wrinkled her nose. "Nasty stuff. Snapping turtles are really boney and sort of awful, but it used to be a big deal in Philadelphia so we had to try it. I guess they make it with stew beef now. Do you think she'll do it?"

"Release Carolina?" He shrugged. "Yeah, I think she will."

"Greta?" Ryan's voice sounded from behind them. *Well, crap.*

She turned, jaw tense, still holding tight to Hank's hand. "What?"

"We still need to talk. Or I do anyway."

She sighed. Losing her temper would feel wonderful, but it probably wouldn't accomplish anything besides making her feel wonderful. And she *so* wanted to get rid of him.

Hank raised an eyebrow. "Want me to bash him now?" he murmured. "I can't guarantee anything in terms of results, but I'd have fun doing it."

She shook her head. "Give me ten minutes, okay?"

"If you say so." He gave her hand a quick squeeze, then turned toward the back door.

Greta gestured toward a garden bench—not, thank god, the bench where she and Hank had done their owl imitations—and sat. "This is the last time I'm doing this, Ryan. Whatever you think you need to say to me, you should say it now. After this, we're done."

He sank down beside her, rubbing his hands on his thighs as if he were wiping off sweat. Nervous? Ryan was nervous? That made no sense at all—she didn't think she'd ever seen him nervous in the entire two years they'd been married.

"I thought you might have hurt yourself," he blurted.

She blinked. Definitely not what she'd been expecting—not that she'd been expecting anything in particular. "Hurt myself? When?"

"When you left. When your mother called me. I thought...you know. You might have been upset."

The penny slowly dropped. Greta stared at him. "You thought I'd try to kill myself? Over you?"

"Well..." He had the grace to look somewhat embarrassed, staring down into the dirt so that he wouldn't have to meet her gaze. "I mean, I didn't know what had happened to you. And I was worried. I thought, you know, I'd made you so unhappy..."

For a moment, she was furious. *Over you? Kill myself over you?* And then a giggle worked its way loose. "You thought..." Another giggle, then another. "You thought I..." And then she was whooping, resting her head against the back of the bench, laughing so hard she could hardly catch her breath.

Ryan stared, his mouth partly open, his forehead furrowed. "Damn it, Greta. That's not fair."

It took her a few more moments to stop, and then she shook her head, gasping. "What's not fair?" She wrapped her arms around her waist, concentrating on breathing. At least she'd managed to slow the laughter down to the occasional eruption of snickers.

"Laughing at me. I was really worried about you. I didn't know what might have happened. It's not funny anyway. I thought I might have driven you to it, that it was one more thing I'd screwed up. I was...frightened for you." He suddenly looked a lot like Hyacinth, chin up, lower lip extended.

Greta closed her eyes for a moment, steadying herself. "Okay, you've got a point. Maybe it's not all that funny. But honestly, Ryan, what was the first thing I did after you came home that day when Dorothy dropped her little bombshell?"

He sighed. "You threw something at me."

She nodded. "I threw my copy of *Larousse Gastronomique*, which I'd picked up because I was thinking of going back to work at that point. It's a very heavy book."

"You missed."

"Lack of practice." She shrugged. "People who throw things do not kill themselves, Ryan. They're more inclined to murder than suicide. That's what I was contemplating at the time."

"I didn't understand that was how you felt. We didn't really talk. Besides, it's been months. I wasn't sure how you were feeling now."

"You didn't know how I felt." She closed her eyes for a moment, then shook her head. "You didn't ask. And I didn't ask. We just sort of let it go, didn't we? We really weren't very good at being married, Ryan."

He shook his head slowly. "I guess not."

She put her hand on his arm. "Go back to Dorothy, okay? I think she knew what she was talking about when she said we weren't right for each other. I don't know whether she's right for you or not, but I'm pretty sure I'm not. And she'll look a lot better at company dinners than I ever did."

Ryan stared down at his hands. "Dorothy's gone."

"She left you?" Greta blinked. "That does surprise me." Dorothy seemed to have had their entire future worked out.

"I told her to go." He looked up at her again. "That whole thing with inviting you to lunch and then telling you about her and me—that was a shitty thing to do."

*Yep.* She shrugged. "I hope you gave her a good severance package. She might have grounds for a harassment suit."

"She got a great severance package." He paused. "Dad gave it to her."

*Okay, tricky.* Ryan's father hadn't been one of Greta's biggest fans. In fact, she was willing to bet he'd been expecting somebody more like Dorothy to be his daughter-in-law. But his company was definitely big time. And Ryan was one of his shining stars. Or he had been. Scandal would not be something he'd be crazy about. "Did your father send you here to find me?"

"What?" Ryan stared at her, shaking his head. "No. He doesn't know where I am."

"But he's unhappy with you?"

"You might say that." He rubbed his eyes. "I'm on leave of absence for a few weeks. He wants to make sure there are no repercussions."

"Repercussions?"

"I guess Dorothy talked a lot about the two of us. A lot of people around the office knew we were…seeing each other."

*Screwing each other, actually. Terrific.* Well, she hadn't planned on spending any time around Ryan's office anyway, but it was another reason not to go back to Boston. No telling how many of their friends and acquaintances knew about Ryan's little fling. "I'm sure it will all blow over. You should be able to go back soon."

He shrugged. "Maybe. I don't know. I don't even know if I want to go back. I don't know why I got involved with her anyway, to tell you the truth. She's not nearly as attractive as you are. And she's a real bitch sometimes. You've got a temper, Greta, but you're not a bitch. And you're more fun to talk to than she ever was. All she wanted to talk about was work."

Which was nice to hear, but a little late. "Anyway…"

"Anyway, then your mom called, and I started worrying. And then I got this idea about coming down here and finding you. That it would be something I could do to sort of make it right. So, you know, here I am." He shrugged again, his blue eyes wide. For a moment he looked around ten years old. "And I'm glad I came. Sort of."

*I used to love him. Or something.* Whatever it had been, she didn't feel it now. On the other hand, she did feel a certain amount of sympathy for him. He looked like a lost child all of a sudden rather than the Master Of the Universe his father had always wanted him to be.

"Go home, Ryan," she said softly. "I can't help you. I wish I could in a way. But I really can't. You need to work this whole thing out for yourself and figure out what you want to do next. And you need to do it somewhere else."

He glanced around the garden, regretfully. "Maybe. You know, this seems like a really nice place, a good place to think about things."

She nodded. "Yeah, it is. But I got here first. And it's not big enough for both of us."

"Really?" He gave her one of those winning, boyish smiles she used to find so endearing. "Maybe if I stayed, we could sort of figure things out together."

"No, we couldn't," Greta said firmly.

"No chance at all?"

She shook her head. Endearing smile and all, he was history. "No chance at all."

He sighed. "Okay." He gave her another one of those smiles, this time with a dimple attached. "How about a kiss for old time's sake?"

*You have got to be kidding me.* "Nope."

He sighed again. "All right. If that's the way you want it. Maybe I'll head back to the city." He pushed himself to his feet, his expression stoic.

"Wait." Greta sighed, getting to her feet beside him. She leaned over and brushed her lips across his, running her fingers along his cheek. "Take care of yourself, Ryan."

He nodded. "You too." He turned and started toward the garden gate, then looked back just before he reached it. "If you ever need anything, just, you know, call."

"Right." She folded her arms across her chest, watching him walk away.

"That was interesting."

She turned toward the darker part of the garden. Hank lounged on their bench.

"Were you here for all of that?"

He shrugged. "Pretty much. I thought about making noise

so you'd know I was sitting here, but then I got caught up in the conversation."

She walked deeper into the darkness of the maples. Hank leaned back, resting one shoulder against a cast-iron armrest.

"You shouldn't have been eavesdropping, but I guess it doesn't matter. Are you upset about any of that?"

He shook his head. "Should I be? I hadn't planned on it."

She sank down beside him. "He really is clueless. Believe it or not, he's good at what he does. But he's totally inept when it comes to people. I'm just beginning to figure that out."

"Still. He should have known not to cheat on you."

She sighed, pushing a lock of hair away from her eyes. "He should have. On the other hand, Dorothy was the determined type. A lot more determined than I am. My guess is he never knew what hit him."

Hank pushed himself upright, running his fingers down the slope of her nose. "Do you really want to talk about your ex-husband right now?"

A shivery feeling seemed to circulate from her neck downward, tightening her nipples and spreading to her stomach. *The nose is an erogenous zone? Who knew?* "No, I do not want to talk about Ryan now. Or ever again, as far as that goes."

"Good." He slid his arm around her waist, bringing her closer. "We've got other things to talk about. Or not talk about as the case may be."

"I vote for not." She looped her arms around his neck, drawing his mouth down to hers.

The combination of moonlight and Hank was just as intoxicating as ever. She dug her fingers into his hair, feeling the short, silky strands under her fingertips, then moving her palms along the sides of his head, letting her thumbs skim across the tops of his ears.

After a moment, he raised his head, staring down at her, the corners of his mouth inching up. "You don't play fair, woman."

"Was I supposed to?" She let her lips skate down the side of his throat, then dipped her tongue into the indentation at the base.

He cupped her face in his hands, drawing her back to his kiss. His tongue plunged deep in her mouth, and heat pooled in her abdomen. She brought her thighs together, feeling the throb of desire between them.

After another moment, he rested his forehead on hers. "You know, this hasn't happened to me all that often. I've never run into a woman who could send me from zero to a hundred and twenty in a matter of seconds. Not until now, anyway."

She caught her breath. "It's not all that typical for me either."

He pulled back to look at her again. "We can't stay here, you know. Another five minutes and we'll be down on the grass. And this time we might actually run into Hyacinth, assuming she decides now is the time to release Carolina."

"Oh." Suddenly, she felt a little less excited than she had a moment ago. "Poor Hyacinth."

"Poor Carolina. She's a turtle. She needs to be out and around." He stood up, extending his hand to her. "We, on the other hand, could be inside and down."

She grinned up at him, allowing him to pull her to her feet. "That sounds like a good idea to me."

"Shall we?" He draped his arm across her shoulders, walking her toward the kitchen door.

"We shall." *Oh, most definitely.*

As they reached the door, he turned, staring down at her. "You're sure it's only two more nights?"

She nodded. "Yeah." *Damn it.*

# Chapter Seventeen

They used Greta's room this time. The moonlight was brighter there, and unless Hank was very much mistaken, she had a better mattress. Not that the mattress mattered all that much. He'd have been willing to make love to her on the hardwood floor if she'd indicated a preference.

Now he lay beside her, holding her loosely against him, wondering if it was too soon to try for a rematch. His body was showing a lot more resilience than usual. Amazingly so, given recent history. In spite of a sprained foot and several days of sleep deprivation, he still felt as randy as a fifteen-year-old.

Oddly enough, though, in spite of his crying need to make love to her, he also felt this crying need to have The Talk. In fact, he felt both needs simultaneously, and at the moment, amazingly, The Talk seemed to be winning.

"Hey?" he murmured.

Greta stirred in his arms, her skin silver in the moonlight. Her eyes stayed closed, but the corners of her mouth turned up in one of those sensuous smiles that made his groin go on high alert. "Hmmm?"

He took a breath. "Are you sure you have to go back?"

Her eyes opened slowly as the grin diminished. After a moment, she nodded. "Yeah." She sighed. "Yeah, I really think I do. Unfortunately."

"The thing is…" He paused, thinking how to say it. "The thing is, you seem to be doing really well here, all in all. I mean, okay, you've got no clothes or personal possessions, but other than that…"

She grinned again. "Other than that…"

"You've got the beginnings of a successful business with Alice. You've been pretty much adopted into the Dubrovnik family. And you're cooking rings around everybody else in the county."

"It's a small county," she murmured.

"Granted. But still. And you've apparently taken care of any lingering problems with your ex, for what that's worth." *And you can have me in your bed whenever you want.* He decided not to share that fact with her just yet. It might be enough to scare her off.

She sighed. "Yeah. I guess I have."

"So the thing is, Greta, why can't you stay?" With me. *Oh steady there, Doc.*

"Because I've only been here for a few days." She turned to him, her expression suddenly serious. Bummer—he wanted that smile back. "I'm not taking the easy way out this time around. I need to go home and face my mom. I need to tell her all about Ryan, and I need to explain about why I didn't tell her before, and I need to take my lumps because she won't be happy. But for once, I need to show that I can follow through on something, that I can do the right thing. That even if she's mad at me, I won't fold. I've always let Josh look after Mom—he's Mr. Responsible. And I just sort of ran off and did my thing. When I screwed up, everybody just shrugged and said 'That's Greta for you'. I'm tired of being That Girl."

"I like That Girl," he said softly.

"You don't really know That Girl," she murmured.

"What about what you've got here? The baking and the cooking and the rest of it?" *Including me.*

She shook her head. "What I've got here is terrific. But it's sort of like a vacation. Like I'm using it to avoid the rest of my life. If I stuck around and kept baking, I'd never be sure whether I was doing it because I wanted to or because I was trying not to do something else. I've got a whole set of decisions I have to make—this job possibility in Boston that I haven't really considered, how I'm going to tell my mom about breaking up with Ryan, what I'm going to do now. This has been a great week, but I can't hide out in Tompkins Corners forever."

Hank lay still for a moment, trying to marshal his next set of arguments, when someone hammered on the door.

Greta propped herself upright on her elbow. "If that's Ryan, I swear I'm going to kill him."

"If that's Ryan, I'll help." He pushed himself to his feet, heading for the door. "Who is it?"

"It's Nadia," she snapped. "Open up."

"If this is some kind of freakin' bed check, I'm not going to be happy." He pulled on his jeans, opening the door a crack. "What?"

Nadia stood in the middle of the hall dressed in a lavender silk kimono, her hair hanging long and slightly wild around her face. "Have you seen Hyacinth?"

"Hyacinth?" He shook his head. "Not since right after dinner. She was going to take care of her turtle."

"Take care of it how?"

"Turn it loose. Isn't she around?"

Nadia shook her head. "She's not in her bed. Alice thought I tucked her in, and I thought Alice did."

Greta appeared at his shoulder, pulling down her T-shirt.

"Did you check the shed? She was down there with Carolina. Maybe she still is."

Nadia sighed. "No. She's not there or anywhere else around the house. Did she say anything about where she might go to set this turtle free?"

Hank shrugged. "Not that I know of. Would you like us to do a search around the garden?"

"I suppose." Nadia rubbed a hand across her lips. "I don't know where she can be. It wouldn't take that long to release the turtle in the woods and come back. Unless she's gotten lost."

"She wouldn't let it loose in the woods around here," Greta said slowly. "She'd take it back where she found it in the first place. Or anyway, she'd take it near water. She told me once that box turtles liked moisture."

Nadia's eyes widened. "Oh my god, if she's gone into marshland somewhere, she might have gotten caught in quicksand or something worse!"

"There's not much quicksand around here," Hank soothed. "The only boggy land I know of is near Tompkins Lake."

"The lake isn't any better." Nadia looked almost tearful. "It's very deep. The child can swim, of course, but I don't know how far."

"Let's try searching around the lake." Greta turned back toward the room. "We need to get dressed. Where's Alice?"

"Searching through the garden again. I'll go get her. The two of us are going with you. Wait for us." Nadia headed for the stairs, traveling much more quickly than Hank would have guessed she was able to move.

Greta sighed. "You don't suppose Hyacinth's run away, do you? Taken Carolina and hit the road?"

"I don't know. Traveling with a turtle doesn't exactly strike me as easy. Or fast." He fought down the image of Hyacinth walking along beside the road with Carolina on a tiny leash.

"How boggy is it by the lake?"

"Not very." He shrugged. "But there are lots of woods around there. Which is what would make it good turtle habitat. Box turtles live on land."

Greta dug her general store sneakers out from under the bed. "These aren't going to be great in mud, but it's better than going barefoot."

"Definitely." He paused for one more longing glance in her direction. Even in T-shirt and shorts, with uncombed hair and an absence of makeup, she was a knockout.

*You're falling in love with her.* He closed his eyes. Maybe, although on less than a week's acquaintance he didn't think that was likely. But even if it turned out to be true, love would have to go on hold for now. After all, she was leaving, right?

Greta watched Alice and Nadia walk toward the shore of the lake. Alice looked her probable age for a change, which wasn't reassuring. Her eyes were sunken, and she clutched her walking stick in a way that emphasized her swollen joints. Nadia wore what looked like the first clothes she'd been able to lay her hands on, a wrinkled skirt and an oversize T-shirt. For once, she had no pashmina over her shoulders, although she could probably have used it in the cool night air.

Greta turned toward Hank, bringing up the rear and carrying a heavy flashlight and a blanket to wrap around Hyacinth once they found her. "Where's the bog?"

"All around the lake but back in the woods. We need to start by calling her. Maybe she's just gotten turned around." He stepped to the water's edge beside Alice and Nadia. "Hyacinth," he called. "Are you here?"

"Hyacinth," Alice yelled at the top of her lungs. "It's Grandma. Can you hear me?"

Nadia joined in, calling in a surprisingly rich contralto.

Greta wandered up the beach a little way, listening. "Hyacinth?" she called. "It's Greta. Are you here?"

For a moment, she thought she heard something, a distant squeaking, like a tree in the wind. Then she decided it actually was the wind after all. "Hyacinth," she called again, moving down the beach. "Hyacinth, can you hear me?"

The shouts of the others faded slightly. Greta closed her eyes, listening. "Hyacinth?"

The squeaking came again, closer now that she'd moved down the beach. Not the wind, given the stillness of the water. "Hyacinth," she called again. "Yell if you can hear me."

This time the squeak was very definite and very recognizable. "Help," Hyacinth called.

Greta turned on her heel. "Hank," she yelled. "Alice. Nadia. She's over here."

She turned back again, moving toward where the "Help" had come from. Or where she thought it had come from.

Hank's footsteps thumped behind her. "Where is she?"

"I'm not sure." She turned toward the woods on the lake shore. "Hyacinth, call again so we can find you."

"Help, help, help." This time the voice was more definite. To the left, away from the lake.

Alice appeared at Greta's side. "She's in the woods. Damn it. She knows she's not supposed to go in there. It's full of poison ivy."

"Terrific." Hank sighed, turning on the flashlight. "Keep

yelling, Hyacinth. We're coming."

He shone the light into the dense wall of trees in front of them. "There's a path there, over to the right."

Greta followed his pointing hand, stepping carefully between the tree trunks. Something swished through the leaves beside her, and she caught her breath. *Squirrels. Rabbits. Field mice. Not bears. Definitely not bears.* Nadia and Alice trudged ahead of them.

Hyacinth's voice was nearer now, high and slightly shrill, as if she'd been calling for a while.

"Over this way," Hank muttered, pushing aside what she hoped were bushes rather than a massive pile of poison ivy.

"Over where?" She paused, staring around at the trees. Hyacinth's voice seemed to be near, but she couldn't see anything except tree trunks.

"Up here," Hyacinth yelled.

Greta bent her head back as Hank shone the light up to the forest canopy. And then they saw her.

Hyacinth clung to the trunk of a remarkably spindly white pine. She seemed to be at least ten feet up, her legs and arms wrapped tight.

"Oh my lord," Nadia whispered.

Beside her, Alice huffed out a breath. "How in the blue blazes did you get up there? No, the real question is *why* are you up there?"

"I wanted to let Carolina go," Hyacinth muttered.

"In a freakin' tree?" Alice sounded more annoyed than worried, although Greta was betting she was both.

"No." Hyacinth sounded like she was pouting. "I let her go in the forest. And then I climbed the tree because there was a bear."

"A bear." Alice narrowed her eyes.

"Yes. I thought so, anyway. I mean I heard something that could have been a bear, and I got scared. Only now, I'm up here." Hyacinth's voice wobbled a little on the last word.

"You can climb down now, dear," Nadia said in a reasonable voice. "There are no bears around. We checked."

"I can't." Hyacinth's voice was definitely wobbly now. "I don't know how. I'm afraid."

Alice closed her eyes. She looked like she was counting. "Now what do we do?"

"Talk her down." Hank shrugged. "I'll train the flashlight on the trunk and we can tell her how to climb down again."

"Hyacinth, dear," Nadia called, "Hank's going to shine the light on the tree so you can see what you're doing. You can just climb down on the branches."

Hank shone the light up the dark trunk, the branches standing out jaggedly against the night sky. The entire tree looked remarkably frail, as if it might break in half in a high wind.

"Come on, Hyacinth," Alice called. "You climbed up. You can climb down the same way."

Above them, Hyacinth seemed to glance down and then fasten herself more tightly to the trunk. "No," she whimpered. "It'll break."

"You'll be fine," Alice said. "Just get started. Once you're climbing down, you won't have any trouble." She sounded like she was gritting her teeth.

This time Hyacinth didn't bother to answer but pressed her face more tightly to the tree trunk.

"Damn it," Alice muttered.

"Hyacinth, sweetheart." Nadia leaned forward, resting her

hand on the trunk. "You can do this. I believe you can. So does your grandmother. What's the matter, honey?"

"I can't look down," Hyacinth mumbled. "It's too far. It shakes when I move."

Alice folded her arms across her chest. Her teeth were definitely gritted now. "What do we do? Call the fire department? If she were a cat, I'd use a can of tuna, but that wouldn't work with Hyacinth—she hates fish. Maybe we could try cookies."

Nadia rubbed a hand across her face. "You can't tempt her down, Alice. She's really frightened. And the longer she stays up there, the more dangerous it gets. After a while, she'll be too tired to hold on. Or the stupid tree really will break. It looks pretty fragile to me." She stared back up into the tree again, chewing on her lip.

"Well, we can't drag her down and I don't have a ladder that tall. What do you suggest, Nadia?"

"I could try climbing up there, but I'm not sure the tree would hold me." Hank shook his head. "Maybe I could get partway up and get hold of her somehow. Or maybe I could catch her if she lets go."

Greta rubbed her hands along her thighs, drying off the sweat, then kicked off her shoes. "Keep that light on the trunk, okay?"

Hank narrowed his eyes. "Why? What are you going to do?"

"Just keep the light there. I don't want to try this in the dark." She stepped to the tree, placing one bare foot in the crook of a limb a couple of feet off the ground.

"Greta, it won't hold you either. It's too flimsy." Hank's voice was urgent.

"Wait just a minute there," Alice snapped. "We need to

discuss this."

"It'll hold me. I'm not going all the way up." She placed another foot on a higher branch. "I'm the lightest one here after Hyacinth. If anyone's going to go up, it has to be me."

Above her the tree swayed slightly with the impact of her feet. Hyacinth whimpered again.

"Don't worry, Hyacinth," Greta called. "It's all right. I'm coming for you."

"It's shaking." Hyacinth cried. "Stop it! You're making it shake."

"It'll hold us both," Greta soothed, hoping to god that she was right. The branches seemed fairly rickety. She tried to keep her feet close to the trunk as she pushed her foot to a higher branch.

"What do you think you're doing?" Alice hissed. "You can't carry the child down from there. The damn tree's going to split. Both of you are going to break your necks."

Greta ignored her, as well as the voice at the back of her mind telling her to stop and think, while she inched up the trunk until she was maybe three feet below Hyacinth. She could see the soles of her shoes where her ankles were clasped around the tree. It trembled slightly whenever either of them moved. "Okay, Hyacinth," she said quietly, "we're going to climb down this tree together. But I can't climb any higher. The tree's too skinny. You're going to have to come down until you're next to me."

Hyacinth whimpered.

Greta tightened her grip on the trunk, trying to hold herself steady. "It's okay. This will work. But you need to come down here opposite me."

"The tree's not strong enough," Hyacinth moaned. "It'll

break with both of us up here."

Greta sighed. "No it won't. It's thinnest up where you are now. If you come down further, it will be sturdier. The trunk gets thicker the lower you go. It's going to be all right." *Right, Greta, now convince the tree.*

After another moment, she saw Hyacinth's right foot move. Slowly, she brought her heel away from the trunk, fumbling for a moment until her toe was tucked into the base of a lower branch.

"That's it," Greta murmured as the child brought her other foot down. "Now put your hands on a couple of the branches and hold on while you bring your feet down to the next footholds."

Hyacinth paused for a moment, as if she was gathering her breath, and then she moved her feet down slowly to the next set of branches. The tree trembled faintly, as if it were frightened too.

It seemed to take a very long time for Hyacinth to climb down to meet her, although it was probably only a matter of minutes. But eventually the two were more or less opposite each other, with Hyacinth hanging on to the trunk for dear life.

Greta was hanging on tightly herself. The tree shook beneath their combined weight.

Hyacinth blew out an unsteady breath. "Are you going to carry me down?"

Greta shook her head. "We're going to climb together now. I'll start and then you follow."

Hyacinth bit her lip, but then she nodded. "Okay."

"Okay. See where I have my hands? That's where your feet will go next, as soon as I get down a little farther." She dropped down to the next set of branches, then watched as Hyacinth set her feet carefully into the crotches of the branches she'd just left.

"See how it works?" Greta gave her the brightest smile she could muster. "We're much closer to being down now. We'll just keep going like this until we've gone all the way. Okay?"

Hyacinth nodded, watching her with wide eyes.

"Okay, then, here we go again." Greta felt around below her for her next toehold, careful to keep her gaze on Hyacinth as the tree swayed beneath them. "Just put your feet where my hands were, and you'll be fine."

The time it took to climb down three feet of trunk seemed agonizingly long. Greta kept murmuring encouragement while she tried to keep her bare feet from slipping off the branches. If she fell, she had a feeling Hyacinth would not be easy to pry loose. Of course, if she fell, she'd probably have other things on her mind herself.

Finally, when they were a few feet from the ground, Hank stepped up beside the trunk, reaching his arms up for Hyacinth. "Okay, kid, I've got you," he said, taking hold of her hips.

Hyacinth gave a small sob and turned, throwing her arms around his neck. Hank looked faintly surprised, but he wrapped his arms around her waist, turning toward Alice. "Here you go. Here's your grandmother."

Hyacinth transferred her embrace to Alice, clasping her arms around her waist and burying her face in Alice's stomach. "I'm sorry," she mumbled. "I'm sorry. I was so scared, Grandma."

Alice stroked her hair a little awkwardly. "Okay, you're all right now. Let's get you back home. We can talk about it tomorrow."

Nadia stepped next to her sister, wrapping her arms

around her so that Hyacinth was caught in between them. "Oh, child, we were so worried. Don't ever do that again."

Hyacinth shook her head, apparently too relieved to talk.

Alice transferred Hyacinth to Nadia, stepping away to where Greta was leaning against the tree trunk trying to get her breath as she pulled on her shoes. "That was a damn fool stupid thing to do."

"Maybe. In retrospect." Greta rubbed a hand across her face. "But it was all I could think of."

"You could have hurt my granddaughter." Alice kept her voice low, and it sounded like she was managing not to yell by sheer will. "Would it have killed you to have taken five seconds to tell us what you had planned?"

Greta shook her head. "I'm sorry."

"You were lucky. And it turned out all right. That's the only thing that's keeping me from having your head on a platter." Alice took a shuddering breath.

"Alice," Nadia called. "Time to go. Hyacinth needs to get to bed."

After another moment, Alice nodded, then turned her back on Greta, stalking stiffly across the clearing to where the two stood.

"Come on." She draped an arm across Hyacinth's shoulders. "Let's go."

Nadia draped her own arm across Hyacinth, who wrapped her arms around her two elderly relatives. The three of them managed to shuffle off toward Tompkins Corners without a backward glance.

Greta kept her gaze on the mass of pine needles underneath the tree, trying not to feel the ache in the middle of her chest. The disappointment. The guilt. *You've felt like this before. So what?* Yeah, she had. Every time she'd rushed into something when she shouldn't have. She just wished she didn't keep doing things that made her feel this way.

Hank still stood where he'd been when he'd handed Hyacinth over to Alice. Greta brushed the remaining pine bark and dust off her knees, fighting back the numbing wave of regret. After all, she'd actually gotten the kid down in one piece.

"Alice was right in a way. That was an amazingly nutty thing to do," he said quietly.

Greta stiffened, not looking up. "Thanks for sharing."

He shrugged. "Still, it worked. I'm sort of bowled over by your audacity, but it did work."

"So you think Alice was right?" She straightened. "That it was another example of my chronic lack of judgment?"

"Nope." He shook his head. "I think Alice is upset and suffering from the effects of seeing her granddaughter stuck at the top of a pine tree. My guess is she'll feel a lot different tomorrow morning. If you hadn't done it, Hyacinth might still be up there. And given how scared she was, she definitely needed to be brought down. It paid off."

Greta folded her arms across her chest. "So what are you saying exactly?"

He sighed. "Maybe that this whole impulsive thing you're worrying about isn't always bad. Maybe you should give yourself a break."

She closed her eyes for a moment, then shrugged. "I guess it's not always bad. But the fact that it worked this time doesn't really get me off the hook."

He frowned slightly. "Why did you do it, by the way? I mean, why didn't you take a few moments to explain what you had planned before you took off up the tree?"

She shrugged again. "I'm afraid of heights."

He stared at her blankly. "Say what?"

"I'm afraid of heights. If I'd stood around and talked about it, I wouldn't have been able to do it. I figured if I got myself up there, I'd be able to get us both down."

He shook his head slowly. "You could have been stuck up there too. You realize that makes no sense."

"Now it doesn't. Then it sort of did."

Hank sighed. "Come on." He pulled her against him, wrapping his arm around her shoulders. "We can talk this all out later. Or not. But at any rate, it's time to go back to bed."

She nodded, leaning against him. "Sounds like a plan."

"Nope." He rubbed his cheek against her hair. "No plans. No analysis. We just go back to bed and take it from there."

She gazed up at him, the dark green eyes, the brush of sandy hair turned to silver in the moonlight, the slight scrape of beard on his cheeks. She could have all that if she wanted it.

And she did want it. Very much.

Unfortunately, it didn't look like she could let herself take it.

"I think I need to head back home tomorrow," she murmured.

There was a long pause. Then Hank sighed. "Whatever you say, Greta. But keep in mind, Promise Harbor isn't that far away."

*That's what I'm counting on. Sort of.*

# Chapter Eighteen

For her last breakfast on her last day at Casa Dubrovnik, Greta made French toast with blueberries and whipped cream cheese. She'd sort of been saving it, knowing it qualified as a finale dish, at least the way she did it.

Of course, she hadn't figured her last day would be quite such a final finale. She hadn't talked to any of the Dubrovniks since last night. The Hotel Grand had been dark and still when she and Hank had finally gotten back. For a few moments, she'd actually considered sleeping in the garden, but Hank had a key to the front door along with his room key.

Now he sat alone at the kitchen table, slicing into his French toast with gusto. "I don't suppose you could just box me up the rest of this for a midmorning snack."

She shook her head. "It wouldn't taste as good if it sat out on the table all morning. Plus this is the end of the bread. I'll need to bake some more before I can make your sandwiches. Maybe I'll just grab some from the store."

He paused, his fork halfway to his mouth. "Hell. I'm going to have to go back to making my own freaking sandwiches."

"You can handle it." She managed to give him a tight smile. "You did your own lunches before I showed up. I have every confidence in you."

"Yeah," he said slowly, "but the company's going to suck."

She turned back to the stove, slicing the last few pieces of bread. No way was she going to start feeling crappy this early in the morning. Of course, she might not have a choice.

The door swished behind her as Nadia entered the kitchen, slipping her pink pashmina up over her shoulders. "Good morning," she trilled. "French toast? How lovely." She settled at the table opposite Hank, smiling beatifically. "And how is everyone this morning?"

"Late." Hank pushed himself to his feet, wiping the last bit of cream cheese from his lips. "Thanks for the breakfast." He paused. "For all the breakfasts, actually."

Greta took a deep breath, ordering herself not to get teary. "You're welcome."

She watched him head for his truck, trying not to think about the fact that this might well be the last time she'd see him.

"You're leaving?" Nadia picked up her coffee cup. "I thought you'd have worked through that by now."

"There's nothing to work through. I said I'd be here a week, and it's been almost a week." Greta placed a plate of French toast in front of her. "I've enjoyed it—well, most of it. But it's time to go back to the real world and face the music. I've got some decisions to make."

One of Nadia's black eyebrows arched up. "Not the real world as in the husband, surely. Or the ex-husband, to be more accurate."

"No. Ryan's gone back to Boston. I'm heading for Promise Harbor." She managed not to sigh. "Where I'm from."

Nadia took a bite of toast, nodding approvingly. "So even though the idea of opening your own bakery service in our kitchen appeals to both you and me and undoubtedly Alice if it was explained to her, you're still leaving?"

Greta dipped another piece of bread into her egg mixture. "Alice might not be all that enthusiastic about me sticking around after last night."

"Last night Alice lost her temper." Nadia shrugged. "She does that regularly. She probably won't apologize, and she will probably assume that the entire confrontation wasn't serious enough to rate discussion."

Greta turned, resting her hip against the counter. "Do you feel that way too?"

"I feel you did a courageous and slightly foolhardy thing. But you wanted to rescue my grandniece and you did. We could all have stood around and debated what to do for an hour while Hyacinth grew colder and stiffer and more and more frightened. But instead, thirty minutes later we took her home. I'm grateful to you." She took a sip of coffee, smiling appreciatively. "And Alice will be too, once she's had the chance to stop being so frightened over Hyacinth's brush with injury or worse."

As if she'd heard her name, Hyacinth breezed into the kitchen, smiling happily. If she had any lingering terrors from the night before, they didn't show at the moment. "Good morning. What smells so good?"

"French toast with blueberries and whipped cream cheese. There's also syrup if you want it." Greta turned back to the stove.

"Yes, please." She plopped into her chair next to Nadia. "Can we go to Promise Harbor today? I need to go to the library."

"I suppose." Nadia shrugged. "I need to do some grocery shopping anyway."

Hyacinth's forehead furrowed. "Why doesn't Greta do the shopping? She's cooking."

"I won't be cooking after today," Greta explained, placing

240

Hyacinth's French toast in front of her. "This is my last day at the hotel."

Hyacinth's smile was instantly transformed into a mask of tragedy. "No. You can't leave. Aunt Nadia, don't let her leave."

"I'm afraid it's not my decision, dear," Nadia said calmly. "My, this French toast is exquisite. Are the blueberries local?"

"Aunt Nadia." Hyacinth raised her voice. "You can't let her leave. You have to do something."

"My dear, Greta has decided to go back home. In fact, she decided that when she came here a week ago. She never promised to stay longer than that. And we must respect her wishes. Now eat your French toast before it gets cold." She gave Hyacinth another bland smile and returned to her own breakfast.

Greta kept her back to the table, dipping slices of bread in her milk and egg mixture. She had a feeling if she looked, she'd see Hyacinth doing puppy eyes, and she wasn't sure she could stand it.

On the other hand, the fact that Alice hadn't yet appeared might say a lot about her feelings at the moment. And Alice's opinions seemed to have a great deal of weight all of a sudden since they seemed to mirror those Greta always encountered after one of her fiascos.

She sighed, and glanced back at the table. "Would either of you like more French toast?"

"I'm going to go and harvest the mint for my foot cream," Nadia said, still smiling. "Would you like to help me, Hyacinth?"

Judging from Hyacinth's expression, the answer was no, but Greta figured she wouldn't actually say so. "Maybe later."

"Not too much later, please." Nadia's voice had taken on a certain edge, but she smiled again. "I'll see you at lunch if not before, Greta. I trust you're not leaving before then."

"I'll be here through dinner," Greta explained. And afterward, since she'd begun to think about grabbing one more night with Hank. Who knew? She might actually find a way out of this particular trap she'd set for herself.

Or not. As Nadia left the room, Alice entered, looking as if she were carrying a storm cloud over her head. She glanced at the table, where Hyacinth was making a desultory effort to finish her last piece of toast.

"Go and help your Aunt Nadia," she said flatly.

Hyacinth's lower lip jutted out fiercely. "I haven't finished my breakfast."

"Yes you have. You're just playing with the food now. Go."

Hyacinth pushed herself to her feet, still pouting. "All right, but I'll be ravenous by lunchtime."

"Good. You can do justice to the food by then." Alice plopped into a chair, making little shooing motions with her fingertips.

Hyacinth threw one more tragic glance in Greta's direction, then stomped out of the room.

Leaving her alone with Alice. Not necessarily something Greta was looking forward to. "French toast?" she asked a little stiffly.

Alice nodded. "Two slices. What are you doing for the store?"

"Banana bread. I've got it ready for the oven."

"What are you going to do—sell slices?"

Greta shrugged. "Yeah. Unless you want to try selling the loaves, which I wouldn't suggest. Don't worry. Everybody loves banana bread."

"Slices are all right," Alice said sourly. She stared down at her coffee cup for a moment, then looked up at Greta again. "Thank you for saving my granddaughter." She sounded as if the words were being extracted with pliers.

Greta stood very still, waiting for the *but* that she was sure would be coming. After a few moments, she realized it wasn't. "You're welcome. I was glad to do it."

Alice fixed her gaze on the corner of the room. "I behaved badly last night. I should have thanked you then. I apologize."

"Don't mention it." In fact, Greta meant that literally. She really wanted Alice to stop talking about it.

Apparently, Alice felt the same way. She started eating her French toast with enthusiasm. "Very good. Too bad we can't serve it in the store."

"That would require plates and forks, which would also require a dishwasher." Greta shrugged. "You could consider serving breakfasts if you're still interested in opening the dining room."

Alice gave her another narrow-eyed stare. "You're leaving? Today?"

Why was everybody asking her that question? Wasn't it obvious? "Yes, I'm leaving. Today."

Alice arched an eyebrow. "For how long?"

"Excuse me?" Greta froze in the act of putting the banana bread into the oven.

"How long do you plan to be gone before you come back here and get started on the whole breakfast pastries business? Surely it won't take you that long to explain everything to your mother and take whatever you have coming from the town gossips. In fact, if you'll leave behind a list of the things we need to do to get started, I can get the whole thing underway while you're off doing penance." She sliced another piece of French toast.

"I…don't think I'm ready to do that yet." Greta pushed the bread into the oven, slamming the door, then sank down at the table. "In fact, I don't remember discussing this whole idea with you." Mainly because they hadn't ever done it.

Alice shrugged. "You didn't have to. Nadia dropped a few details, but it doesn't take a genius to see how the whole thing would work. I'd already been thinking about something along that line, but I didn't have a cook before. Now I do."

Greta took a couple of deep breaths. She felt a little dizzy. "I was just sort of brainstorming with Nadia. I haven't really gone any farther than that. I mean, I have to sit down and think the whole thing through, maybe write out a formal proposal." Which would give her some time to actually consider the idea carefully and in detail for once before jumping in with both feet.

Alice shook her head. "You can do that if you need to—maybe it'll help you get it straight in your mind. But I can see how this is going to work. Can't you?"

Greta rested her head in her hands. "I've got some very questionable history on things like this. I've rushed into a lot of things in my life and screwed up royally. How do I know this isn't going to be another disaster?"

"You don't." Alice walked to the coffeepot to pour herself another cup. "I'd say our chances are decent to make back our outlay, but that's without knowing how much our outlay is going to be. I'll need to get somebody from the county in here to inspect the kitchen, and he'll probably want some changes. Hell, it hasn't produced anything but family meals for years. And I'm not sure Nadia's cooking even qualifies as meals."

Greta nodded slowly. "You'll have to do some updating. And they'll probably require some equipment replacement. And as I said, you'll need a dishwasher."

"Right. So there will be some expenses involved. Which, in turn, will mean we'll have to expand to as many stores as we can reach. How are you on salesmanship?"

Greta shrugged. "I'm decent, I guess. I believe in my own stuff."

"As well you should. So are you ready to go with this?"

She closed her eyes. "I can't make a decision like that, Alice. I just can't. It's too big, and it's too important. I need time—for once, I need to actually weigh pros and cons before I get invested in this. I've made too many mistakes because I didn't stop to think about what I was doing."

"You also rescued my granddaughter from a fifteen-foot pine tree," Alice said quietly. "You didn't stop to think and you got her down."

"One of my rare successes," Greta muttered.

Alice sighed. "All right. I have to open the store. Bring me some banana bread when it's ready. And you might spend some time thinking about the future."

Greta gathered the dishes in the sink after she'd gone. She could pretty much guarantee she'd be thinking about the future from now on. She just couldn't guarantee she'd be able to come to any decision. From being somebody who jumped into anything that presented itself, she'd suddenly changed into somebody who couldn't make a decision to save her soul.

*Maybe I need to talk to my mother.* She closed her eyes. Talking to her mother was probably the first thing she needed to do.

Fifty minutes later, she started slicing up the banana bread, covering it in squares of plastic wrap. *If we were to do this full time, we'd need more help. It takes me too long to wrap these suckers as it is.*

She paused. *If we were to do this full time...* Her shoulders ached with tension. *What if it all goes south? What if I make another mistake? And this time it would break my heart in more ways than one.* She took a deep breath, arranging the slices of banana bread on a sheet pan, and headed for the store. She wasn't going to do anything now. She didn't have to. She'd have other chances—no matter what Alice said, she didn't have to make up her mind this very minute.

And she had other possibilities she could consider. She could always go to Boston and work in Mary Ellen's bakery. Or go back to Promise Harbor. And move in with her mother.

She closed her eyes. Okay, so she didn't necessarily want to do that. There might still be other possibilities.

The customers in the general store were lined up four deep this time, watching her like pigeons eyeing a bag of peanuts. She placed the tray in front of Alice. "Here's the first batch."

Alice frowned. "Best get the next batch out as soon as you can. We've got a lot of hungry people this morning."

"You're leaving?" somebody called out. "Whose idea was that?"

"Mine," Greta muttered, turning back toward the door.

She let Hyacinth take the next tray of slices out to the store once she'd finished wrapping them. Nadia was busy processing mint at the sink when Greta came back in. "Do you need to wash anything in here?" Nadia frowned. "We'll need to work out logistics once you start cooking larger batches, but I expect we'll also need to invest in a dishwasher and perhaps some more prep space."

Greta bit her lip as her stomach gave another twinge. *Other possibilities, damn it!* She headed back toward the door to the hotel. "If anybody wants me I'll be in the lobby." Or somewhere. Basically, anywhere she wasn't being pressured to commit

246

herself one way or the other.

She wandered out to the front porch of the hotel. The wooden rockers looked as if they'd been worn smooth by generations of butts. Sighing, she slipped into one of them, then closed her eyes and began to rock slowly.

If she stayed, she'd make little or no money for a while, maybe a long while. And she might have to invest some money herself. All their profits would have to be plowed back into the business. If she stayed, she'd be living with the Dubrovniks. Hell, she'd probably become a Dubrovnik herself. If she stayed, she'd have to explain to her mom why she was willing to commit herself to a group of relative strangers who couldn't promise her much beyond a kitchen and a starting place, although she'd only known them for a week.

If she stayed, she'd have to figure out what to do about Hank.

That last thought really made her shoulders clench. She'd only been divorced for a couple of weeks. She'd only been on her own for two or three months. How could she be ready to jump back into a relationship so soon? Was she actually jumping into a relationship or was she just doing the rebound thing?

Her stomach gave another twinge.

The easiest thing to do would be nothing. To get into her car and drive back to Promise Harbor. To pretend the last week had been a really nice vacation and then get ready for the rest of her life without Tompkins Corners.

The Rest Of Her Life. Her whole body ached all of a sudden. She wondered if she was coming down with the flu.

*Oh yeah, Greta, the rockin' pneumonia and the indecisive flu.*

A car pulled in to one of the parking spaces in front of the hotel, and she opened her eyes. And stared.

Her mother climbed out of the driver's seat of her Accord. Owen Ralston climbed out of the passenger's side. Before Greta could gather herself for a dash back inside, her mother glanced up and saw her.

Greta licked her lips. "Hi, Mom," she croaked. "Long time, no see."

When Greta hadn't shown up at the site by lunchtime, Hank finally decided to head back to Casa Dubrovnik. It wasn't just that he hadn't brought any lunch with him this time. He hated to admit it, but he'd begun to worry that she might have taken off. He didn't think she'd leave without talking to him, but he was afraid she might. She'd been sort of antsy ever since last night.

He gave Marty an hour for lunch, with strict orders to sieve dirt if he got back first. Hank really hoped that didn't happen since he didn't trust Marty to do anything on his own, but he didn't know how long it would take for him to track Greta down.

And if she'd left, he *would* track her down. Of that, he was absolutely certain. Of course, what he'd do when he found her was another question.

He started to head toward the carport where he usually parked, but he slowed when he reached the front of the hotel. Greta was standing on the porch, talking to an older man and woman. She looked...nervous. On impulse, he pulled his truck into a spot down the street and climbed out.

Greta glanced up as he mounted the steps. Her eyes widened slightly. *Terrific.* Now he was making her nervous too. He gave her what he hoped was a reassuring smile.

"Hi," she murmured, rubbing her hands on her thighs. "Um...this is my mom. Mom, this is Hank Mitchell. Professor Hank Mitchell. He's an archaeologist and he lives here at the hotel." Her smile looked more like a grimace.

Mrs. Brewster—he assumed that was her name anyway—gave him a slightly more genuine version of the same smile. "Pleased to meet you, Professor."

"Likewise." He glanced back and forth between them, trying to figure out what was going on. "Are you taking Greta back to Promise Harbor?"

Amazingly enough, Mrs. Brewster's face turned faintly pink. "No, we're actually going the other direction. That is..." She turned toward the man sitting in one of the rockers at the side. "This is Owen Ralston. My friend, Owen Ralston. We're just...headed toward the coast."

Ralston leaned forward, grinning as he shook Hank's hand. "Vacation," he said. "Need to get away. From those old hens in the harbor."

Oddly enough, Hank was pretty sure he knew what Ralston was talking about in spite of his somewhat elliptical phrasing. "Taking some time off would give them time to find something else to talk about, I guess."

"Damn right," Ralston said placidly.

Greta ran her fingers through her hair, leaving it standing more or less on end. Hank discovered he liked it that way. "How did you know I was here?" she asked.

Mrs. Brewster shrugged. "Ryan told me."

Greta's expression became guarded. "Ryan's in the harbor?"

"So far as I know, he's in Boston. But he stopped by long enough to tell us you were here before he drove on home."

"Oh." Greta blew out a breath. "Well, good. I mean, I was coming home today, honest."

"And, of course, you wouldn't have found me if you had," Mrs. Brewster said briskly. "Since Owen and I are going to Greenbush Island for the weekend."

"Oh," Greta repeated. "I just... Could I maybe talk to you for a minute?" She sounded a little desperate.

"You mean in private?" Mrs. Brewster shrugged. "Why not. You boys can take care of yourselves, can't you?"

"Sure." Hank gave them both another reassuring grin. "Don't worry about us. We can wait."

"Good." Mrs. Brewster turned back to Greta. "Well, then, shall we go inside? I assume they've got a lobby here."

"More or less," Greta mumbled. She held the screen door for her mother and then followed her.

Hank glanced back at Owen Ralston. "They may be a while. Would you like some iced tea or something?"

Ralston shook his head. "Nope. Good time for a nap." He settled back in his chair, closing his eyes.

Hank watched him for a moment, then dropped into the chair next to him. All of a sudden, a nap seemed like a fine idea.

# Chapter Nineteen

Greta was trying not to babble. She had a feeling if she opened her mouth, the torrent of words that came out would bury them both. And her mother didn't look like she'd enjoy that much.

Her mother looked around the lobby of the Hotel Grand with narrowed eyes. "You're staying here? Seriously?"

"It's fine," Greta said quickly. "The rooms are really…nice."

Her mother looked unconvinced. "Ryan said you were cooking."

"I am. I get a free room in exchange for cooking the meals and preparing some pastries for the store."

Her mother's eyes widened. "Why do you need free room and board? What happened? Did you lose all your savings?"

Greta gritted her teeth. "No, Mom. It was just a short-term deal. Alice only takes cash and all I had were credit cards. Besides, it's been fun. I like cooking."

"But you're leaving now?" Her mother settled into the leather chair. At least it didn't send out a puff of dust.

"I guess so," Greta said slowly. "I mean, I was going back so I could talk to you, but here you are." She narrowed her eyes slightly. "With Owen Ralston."

"Here I am," her mother said hurriedly. "So talk."

"I'm really sorry, Mom." She sighed. "I should have told you about Ryan and me when it happened. I meant to. And then I got to the harbor, and everything started with the wedding..."

Her mother held up her hand. "How long ago did you and Ryan separate?"

Greta sighed again. "Three months, more or less."

"So it wasn't really the wedding that was the problem, was it?"

Greta's heart gave a hard thump. She shook her head.

"Then tell me—why couldn't you talk to me about it? What were you afraid I'd say?" Her mother frowned. "You couldn't possibly think I'd be on Ryan's side, could you?"

"No, it's not that." She paused. "Well, not exactly. It's just that I thought you'd be...disappointed. Again."

"Disappointed in you?" Her mother's eyebrow arched.

Greta nodded. "I was afraid you'd think I'd made another rotten decision, jumped into something without thinking, and then gotten burned. Just like the purple hair and the prom dress that was too tight and all those other times I did stuff you said I shouldn't do." She sank onto the couch opposite her mother. "I should have listened to you when you told me I was rushing into the marriage, Mom. I'm sorry I didn't. I wish I could promise I'll listen from now on, but I don't think that would be honest."

Her mother sighed. "Now would be a great time for me to say I told you so. It's probably the best chance I'll ever have, in fact. But I wouldn't be much help to you if I did. What happened, Greta?"

"He...hooked up with somebody else. Sort of. I guess it wasn't permanent, but when I found out about it, I was really hurt. I kicked him out, and then I realized I didn't want him to come back even if he said he was sorry and wanted to." She rubbed a hand across the back of her neck. "And I was really sort of embarrassed about the whole thing. That he'd found somebody else—or let somebody else find him. It didn't say much for our marriage that he did."

Her mother's jaw tightened. "I thought it was probably something like that—the rat bastard."

Greta blinked. "Mom?"

"Well, he was, Greta. Even if he says she seduced him, that's really no excuse. He was weak enough to let it happen. So what have you been doing since then?"

Greta shrugged. "I worked for one of my friends in Boston at her bakery—sort of a temporary fill-in, only she started talking about making it permanent and full time. I'm supposed to decide if I want to go on working for her now."

"So you're going back to Boston?" Her mother sounded like she was keeping her voice carefully neutral.

Greta shook her head. "I don't know if I am. There's this...possibility here."

"Cooking for this place?" Her mother looked around the lobby again, pursing her lips. "Really?"

"It's more than that. I'd be baking pastries to sell here and at some other general stores in the area. We've been brainstorming about the details, but it seems doable." *And I like it here. And they like me. And there's Hank.* She licked her lips. Not what she should be thinking about.

"What do you want to do?" Her mother narrowed her eyes.

Greta took a deep breath. "I want to not rush into any more stupid decisions. I want to...not make any more mistakes."

Her mother folded her arms across her chest, shaking her head. "Good luck with that. It's not something I've ever been good at myself."

"But you've been better at it than I have," Greta said slowly. "You and Josh. Especially Josh. I know I've let you down."

"Oh Greta, for pity's sake! Will you listen to yourself?" Her mother snorted. "Your brother's fiancée took off with another man. From what I can deduce, your brother's been doing who knows what with Devon Grant. And I'm the one who pressured Josh and Allie into deciding to get married in the first place. I wouldn't say anybody in our family is ready to be declared infallible."

Greta fought down a totally inappropriate grin. "Well, there is that."

"And so I repeat—what do you want to do?" She leaned forward. "Go back to Boston? Go back to Promise Harbor? Stay here?"

Greta stared down at her feet. Her stomach clenched tight. *Decision time, Greta.* "I really think...I'd like to stay here." She took a breath. That was a lot easier than she'd thought it would be. "We've got some definite possibilities. So far the stuff I've baked has sold like gangbusters, and Alice seems to feel there's a market beyond Tompkins Corners. And there's a possibility that we might do something with the dining room too, maybe make it a bed and breakfast." She took a quick glance around the lobby, managing not to shudder. "Of course, that's sort of in the future."

Her mother shrugged. "Sounds good to me. I can think of a couple of places in the harbor that could benefit from having decent baked goods for a change. The Promise Harbor Inn's croissants remind me of potholders."

Greta smiled again, then let the smile dim. "Of course, I might screw it up again."

Her mother nodded. "You might. Or somebody else might.

Or we might be hit by a freak hurricane that will wipe out your kitchen. Anything could happen, Greta. But that doesn't mean you shouldn't give it a try anyway."

The door to the general store swished open, and Alice leaned into the room. "Are you making lunch today, or are we on our own?"

"Oh lord, I forgot all about it." Greta glanced back at her mother. "Have you and Owen eaten?"

She shook her head, her cheeks turning pink. "We were going to have lunch on the road."

"Then come on into the dining room, and I'll fix everyone something." She turned toward Alice. "Alice, this is my mother, Sophie Brewster. Mom, Alice Dubrovnik—she owns the hotel. Hank's outside too, along with Mom's friend Owen."

Alice and her mother nodded at each other a little warily before Alice headed back to the store. Greta walked toward the kitchen door but turned back for a moment. "Mom, about Owen..."

Her mother narrowed her eyes. "Don't go there, Greta. Just don't."

Greta bit her lip to keep from grinning. "Well, anyway, thanks, Mom. Really. Thanks."

Her mother sighed. "Don't mention it, sweetheart. At least I can offer good advice for one of my offspring."

Lunch had been both delicious and surreal. Greta made some kind of cold vegetable soup that everybody slurped up, along with sandwiches and mint iced tea. Nadia was more Nadia than usual, with a lavish paisley shawl and golden hoop earrings. Hank half expected her to start telling fortunes. Alice delivered several zingers in her customary dry monotone. Hyacinth described her newest find, a couple of house finches currently at the bird feeder.

Greta's mother sat through it all with a faint smile, making some friendly comments to Nadia, more of them to Hyacinth, fewer to Alice. If she was overwhelmed, she didn't show it. Her friend Owen said little. Every once in a while they exchanged smiles. Hank wondered if Greta had noticed, but he didn't feel like calling it to her attention.

In fact, she seemed to be avoiding his gaze as much as possible. He couldn't decide if that was a problem or not. Probably it was, but he didn't feel up to analyzing it at the moment. He also didn't feel like going back to the dig. God help him if Marty decided to do some excavating on his own, but he had a feeling the kid was more likely to take the opportunity for a quick siesta than to do any unsanctioned digging.

Finally, Greta's mother and her friend went back to their car again, giving Greta a list of unsolicited instructions for things she needed to do around the house when she went back to Promise Harbor. Or at least Greta's mother did that. Her friend Owen settled back in his seat, closing his eyes again. The ability to nap whenever you had a chance was very useful, at least from Hank's point of view.

Finally, they were gone. Greta stood on the front porch, staring down the road after them. *Now or never. Hopefully the former.*

He stepped beside her. "So what's it going to be—stay or go?" He hadn't meant to be that direct about it, but he really wanted to know.

She glanced back at him, her lips turning up in a faint smile. "Stay, I guess. I mean, there's no point in going back to Promise Harbor to talk to my mom when she's currently off having a spa vacation with Owen."

He felt as if his knees had quite suddenly turned to applesauce. He reached a hand to the porch railing to keep from collapsing in sheer relief. "And long term?" His voice sounded a little choked, but maybe she wouldn't notice.

She sank down slowly on the top step. "Long term I may give Alice's idea a whirl. I'm starting to think it might be possible after all."

"More than possible, I'd say. Highly probable." He slid down beside her, hoping that he'd get enough muscle control back to be able to stand up later.

"Possible," she said firmly. "I'm not taking it farther than that. And I'm going to be doing this on a month-by-month basis, maybe even week-by-week."

"Still. You'll be the head chef of the Hotel Grand, Tompkins Corners, Massachusetts. That's got to count for something."

She glanced up at him, and he grinned. For a moment the corners of her mouth trembled as if she might smile herself, but then she turned back to the road again. "I don't know how this is going to work out. I mean, I was only going to stay for a week. All of a sudden, I'm here for the foreseeable future. It's a little scary."

He wasn't sure if she was talking about Alice or him, but he decided to assume it was the latter. At least, he could do something about that. "I never thought of myself as a scary man."

"You're not. Exactly."

"Just sort of." He stretched his arm around her waist. The worst she could do would be to push him away, but he was really hoping she wouldn't.

She didn't. Instead, she sighed, leaning her head against

his shoulder. "I've only been divorced for two weeks. And this all happened really fast."

"So we can slow it down a little now. But *fast* doesn't necessarily mean *wrong*."

"No it doesn't." She looked up at him, her brown eyes dark.

"What's really bothering you, Greta?" He took a deep breath. "Were you toying with my affections? Was this supposed to be over by now?"

She narrowed her eyes. "You're kidding, right?"

"Partly. Maybe mostly." He sighed. "Are you scared because what was going to be a fling turned out to be more than that?"

She closed her eyes for a moment. "Partly." Her lips quirked up. "Maybe mostly. It's definitely beyond the fling stage by now."

"I repeat. We can take it slow if that's what you want." Although slow didn't sound all that appealing all of a sudden. As a matter of fact, he decided he'd really like to carry her up the stairs and maybe stay there for a couple of days. Assuming Alice would provide room service. "We can take it at whatever speed you want, provided you're willing to keep going."

She licked her lips. "I'm willing. Most definitely willing."

He touched his lips to hers, lightly, then more firmly, smelling lavender and sage, sweet and savory. *Greta. Oh my, yes.*

She pulled back slowly, then dropped her head on his shoulder again, smiling. "You're a really great guy, Doc. I'm very glad I didn't leave you in that hole a week ago."

"Needless to say, so am I." He rubbed his hand up and down her arm. "Do you need to go back to Promise Harbor for anything? We could go over there now, after I check to make sure Marty hasn't decided to dig a tunnel to nowhere. Maybe

Barney's wouldn't be such a bad place for dinner. You could tell your buddy Bernice you're in the bakery business."

"What I intend to tell my buddy Bernice has nothing to do with baked goods." She blew out a breath. "I should probably talk to Alice before we take off. I need to let her know I'm staying."

"I have a feeling she's figured that out." He nodded toward where Alice stood in the doorway.

"You fixing dinner tonight, or do I need to pull one of the frozen pizzas out of the store?" She didn't look all that excited about the prospect.

"We never did discuss days off, did we?" Greta pushed herself to her feet. "I'm thinking weekends would be good."

"I'm thinking we'll discuss this later." Alice shrugged. "So what about tonight?"

"Go for the pizza, Alice." Greta grinned. "I need to pick up my stuff back in Promise Harbor."

Alice sighed. "First thing Monday morning, we hash all of this out. I guess pizza won't kill us for one night. Considering that Nadia was ready to take over the cooking again."

"Monday it is." She watched Alice head back inside, then peered beyond her into the hotel, her eyes widening. "Oh my lord."

Hank pushed himself to his feet. "What?"

She nodded toward the lobby, stepping through the front door. "That."

Hyacinth stood on a footstool, wearing the Bridesmaid Dress from Hell Greta herself had been wearing when she first arrived. The neckline dipped almost to her waist, exposing the white T-shirt underneath. The puke-green ruffled skirt was bunched up to her elbows. She looked a little like she was wearing an exercise ball.

"This is the most wonderful dress in the world," she said dreamily.

"It's a little big," Greta murmured.

"I'll grow into it."

Nadia stepped through the door to the family apartment, her garden basket on her arm. "Come on, Hyacinth. We need to pick some rosemary." She narrowed her eyes. "Put the dress back for now. We'll cut it down later."

Hyacinth sighed. "Do we have to cut it down?"

"Only if you want to be able to actually walk around in it. Which is always handy." Nadia took a handful of ruffles, lifting the dress up toward the little girl's head. "Hold still and I'll pull it loose."

Hyacinth glanced back at Greta. "Thank you for the dress. It's lovely. I'm glad you're staying."

Greta nodded. "Me too."

Nadia sighed. "All right, let's go." She cast a quick grin in Greta's direction. "Have a nice trip, my dear. See you tomorrow."

Greta stood watching for a moment, then shrugged. "You know, she's right. That dress was absolutely ghastly, but in a lot of ways it was the most wonderful dress in the world."

Hank slid his arm around her waist, trying to control his idiot grin. "In that it brought you to Casa Dubrovnik, I'm inclined to agree. Want to head to Promise Harbor? What do you need to bring back, by the way?"

She shrugged. "Just my suitcase mostly. I need my clothes. I'm out of underwear."

He gave her a long look. "If you bring back your suitcase, does that mean no more braless days?"

"Probably." The corners of her lips edged up again. "Then again, I'm open to negotiation. And bribery."

He pulled her into his arms, feeling her warm, braless breasts soft against his chest. "Woman," he murmured, "I so like the way you think."

# About the Author

Meg Benjamin is an award-winning author of contemporary romance for Samhain Publishing. Her books have won an EPIC Award for Contemporary Romance, the Romantic Times Reviewers' Choice Award, the New England Romance Writers Beanpot Award, and the Holt Medallion, among other honors. Meg lives in Colorado. Her website is www.MegBenjamin.com and her blog is http://megbenj1.wordpress.com. You can follow her on:

Facebook: http://facebook.com/meg.benjamin1

Pinterest: http://pinterest.com/megbenjamin/

Twitter: @megbenj1

Meg loves to hear from readers—contact her at meg@megbenjamin.com.

# You're invited to the wedding of the year

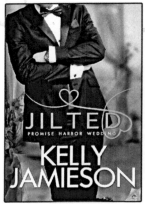

Book 1

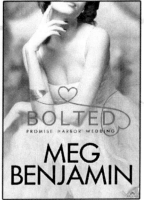

Book 2

Book 3

Book 4

Don't miss any of the books in the
Promise Harbor Wedding series

PUBLISHING

*It's all about the story...*

Romance

# HORROR

www.samhainpublishing.com

CPSIA information can be obtained at www.ICGtesting.com
Printed in the USA
BVOW04s2248030414

349480BV00002B/9/P

9 781619 217010